SKIES

OF

DEFIANCE

A **Kate Barrett** Thriller

Cam Shaw

SKIES

OF

DEFIANCE

A **Kate Barrett** Thriller

Cam Shaw

2023

CAM SHAW
AUTHOR

First Edition ISBN: 978-0-6458750-8-9

First published by Cam Shaw

Editing by Karen Guest

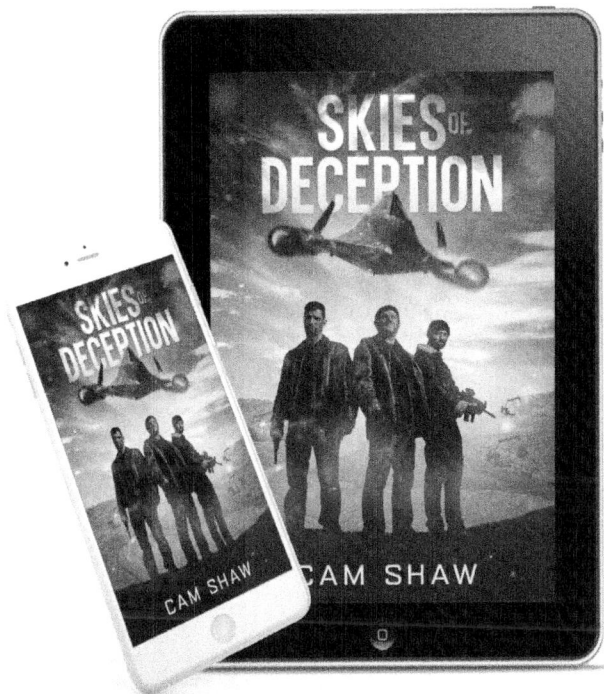

Sign up for my monthly newsletter to receive a digital copy of the novella—*Skies of Deception*—obligation free and exclusive to subscribers.

This title is not available in any store!

www.camshawauthor.com

Other titles by Cam Shaw

For Paul

Who is dearly missed.

"You may have to fight a battle more than once to win it."

—*Margaret Thatcher*

PROLOGUE

Rocky Mountains, Canada
25th December 2020
8:54 am Mountain Standard Time

On a snow-covered mountain, high in the Canadian Rockies, a solitary figure wearing snow-coloured fatigues lay flat on the ground between a clump of giant fir trees. The wind howled around him, causing snow to spill from the surfaces of nearby drifts and form swirling, erratic clouds of white dust which only assisted his camouflage. The freezing cold and the swirling snow were of no concern to him as he held a set of military-grade binoculars to his eyes.

A few minutes later, he tucked the binoculars away into a pocket inside his jacket, got to his feet, and tugged at the fur-lined hood of his jacket, pulling it over his eyes to protect them from the lashing snow.

He then began trudging through the deep snow towards the concrete-walled building at the bottom of the valley. After an arduous walk through the deep snow, he reached the laboratory compound and pulled out a pistol as he crept against the chain-link, barbed-wire-topped fence. He reached a small gate positioned within it and stopped.

Brushing away the built-up snow from the padlock securing the gate, he produced a small amount of C-4 plastic explosive from a pocket of his multi-pocketed trousers and spread it carefully over the lock with his thumbs. He then backed away from the gate as he ejected the clip from his pistol and exchanged it for a secondary clip containing tracer rounds.

This was a trick he had learned from his father, who had once told him that tracer rounds were constructed with a small pyrotechnic charge in their base. These charges would detonate upon firing, enabling the shooter to *see* the bullet's trajectory for a more precise shot. It was a technique commonly used amongst elite snipers—although this man was no sniper. He was using the pyrotechnic charge at the base of the bullet to detonate the plastic explosive.

Standing several metres from the gate, he raised the pistol, took aim, and fired. The tracer round lit up immediately—a bright orange streak of light trailing behind it as it speared towards the plastic explosive. The round detonated the C-4 with a deafening explosion, blowing the padlock into pieces and taking the gate clean off its hinges.

He sprinted through the subsequent cloud of snow produced by the explosion, using it as camouflage, and entered the compound. He ran towards a wall of the building and put his back against it.

He waited, quickly swapping the tracer round clip for a standard one and screwing a silencer onto the end of the pistol.

He did not have to wait long.

Within seconds, two guards armed with rifles burst out of the nearby fire exit door to investigate the explosion. He fired two quick shots. Each one hit its target, dropping the men face-first into the snow.

As soon as they hit the ground, he entered the laboratory through the door the guards had left open.

With his pistol raised, he walked down the dimly lit corridor until he reached a junction in the corridors. With his back to the wall, he quickly glanced around the corner, scanning for any other guards.

Clear.

He spun around the corner and entered the room to his left and quietly shut the door behind him. He found himself in a large laboratory-like room, filled with high-top, stainless-steel tables covered with petri dishes, microscopes, flasks, and beakers.

On the opposite side of the laboratory was a solitary, isolated room with heavy-duty, soundproof glass for walls. Inside this room was a large, long-haired, scruffy-looking scientist wearing a white lab coat sitting at a desk, bobbing his head in time with the music blaring through his headphones.

The camouflaged man walked up to the glass and tapped it with the silencer on the end of his pistol.

The scientist didn't respond and continued nodding to the music while mixing chemicals in the test tubes in front of him—oblivious to the tapping on the window behind him.

Taking a few steps back from the glass, the camouflaged man fired a shot, causing the glass to explode and the scientist to spin around in his chair so quickly that it caused him to lose balance and fall off it.

"What the…?" he spluttered as his hands crunched into the shards of glass on the polished floor beneath him.

"When someone is knocking at your door, it's polite to answer it," the camouflaged man said. "Stay down."

The scientist froze as he lay on the floor with the headphones skewed to one side on his head and blood oozing from the cuts to his hands. "Who the hell are you?" he asked, his voice quivering with fear. "What do you want?"

"I'm here for the product," the camouflaged man said, pointing the pistol at the scientist's head. "Where is it?"

The scientist raised his bloodied hands in the air. "Woah, Woah, Woah. What product? What are you talking about?"

"You know *exactly* what I'm talking about. The fucking product!" he shouted, cocking the pistol

"Okay, okay, okay!" the scientist said, raising his hands higher into the air. "I'll show you! Just don't kill me! Please!"

The camouflaged man motioned for him to get up with his pistol. "On your feet. Now."

The scientist whimpered as he got to his feet. "You're going to kill me, aren't you?"

"Move!" the camouflaged man shouted.

The scientist reluctantly turned around and opened the door of a large steel refrigerator behind him. As he slid out a rack of vials inside it, he felt the cold barrel of the pistol push into his left temple.

The scientist froze again.

"Thank you," the camouflaged man said.

The pistol fired and blood sprayed out of the scientist's head, splattering the walls as his body slumped to the ground.

The camouflaged man holstered the weapon and removed the rack of vials the scientist had started to slide out of the refrigerator, setting it down on the bench. He carefully picked up a vial and inspected the label—

—*White Cloud.*

OSCAR

The world had changed. Everyday life had become painful and unspeakable; but it was something Kate Barrett, along with the rest of civilisation, had been through before. The 9/11 terror attacks in New York had once created undeniable fear in the western world, and the feeling today was extraordinarily similar. Although the 2018 White Cloud aircraft attacks differed greatly from those that had occurred in New York. They were on a *global* scale, causing humanity's eyes to be well and truly opened to the devastating, and horrific, capability of evil.

Nowhere felt safe anymore.

If White Cloud could fly aircraft into the world's landmarks, holy places of worship and wherever else they desired, civilisation desperately needed to change to counter-act that evil. It simply couldn't return to the way life used to be. If it did, humanity would only leave itself vulnerable to further attacks.

White Cloud had left an open wound in the lives of millions. Tens of thousands of people had perished, not only in the air but also on the ground where the aircraft had crashed. Countless families had lost loved ones, and if anyone was lucky enough not to have lost someone close to them, they surely knew of someone who had.

Three years after the attacks, the ripples of fear were still evident. No one was brave enough to fly anymore, causing airlines to work hard in an effort to regain the public's trust. Subsequently, this caused many of the low-cost airlines to cease trading and the larger airlines to ground much of their fleets.

The world was still in lockdown while its inhabitants licked at their wounds and cleaned up the Earth's rubble-covered surface.

For Kate Barrett, though, her situation was entirely different from everyone else's. Shortly before the White Cloud attacks had begun, she had united with the vigilante group, Viribus, and together, they'd stopped White Cloud from achieving total annihilation of the planet.

It was her husband, Sol, who White Cloud had manipulated to assist them with the attacks. And it was Kate who fired the bullet into the helicopter that Sol and the White Cloud leader, Nikolai, were escaping in. The helicopter subsequently ignited, killing them both.

For a passive and a humble ward nurse, this was something she continued to live with, and it weighed heavily on her conscience.

After they prevented White Cloud from completing their heinous plan, Kate and two other members of Viribus, Alaina and Matt, went into hiding at the Shoalwater Bay Military Training Base on the east coast of Australia. The base commander, Major Richard Barton, advised against pursuing the remaining White Cloud members and to stay in place.

It had proved good advice, as seven months later, Kate gave birth to her twin boys, Liam and Kane.

Her life changed again.

In return for her protection and accommodation, Major Barton engaged Kate and the others to accompany some of the more experienced trainee pilots on training flights around Shoalwater Bay. He didn't have the time to babysit the trainees while they got their hours up to qualify for their solo licence, so hiring Kate and the others to do the task for him seemed logical.

It had just gone three o'clock on a summer's afternoon as the light aircraft carrying Kate and trainee pilot Jesse Delaney took to the sky. The temperature outside was finally beginning to drop after peaking at a sweltering 44 degrees Celsius, but it was still hot. For Kate, sitting in the climate-controlled cockpit of a Piper Cherokee while being flown around Shoalwater Bay was a good excuse to escape the oppressive summer heat.

Jesse sat beside her, concentrating on the instruments in front of him. They were shoulder to shoulder in the cockpit of the small propellor-driven aircraft—well and truly invading each other's personal space. Jesse was extremely well built and barely fit into the small cockpit.

Jesse had been at the Shoalwater Bay Military Flight School for almost five years, and it was obvious he liked to go to the gym in his spare time. Kate could see his rippling biceps bulging under his short-sleeved white pilot shirt as he made minor corrections with the control stick and couldn't help but notice his scent. The intoxicating aroma of sandalwood with a hint of musk permeated the air conditioning system of the aircraft—he smelled amazing.

Kate stole a glance at him as he focused intently on the aircraft's instruments. She thought it rather fortuitous this would be one of his last flights in this aircraft before graduating to a larger one—he was rapidly outgrowing this cockpit.

She took her eyes away from his quivering muscles momentarily and gazed out of the window at the brilliant blue water of the Great Barrier Reef below her.

A strange-looking vessel on the horizon caught her attention, and she squinted, trying to focus on it.

It was white.

Large and white.

"What's that?" she asked, pointing a finger at the white blob in the distance.

Jesse took his eyes off the instruments for a second and looked to where she was pointing, narrowing his eyes to focus, just as she had done.

"Looks like a ship of some sort," he said.

"No shit," Kate replied. "It isn't a normal ship, though, is it?"

"You might be right. Let's go and take a closer look, shall we?"

Jesse banked the aircraft left, and as they drew closer, Kate's eyes widened as the realisation of what the white ship was sunk in.

"Turn around!" she screamed.

"Why? What's wrong?" Jesse asked.

"Just turn around! Get me back to base NOW!"

Jesse did as he was told and rolled the aircraft hard to the left, turning it completely around and advancing the throttle lever as far forward as it would go.

The aircraft responded and sped up.

Jesse glanced at Kate as he lined up the runway in front of him. She was sweating profusely and becoming increasingly pale.

"What's wrong?" he asked.

"I don't have time to explain," she said. "Just concentrate on the landing. I'll tell you later."

He didn't ask any further questions, and after a bumpy landing and short taxi, he brought the aircraft to a stop in front of the hangar. Kate threw the door of the aircraft open and leapt out, sprinting inside the hangar.

She bustled her way into a briefing room and saw Matt standing behind a desk, staring at his laptop screen in shock. Alaina sat next to him, doing the same.

They snapped their heads around to look at her as she entered the room.

"Is that who I think it is?" Kate asked.

Matt nodded his head slowly.

"Why? What did *you* see?" Alaina asked.

"An enormous cargo ship with *White Cloud* written down the side of it. That's why I came back. And by the look on both of your faces, I'd say you guys have seen something as well. Am I right?"

Alaina nodded and turned Matt's laptop around so she could see what was on the screen. "This happened just before you came through the door," Alaina said.

A notification flashed on the screen.

Activity detected in the area.

"We need to get out of here," Matt said. "They've found us."

Major Barton entered the room. "What's going on? Why are you back…"

"Not now, Major," Kate snapped, cutting him off. "Where are the boys?"

"Playing with Sarah and a bunch of Lego," the Major replied. "Right where you left them."

Alaina stood up and snapped her laptop shut. "Matt and I will start loading Moose. You fetch the boys, and we'll get the hell out of here."

Kate ran out of the hangar dressed in the olive-green flying suit the Major had lent her earlier and sprinted towards the front office. The Major scurried behind her, trying to keep up.

"Where are you going?" he shouted after her.

"I don't know yet, Major!" she yelled over her shoulder. "But we need to move! Something is going on with that ship, and we need to find out what that is."

She barged through the door of the office, expecting to see her boys happily playing with Lego on the office floor—but they were nowhere to be seen. "Sarah!" she shouted.

No response.

"Sarah!" the Major repeated as he entered the office behind her.

Nothing.

"They were here 10 minutes ago," he said.

The sound of a car door being slammed attracted their attention. They turned their heads towards the noise and leapt over to the office window. Parting the blinds, Kate saw two boys—her boys, Liam and Kane—staring back at her through the rear window of the Major's black Volkswagen Golf GTI, with tears staining their cheeks.

The Golf then started its engine and screeched its tyres as it sped away.

Kate ran out of the office towards the massive C-17 Globemaster III cargo aircraft the crew affectionately called *Moose* parked on the apron outside the hangar and leapt up the rear cargo ramp in double-quick time.

"I need the van!" she yelled, entering the aircraft's yawning chasm of a cargo bay.

"What for?" Matt asked as she pushed past him and got into the driver's seat of the van.

"Someone has just kidnapped the twins," she said, slamming the door of the van behind her and starting the engine.

Matt looked at her with confusion on his face. "Kidnapped the twins?" he asked.

"Yes!" Kate screamed back at him. "Get in the van!"

Matt and Alaina quickly grabbed some of the hard-plastic cases they were already loading into Moose and jumped into the back of the van.

Matt went to close the rear door as the Major appeared in the opening of the aircraft's cargo bay, out of breath and panting. "Jesus Christ, you guys run fast!" he said, leaning on the side of the aircraft.

"Get in!" Matt shouted, holding the door open for him to get in.

"Hurry up, Major!" Kate yelled from the front.

He ran up the ramp, leapt into the back of the van, and Matt slammed the door shut behind him.

Kate threw the van into reverse and shot out of the aircraft backwards, tyres squealing in protest as they contacted with the apron surface. She stopped the van, changed gear, and then stamped on the accelerator. The van responded and surged forward, hurtling down the long, straight main road of the base as the Major, Alaina, and Matt held on to whatever they could in the back of it.

Up ahead, Kate saw the Golf smash through the lowered boom gate, sending pieces of red and white striped wood flying high into the air. The old security guard manning the gate shuffled out of his cubicle to see what the commotion was as the Golf ploughed through the barbed-wire fence of an adjacent field and disappeared into a cloud of orange dirt.

Shoalwater Bay, Queensland, Australia
9th February 2021
4:02 pm Australian Eastern Standard Time

Kate blasted the horn of the van as she rapidly approached the now gate-less exit. She raced past the gawking guard and launched the van into the same field the Golf had gone into.

It was typical Australian scenery. Dusty, arid, and grassless, except for some scrub and the occasional silver-barked, leafless eucalyptus tree.

Up ahead, the Golf tried to get traction on the loose surface, spewing out clouds of red dust and rocks behind it that pelted the van's windscreen.

"Alaina!" Kate yelled over her shoulder into the back of the van. "Did you bring weapons?"

"I sure did!" Alaina shouted back over the noise of the dirt and gravel clattering into the van. She clicked open one of the hard-plastic cases with one hand while keeping hold of the van with the other as it bounced over the rough terrain. "We have a shotgun, a rifle, and a pistol. What would you like?"

"Pistol!" Kate said.

Alaina took out a 9mm Glock and stretched over the front seat, handing Kate the weapon.

Kate snatched it from her and wound down her window. "Now take the wheel!"

"Do what now?" Alaina asked.

"Take the bloody wheel!"

Alaina scrambled into the front seat and reached across to hold the steering wheel as Kate cocked the pistol and leaned out of the window.

Rocks and dirt pelted her in the face. She narrowed her eyes and held her breath. The shot had to be accurate. Her children were at risk. All she needed to do was slow the car down, that's all. As long as she could prevent the car from digging into the dirt and flipping over, the twins would be safe.

She ducked back into the van momentarily, realising that if the van could get closer to the car, it would increase her chances of making the shot through the dust cloud.

"Steer towards the car!" She shouted.

"What?"

"Trust me!"

Kate took a lung-filling breath of air and returned her head into the dust cloud that was relentlessly pelting the van. She pressed her foot down on the accelerator as Alaina guided the vehicle towards the Golf and steadied herself against the van door as it inched closer and closer to the car.

She slowly let out the breath she had been holding as the dust cloud cleared for a split second, and the rear of the Golf appeared in front of her.

Kate squeezed the trigger.

The right rear tyre of the Golf burst and immediately began shredding itself on the wheel's rim, causing the car to fishtail wildly across the dirt.

Kate dropped back into the driver's seat, took control of the van from Alaina, and guided it alongside the out-of-control Golf.

She peered through the passenger window and, to her horror, saw the Major's wife, Sarah, staring back at her with a look of terror on her face. Next to her, a man wearing a black hoodie was busy wrestling with the steering wheel, fully occupied with keeping control of the car.

Kate needed to act fast, or the car was going to crash, injuring not only her boys, but Sarah as well. She turned the steering wheel violently towards the Golf again. This time, the car slammed into the side of the van, preventing it from fishtailing—but the car didn't slow down. The hooded man had no intentions of stopping, even though he was driving with only three tyres.

Kate sped up, manoeuvring the van in front of the Golf and began slowly pressing down on the brake pedal, causing the car to collide with the rear of the van.

Her plan worked.

As soon as she felt the two vehicles come together, she slammed her foot down harder on the brakes, forcing the Golf to plough into the rear of the van. Within seconds, both vehicles came to an abrupt stop and Alaina threw open the sliding side door, pointing her shotgun at the cloud of dust engulfing the car behind them.

"Get out of the car!" Alaina shouted.

Kate heard a car door open from somewhere inside the cloud of dust, but couldn't fire her weapon. Neither could Alaina. There was too much risk. She could hear the twins screaming in the car and the distressing noise of Sarah sobbing.

As painful as it was, Alaina and Kate waited patiently for the driver to emerge from the dust cloud, or for the dust to settle; whichever came first.

"Nobody fire," Kate said.

"Why not?" Matt asked.

"Sarah and the twins have been through enough. We don't need to terrify them any further by firing weapons."

"What if he fires first?"

"Then he leaves us no option."

Before the airborne dirt had time to settle, the driver made his move. Bursting from the dust cloud, he ran for cover in the nearby scrub, zig-zagging his way across the ground, making it difficult for anyone to shoot him.

Kate, Alaina, and Matt didn't fire their weapons. Instead, they watched him weave towards a thicket of scrub and disappear behind it.

"We'll find you!" Kate yelled after him before quickly turning her attention to the Golf. Matt remained focused on the scrub while the Major extracted a petrified Sarah from the car. "What happened?" he asked into her ear as they held each other tightly.

"That man burst into the office, grabbed the boys, held a gun to my head… oh, Richard, it was terrifying," she said, burying her head into his chest and sobbing.

"You're safe now," he said as he stroked her hair. "Everything's okay."

Kate threw open the rear door of the Golf and the boys reached up for her with tears streaming down their faces. She threw her arms around them and squeezed.

Alaina opened the opposite door and poked her head in. "Are they okay?" she asked.

"Aunty Awaina!" Liam cried, reaching up and grabbing Alaina around the neck.

Kate picked up Kane and turned to the Major. "Would you mind taking care of the boys for me? We have some *business* we need to attend to."

The Major stared at her for a moment. "Sure," he replied. "Just be careful."

Kate looked down at Kane in her arms and then over at Liam with Alaina. "Mummy won't be long, okay?" she said to both of them. "Aunty Sarah and Uncle Richard will look after you. I'll be back soon."

The boys nodded to her as they wiped away their tears with the back of their hands.

"I think it might be for the best if we make our way back to base with the twins," the Major said. "I'll put the spare on, and we'll take the Golf back. It doesn't seem too badly damaged. We'll meet you there."

"Thanks, Major. Don't let these boys out of your sight, please."

"Don't worry. I won't."

Kate kissed the twins on the forehead and handed them over to the Major. She gave them a wave as she got into the van with Alaina and Matt and drove towards the scrub where the hooded man had disappeared moments earlier.

They scoured the clumps of scrub as Alaina drove around, but there was no sign of the man in the hoodie.

"Keep driving, Alaina," Kate said, looking out the window. "He can't have got far."

"Do you think he's with them?" Matt asked, peering out the window next to her.

"I'm not sure. But we have to find out."

Matt shook his head. "I don't get it. We've been in Shoalwater for three years and haven't heard a thing from White Cloud. What reason would they have to show up now?"

"If I had to guess," Kate said. "I would say they are getting ready to attack again."

"What makes you think that?"

"They know we're responsible for what happened in Peru. The kidnapping of the boys was more than likely a way to get our attention."

Matt took a moment. "You think someone sent this guy to kidnap your boys and use them as blackmail against you?"

Kate nodded. "Yes. It's possible. It's what they do. They kidnapped me to get Sol to comply, remember? They know we're alive, Matt, and if we're alive, it means Viribus is still a threat."

Matt smiled. "You're God damn right we are."

"We need to find this guy and find out exactly where he came from."

They continued scouring the scrubland and half an hour later, the sun dipped below the horizon, plunging the area into twilight and subsequent darkness. As the van bounced over the rough terrain in search of the hooded man, Alaina suddenly squealed and slammed on the brakes, throwing Kate and Matt forward in the back of the van.

"What the hell was that for?" Kate asked, picking herself up off the floor.

Alaina pointed to something in front of her. "Look," she said.

Kate looked at where Alaina was pointing. What she saw chilled her to the core. In the light of the headlights, a tall thin man wearing a black hooded tracksuit stood 20 yards in front of them, holding a machete by his side.

Alaina revved the van's engine, hoping to scare him—but the man didn't move.

It was a standoff.

"That's a fucking big knife," Matt whispered.

Alaina floored the accelerator.

The man didn't flinch as the van sped towards him.

Alaina didn't slow down.

Kate looked away and winced, waiting to hear the man's bones crunching against the front of the van.

"Holy shit!" Alaina screamed.

Kate opened her eyes to see the man leap up onto the hood of the van and run up onto the roof.

She heard his footsteps thump on the metal roof above her and moments later, the machete blade plunged through the ceiling with a metal-on-metal squeal as it pierced the skin of the van, mere millimetres in front of her face.

Alaina slammed on the brakes, sending the man tumbling off the roof and landing with a thud on the dirt in front of them.

They watched the man roll to a stop, and then, for a moment, there was complete silence—except for the noise of the incessant cicadas chirruping outside and the idling diesel engine of the van. Kate looked up at the machete stuck in the roof. "Who the hell is this guy?" she asked.

Alaina quickly switched her foot to the accelerator and headed straight towards the lifeless body lying in the dirt.

"What are you doing?" Kate shouted—but she was too late. Alaina drove the van over the body, causing the van to rock from side to side, and then stopped.

"Jesus Christ, Alaina. I think you got him," Kate said.

"Hang on," Alaina said, throwing the van into reverse and staring into the rear-view mirror. "I'd better make sure of that." She slammed her foot on the accelerator again, and the van surged backwards.

Kate winced, expecting to hear another sickening, bone-crunching thud from underneath the van—but it didn't come.

Alaina brought the van to a stop and turned around to Matt and Kate. "Where'd he go?" she asked.

"I don't know," Kate said, looking out of the rear window, "But we have to find him."

Arming herself with a shotgun and a pistol, Kate threw open the side door and heard rustling emanating from a patch of scrub to her right.

"I know you're injured!" she shouted into the darkness. "It's only a matter of time before we find you! Just come out now!"

The rustling stopped.

Matt and Kate walked towards where the noise had come from, guns drawn and ready to fire. Kate could hear herself breathing—it was far too loud—as was the noise of the giant Australian cicadas chirruping around her. She wished they would take a break.

They stopped walking to allow them to listen for more noises.

"Oh, wait! I forgot!" Matt whispered as he pulled out a torch from his pocket and shone it into the undergrowth.

"You could have done that sooner!" Kate said.

Matt shone the torch towards the area where the rustling noise had come from, and as the torch beam streaked across a clump of scrub, the man leapt into the torchlight, emitting a scream that would haunt them both for years to come. With an arm hanging limply by his side, he charged at Kate and Matt like a wounded zombie.

Kate raised her shotgun, aimed it at the onrushing, zombie-like man, and pulled the trigger.

The shot tore the man's arm from his shoulder, and he fell to the ground. For a moment, the screaming stopped. As did the chirruping cicadas.

Matt shone his torch at the body and dry retched.

"Ah, shit. I can't stomach body parts not being where they are supposed to be, man."

Kate snatched the torch from him and went closer to the armless man.

She could hear him shallow breathing. He was losing blood fast. "Who are you?" she asked, kneeling beside him.

The man gurgled up some blood and stared at her.

"Where are you from?" she probed.

He sneered a toothy, blood-stained smile back at her.

"Fuck… you," he spluttered.

"Who sent you? Was it White Cloud?"

He stared up at her for a moment before his eyes rolled back into his head, and he stopped breathing.

"Shit!" she said.

"Don't worry about it," Matt said. "Leave him for the eagles and the dingoes. We have more important things to take care of—like getting the fuck out of Shoalwater Bay."

"I totally agree, but we need to find out who this guy is and where he came from," she said. "Just wait a minute."

With the torch in one hand, she patted the other over the body for anything that might reveal the man's identity.

He was carrying nothing.

Kate unzipped the man's hoodie. Underneath was a teal blue shirt with a white pinstripe down the right-hand side. She peeled back the hoodie a little further, exposing the words—*White Cloud*—embroidered on the chest.

She looked up at Matt. "They've found us."

Shoalwater Bay, Queensland, Australia
9th February 2021
6:24 pm Australian Eastern Standard Time

Alaina drove the van across the dusty landscape towards the glow of the lights emanating from the Shoalwater Bay military base. A few minutes later, the van pulled up in front of the hangar and Kate jumped out, closely followed by Matt and Alaina.

Together, they entered the hangar and swung open the door of the briefing room—only to be met by the barrel of a revolver.

"Jesus Christ!" Kate shrieked.

"Oh, it's you," the Major said, immediately un-cocking the weapon and lowering it. "Thank God for that. I didn't think you would make it back alive."

"Oh, ye of little faith," Kate replied with a hand on her chest, trying to calm her heart down from the scare.

She entered the room and saw Sarah sitting with the twins on the floor, entertaining them with a different pile of Lego. The twins leapt to their feet as they realised who was at the door and ran to her side. Kane grabbed her right leg, Liam grabbed the left. She cupped the backs of their heads with her hands and ruffled their hair.

"I assume you got him?" The Major asked, placing the revolver down on a nearby table.

"Yeah, we got him," Kate replied.

"He was White Cloud, wasn't he?"

"Yep."

The Major sighed and nodded. "These guys are bloody pests," he said, staring at the floor and taking a moment to think. "Sarah, would you mind taking the boys somewhere else, darling? I need to talk to Kate in private. The boys don't need to hear what I have to say."

Sarah nodded. "Yes, of course," she said, getting to her feet. "Come on, boys. I'm sure we have some more Lego in the other offices somewhere. Can you help me find it?"

The twins looked up at Kate as they clung to her legs.

"It's fine, boys," she said, looking down at them. "I won't be long. I just need to talk to Uncle Richard, and then I'll come and give you big cuddles."

The boys reluctantly let go of her legs and returned to Sarah, who ushered them into a back office as Matt and Alaina sat down at the table with the revolver upon it.

Once the twins were safely out of earshot, the Major turned to Kate. "Three years ago, you landed in Shoalwater Bay, hell-bent on invading Hong Kong to find Tao. Do you remember that?"

"Yes, I do," she nodded. "And you stopped me."

"That's right, I did—and with good reason, I might add. But now the game has changed. They have found you. And they know you are the face of Viribus now, which means they won't stop until you are out of the picture. You and I both know that the appearance of this ship means something is coming—and none of us know what that is yet—but it is safe to say, your children are strictly off-limits."

She nodded in agreement. "They won't get anywhere near my boys without a fight, Major. I can guarantee you that."

"I once deterred you from going to Hong Kong for this very reason, but after today, I don't think you can wait any longer. You needed to let them make the first move, and now they have moved their chess piece."

"Where do I start?" she asked. "Viribus hasn't been active for almost three years—heck, I don't even know if we still have any operatives out there."

"I'm sure you do somewhere, Kate. You just need to utilise every available resource you have to get Viribus up and running again. Once you do, you can deploy your operatives to find Tao. He is the key to all of this."

"You make it sound easy when you say it like that."

"It *is* easy. You just have to use your resources efficiently. You already have the transport—a C-17 is sitting outside—shit, you even have a pilot," he said, nodding at Alaina. "And Matt can help with the intel. He'll be able to find most of the operatives."

Kate looked at Matt. He grinned back at her with a glint in his eye. She could sense his excitement. Alaina seemed equally enthusiastic sitting next to him. They had been waiting for this day to arrive. She had not.

"However, the greatest resource you have at your disposal right now is sitting at home with your mother," the Major said.

"Alex?" Kate asked.

"Correct. Alexei will be your most valuable asset. He'll enable you to get inside the brain of White Cloud. After all, he was with them for quite some time, wasn't he?"

Kate nodded disappointedly. "Yes, he was."

"He helped Tao to escape White Cloud, didn't he?" the Major asked.

"Yes, he did."

"Then chances are Alex knows something about where Tao may be."

Kate looked at the Major suspiciously. "Are you suggesting he might be in on this?"

The Major shook his head. "Not at all. But it would be prudent of you to discount nothing when it comes to White Cloud or their *ex-members*. They are very good at what they do, and they have people everywhere."

Kate hated to admit it, but the Major was right. White Cloud had proven themselves to be extremely cunning over the years. Even though Alex had pledged his allegiance to her for getting him out of White Cloud alive, she still wasn't entirely sure she could trust him. Admittedly, he had reconciled with her mother, Sue, who seemed to have plenty of faith in him, but that did not mean she had to.

"You need to find out what Alexei knows," the Major continued. "He could very well point you in the right direction. Then you need to find Tao and find out what they are doing."

Kate took a moment to think about this. "But what about the twins? If I go overseas, I can't leave them here."

The Major dismissed her statement with a wave of his hand. "Of course you can. In the morning, my first mission will be to reinforce the base's security protocols. The man we encountered today should never have been allowed to get anywhere near Sarah or the boys. Sarah and I can look after the twins or…" A mischievous smile formed on the Major's face, "You could get Alexei *and* your mother here to look after them for you. Not only will they be familiar faces for the twins, but it also means your entire family will be in the one place and perfectly safe."

Kate smirked. "It also means you can watch Alex, doesn't it?"

The Major chuckled. "You know me only too well, young lady. I will never trust a member of White Cloud, ex or current. The last time I trusted one of them, I got this," he said, pointing at the vertical scar running down the side of his face.

Kate had never asked the Major about his disfigurement, and it seemed rude to point it out.

"We will do whatever we can to support you," he said. "After all, it is more than likely in the best interests of *everyone*."

"Thank you, Major."

"Come. Use the phone in my office to talk to your mother and Alexei. That phone is encrypted, so the call will be completely secure."

Kate followed the Major into his office and sat down at the desk. He handed her the receiver and dialled a number on the phone's base station.

He stopped tapping the buttons. "Now, just type in Alexei's number, and you should be good to go. Let's hope he's home."

Kate dialled her mother's phone number from memory. It rang. A few moments later, Alexei answered.

"Kate! How nice to hear from you! How are those grandchildren of mine?" he asked with a distinctive Russian accent to his broken English.

"They're fine, Alex," she said, with no emotion in her voice. She refused to call him *dad*. Alex had been absent for most of her life. Even though he was now back on the scene and playing happy families like nothing ever happened, the reality was that something *did* happen. Something that Kate held him largely responsible for.

Alex had been the catalyst for the events of 2018, which resulted in her husband, Sol, paying the ultimate price for with his life. She could never forgive him for that. His actions had robbed her of a husband and her children of a father. He did not deserve the satisfaction of being called a *dad*—he wasn't worthy of that accolade. It was only because Alex had put his own life on the line to get her out of a tricky situation in Peru, and that her mother was the happiest she had ever seen her, that she now tolerated him. And, as per the Major's advice, she kept a watchful eye over his movements.

Kate got straight down to business, avoiding the irrelevant small talk. "We encountered some trouble earlier today. Would you know anything about that?"

There was a brief pause on the line. "What kind of *trouble* are you talking about?"

"A *White Cloud* kind of trouble," she said.

Alex sighed. "I was hoping you would not say that. How do you know it has anything to do with White Cloud?"

Kate told him about the container ship she had seen out at sea and the attempted kidnapping of the twins by the man with the White Cloud logo on his shirt.

"I beg your pardon. They did what?" Alex asked.

"They tried to kidnap the twins," she repeated.

Alex went silent for a moment, which only grew Kate's suspicion. "What do you know?" she asked.

"I don't know anything. I promise you. I have had nothing to do with White Cloud since Peru."

"But you still have contacts, don't you?"

"Of course I do. You don't spend 36 years in an organisation and leave with no friends. But you banned me from contacting anyone, remember? I have done everything you told me to do."

"Well, now I need you to do something else. Because now they are threatening *your* family. If you are true to me, true to your grandchildren, and true to my mother, you will supply me with whatever information you can get your hands on."

She didn't give Alex a chance to respond. "I'm sending Alaina and Matt to pick you both up in two hours. Be ready. I'll explain everything when you get here."

She put the phone down and returned to the briefing room. "Alaina, prepare Moose. You and Matt are going to Brisbane to pick up Mum and Alex."

"No problem," Alaina said, getting up from her seat.

"Matt, go with Alaina," Kate said. "But I also need you to engage as many remaining Viribus operatives as you can. Put them on high alert. Instruct them to be vigilant and find out whatever they can about any White Cloud movements. We need to be on guard."

"No worries, Kate. Can do." Matt said, packing away his laptop.

Kate could tell they were excited. Alaina was already outside the room, holding the door open, waiting for Matt to follow her through it. They both enjoyed being a surrogate auntie and uncle to the twins, but it wasn't what they knew.

This is what they knew.

Fly planes, get intel, and hunt White Cloud.

This was what they were trained for.

Kate followed them out to Moose and helped them load the van into the cargo bay. "Be back by midnight," she said, giving them both a hug. "If you're not back by then, I'll send out a search party."

Ten minutes later, the aircraft took off into the darkness, bound for Brisbane.

PAPA

Following the departure of Alaina and Matt, Kate returned to the hangar and found her boys fast asleep on a small two-seater sofa in the office's reception area. Sarah sat next to them and had made the twins comfortable with a few blankets and pillows.

"Thank you, Sarah," Kate said, as she scooped the boys up in her arms. "I appreciate all of your help."

"You're most welcome, Kate. They're no trouble at all. They just ran completely out of energy. It's been quite an emotional day for them."

"For you, too," Kate replied. "You've been through quite a traumatic event as well. You should get some rest, and if you need to talk, please come and find me."

Sarah chuckled. "I won't rest," she said, looking over at the Major in his office. "Richard is far too excited about all of this now. He's going to be up all night."

Kate smiled at her. "Everything will get back to normal soon. I promise."

Sarah gave her a tight-lipped smile. "That depends on what your definition of *normal* is, I suppose. I don't think anyone really knows what that is anymore. I know I haven't known *normal* since… well, since you turned up."

"I'm sorry," Kate said. "I never meant to ruin anyone's life. I'm only trying to make things better for everyone."

Sarah laughed. "You don't need to be sorry! It was you who stopped everything from getting worse! Kate, people are praising you for what you did. You're considered a hero; did you know that?"

Kate didn't know that. She was in hiding. No one knew where she was except for her mum and Alex. She never turned on the television or radio and didn't own a cell phone. She had no desire to know what had happened to the world after the attacks or what the world thought of her. She only thought about her children and close family.

Kate shrugged. "Well, I think I'm ready to have *normal* back," she said.

Sarah smiled warmly again. "I'd like that too, Kate. Richard believes in you just as much as I do. Go and nail these bastards once and for all!"

Kate smiled as she hoisted a boy over each of her shoulders in a firefighter's lift fashion, as she always did when the boys had crashed. "I'll do my best," she said.

The Major escorted her out of the hangar and across the road to her on-base accommodation. It was a normal-looking house, just like the ones you'd find on any regular suburban street, however these houses were normally used for military personnel with their family in tow.

The house had allowed Kate to raise her twins with some regularity while still having the protection of the military-guarded metal fence line surrounding them.

Although that protection was now in jeopardy.

Kate was confident that the Major would do his best to fix that problem, and she believed that security would be tripled by lunchtime tomorrow. However, this did not stop her from feeling uneasy.

Something was stirring in the atmosphere.

She could feel it.

White Cloud wasn't finished. She knew that, and she was sure the Major knew it too.

As she opened the door to the house, her loyal dog, Roxy, ran up to her with her tail wagging. The lumbering Rhodesian Ridgeback licked her legs as she entered and sniffed at the boy's hands hanging behind her back to make sure they were all part of the pack.

"Hey Rox," Kate said, patting the dog on the head. "You're officially on duty now, okay?"

Roxy licked her leg again, as if responding to her pack leader's command.

Kate took the boys upstairs and put them to bed while the Major waited downstairs in the lounge, staring out the window overlooking the front garden as if he too was on guard dog duty.

A short while later, Kate returned downstairs. "You don't have to stay, Major. I'll be fine," she said.

"I think I'll wait until the others get back. I don't want you to be alone."

Kate furrowed her brow a little. "But Sarah is alone, Major, and you should be with her. Don't worry; I have Roxy here. She will surely let me know if there is any trouble coming."

The Major looked down at Roxy, who had fallen asleep on the floor. "That dog doesn't look like it could frighten a thing."

"Looks can deceive, Major. She is just conserving her energy."

He smiled and thought to himself for a moment. "Okay. If you think you'll be alright, I'll go back to the hangar." He reached into his jacket and pulled out a hand-held two-way radio. "But just to be on the safe side, I want you to have this. Use channel one if you need me for anything."

Kate took the radio from him and smiled. "Okay, Major. Thanks."

"I'll see you in the morning."

He shut the door behind him as he left, leaving Kate alone with Roxy and her boys, who were now sound asleep upstairs.

She clipped the hand-held radio to her belt as she walked into the kitchen. There, she opened a cupboard above the kitchen counter and took out a hard, black plastic case. She flicked open the latches of the case, pulled out a pistol and cocked it before sitting on the bottom step of the stairs leading towards the boy's bedrooms.

She stared at the front door in silence. Waiting.

A couple of hours later, the sound of a large aircraft screamed over the house. Kate heard the aircraft's tyres screech on the surface of the base's runway in the distance, shattering the silence.

She looked at her watch.

11:34 pm

Alaina had made good time.

Kate was excited to see her mum and knew the boys would be too when they woke up. She had to admit; she was not as excited to see Alex. On the few occasions she had seen him since the events in Peru, all he reminded her of was the loss of Sol. He was a permanent reminder of that trauma.

Although this time, she hoped he was bringing some vital information she could use to protect her children and stop White Cloud.

Twenty minutes later, the van pulled into the driveway, and Kate heard its doors open. She got up from the bottom step of the stairs and opened the front door.

Sue threw her arms around her and burst into tears. Alex stood behind Sue with their luggage in his hands.

"Good to see you, Mum," Kate said. "I'm sorry we've had to do this."

"It's fine, dear. We all knew this day was coming, didn't we? I'm just thankful you're all okay."

Kate stepped back and held her mother's hands. "Alex told you what happened?"

Sue swept away the tears as she nodded. "Yes, he did. Matt and Alaina filled in the gaps on the way here."

"Okay, good. Come inside. I need to talk to both of you. Where's Alaina and Matt?"

"They're securing some things in van," Alex said in his irritating broken English.

"What *things*?" Kate asked.

"I brought *things* for you," Alex said with a wink. "I do not need them anymore, but you might."

Kate looked at him suspiciously. "*Legal* things?"

"You should not ask questions like those," he said with a smile. "You may not want to know answer."

"Speaking of answers, were you able to get anything?" she asked.

"Sure. But let's go inside to talk, shall we?"

Kate could tell he was nervous. Even though he had the security of being on a military base, he still checked over his shoulder as he entered the house and closed the door behind him.

They went into the lounge and sat on the couch. Sue went into the kitchen to make some tea, like she always did.

Alaina and Matt entered the kitchen from the adjoining garage and sat at the dining room table overlooking the lounge area.

Alex shuffled in his seat and cleared his throat, waiting for his audience to settle. All eyes were on him, apart from Sue, who was busying herself with making the tea.

"Do you remember a man called Mike Royle?" he asked.

Kate recoiled a little at the name. Mike Royle was Sol's colleague and friend—that was until Mike led Sol into the clutches of White Cloud and initiated the entire horrific series of events.

When Kate discovered Mike was involved with White Cloud, she made sure he never showed his face again by beating him to within an inch of his life.

"Yes, of course, I remember him," Kate replied. "I warned that rat-faced idiot what would happen if we ever crossed paths again. Don't tell me he has something to do with all of this," she said.

Alex complied with her demand and said nothing.

"What are you doing?" Kate urged.

Alex looked at her, confused. "You just said not to say if he had something to do with it."

"Jeez, it's a figure of speech, Alex. How is Mike involved?"

"He is *very* involved. White Cloud promoted him to Oceania sector leader to fill the position Sol had vacated."

"No way," Kate said, staring at Alex open-mouthed. "You have *got* to be joking."

Alex looked confused again. "I do not joke, Kate."

"Yes, I know you don't. Another figure of speech— have you not picked up on any Australian sayings while you've been here?" She shook her head. "Anyway, who told you all this?"

Alex looked at the ground. "If I tell you that, I risk never being able to use source again, and under current circumstances, I think we might need them in future. I only tell you this now because we are on secure military base."

"That doesn't mean any of us are safe," Alaina chimed in. "The guy who tried to kidnap the twins got onto the base undetected. It can happen again."

Kate respected Alex's stance. She realised he was taking a risk by being an informant for her. Although if she didn't ask, Alex wouldn't tell. She questioned him from a different angle.

"Did your source say anything else?" she asked.

"No. Nothing. That's all they could give me."

Kate glared at him as he stared at the floor with his hands clasped together between his legs. She could sense there was something else he needed to say.

"You're not lying to me, are you?" she asked.

Alex snapped his head around and looked her straight in the eye. "No. I am not. You have my word. I have nothing to gain by lying, but I have much to lose."

Kate studied his face. He seemed genuine enough, but this face had done many years of deceiving. He was trained in the art. The Major's words popped into her head—*do not trust any of them.*

"So, you're suggesting I find Mike Royle?" Kate asked.

Alex nodded. "All I am saying is he would be weakest link. Put him under pressure, and he will surely squeal like pig in china shop."

Kate frowned at him. "You mean, *bull* in a china shop."

Alex shrugged.

Sue came in and put a cup of tea and two biscuits in front of each of them. "I can't wait until morning, dear. I have to see my beautiful grandchildren," Sue said, touching Kate on the shoulder. "Don't worry, I won't wake them. I just want to see their faces, that's all."

Kate smiled at her. "Okay, Mum."

Sue left the room and went upstairs to the boy's room.

Kate picked up her cup of tea and dunked a biscuit into it, losing herself in thought for a moment.

"You're right, Alex. Mike will squeal, and I think I know how to find him, but that's a phone call that will have to wait until morning." She took a sip of the tea. "Did your source say anything about why that ship is out there?"

Alex sighed. "I do not require my source for that information."

Kate shuffled forward in her chair. "Why not?"

Alex sighed again—deeper this time. "Before I met you in Dubai, White Cloud was already in process of hijacking a ship in Los Angeles. It was their backup plan should the aircraft attacks fail."

"Backup plan?"

"Yes. They always have a secondary plan in case the other one fails. They planned to take over cargo ship, along with captain, and sail it out of Los Angeles. Then they would modify it to carry weapons and vehicles, turning it into sea-going battle station. This way, they could conduct business in international waters where they would be untouchable by authorities and far enough away from Viribus."

"Okay! Brilliant!" Kate said, with a smile on her face and waving her soggy biscuit in the air. "So it's simple! If we blow the ship up, we end White Cloud, right?"

Alex shook his head. "No. It is *not* that simple, Kate. This is why White Cloud has not shown itself for last three years. They have been busy changing ship—installing cannons, anti-aircraft missiles and other self-defence mechanisms. If you go anywhere near it, it will blow you off face of Earth."

Kate thought about this for a moment. "So, you're telling me they have created a warship out of an everyday cargo ship to carry their toys and personnel around in?"

Alex nodded. "Precisely."

"How do you know all this?"

Alex stared at her for a moment and took a nervous breath. "Because I am man who designed it," he said, as a small red laser dot appeared on his forehead.

Shoalwater Bay, Queensland, Australia
9th February 2021
11:57 pm Australian Eastern Standard Time

Roxy jolted from her slumber and began loudly barking at the glass sliding door leading to the backyard. Matt saw the red dot on Alex's head and put the two together—Roxy barking, the red dot. Someone was outside, aiming a weapon at Alex's head through the glass door.

In the blink of an eye, he leapt to his feet, and threw himself in front of the laser beam at the precise moment the bullet shattered the glass door. His shoulder spat out a splash of blood, and he clutched at the wound instantly, grimacing in agony as blood oozed through his fingers.

As she watched Matt get shot, Kate dropped her cup of tea, whipped out her pistol, and began firing it towards where the bullet had come from. Alex ran into the garage as Sue appeared in the doorway from upstairs, her eyes as wide as dinner plates.

Alaina grappled Matt to the floor, removing him from the line of fire, and quickly tore a strip of material from her t-shirt, scrunching it up into a ball, and holding it onto the wound to stem the bleeding.

"Sue! Take over here!" Alaina shouted over the noise of Kate's pistol fire. "Stop this bleeding!"

Sue ran across the room, took the blood-soaked piece of material from Alaina, and pushed it onto the wound. Alaina got up and ran after Alex, following him into the garage.

Kate continued to fire her pistol as she walked through the hole in the back door where the glass used to be, entering the darkness of the backyard.

As her eyes adjusted, she noticed a small-framed silhouette climbing over the back fence—just as she ran out of bullets.

"Shit!"

She unclipped the radio from her belt and pressed the button. "Major? Are you there?" she said into it.

She expected the Major to be asleep, so it seemed only fair to give him a few seconds to respond. However, the Major replied instantly—almost as if he had been waiting by the radio.

"Yes, Kate. I'm here," he said through the radio.

"We've got another uninvited guest," she said. "Matt's been shot. They're getting on the base somehow. There's someone running across the airfield as we speak."

"I thought I heard gunshots. I'm on my way."

"No. That's why I am contacting you. I need you to stay where you are. Lock your doors, arm yourself, and take care of Sarah."

"But—"

"No *buts*, Major. I have enough people here. We can handle it, but you need to alert security immediately."

"No problem, I can do that. Keep me posted."

Alex and Alaina appeared out of the garage behind her, brandishing AK-47 assault rifles.

"Where is he?" Alex said.

Kate's eyes widened at the sight of the weapons in their hands. "Where in God's name did you get those?"

"Don't ask," Alex said. "Where did he go?"

"Over the fence," Kate said, nodding at the rear of the garden.

Alex and Alaina raised their rifles in unison and began firing at the fence, spraying it with bullets. Kate covered her ears as the weapons fired either side of her. The crackling gunshots were unbearably loud. Bullets rained upon the fence and the surrounding garden beds, sending shards of wood and chunks of vegetation soaring into the air.

A few seconds later, Alex and Alaina stopped firing and lowered their weapons to reload as the noise dissipated across the airfield on the other side of the fence.

There was an eerie silence for a moment.

"Holy shit," Kate said, her heart beating in her throat. "Do you think you got them?"

Alex shrugged. "Maybe. Although we should confirm the kill."

They all walked forward to what remained of the fence and peered through the holes where the palings used to be. Kate could see the moonlit silhouette of a person limping away into the darkness and towards the airfield's runway.

"They're injured," she said. "But not dead."

"We need to end them," Alex said. "Or they will only keep coming back."

Kate glanced at Alaina. She hated all this violence. She had got caught up in chasing White Cloud through a genuine need to rescue Sol, not because she wanted to kill people. Kate was a nurse by profession and much preferred fixing people rather than destroying them. A Viribus member once called her *a walking contradiction,* and it was Matt who had quoted Winston Churchill to her—*good men fight bravely in the night to rid the world of evil,* or something to that effect. Whatever it was, it made her realise that at times like these, it's sometimes necessary to do the things you don't believe in to achieve a greater outcome.

"We have to finish these people," Alaina affirmed, recognising Kate's internal struggle. "If we don't destroy them, they're going to keep coming back and killing more and more innocent people. You know that."

"Yes. I know," Kate said. "Alex, go back inside and look after Mum and the boys. We can't leave them unguarded."

Alex nodded his agreement and jogged his way back to the house.

Kate looked at Alaina. "Alright, partner. It's you and me. Let's go."

Alaina kicked at the weakened fence palings and knocked down a section of the fence. The hobbling silhouette had now disappeared into the darkness of the airfield on the other side.

Kate and Alaina watched and listened for the slightest movement or noise as they walked. They had not got fifty metres from the house before gunshots broke the silence once more, and it wasn't friendly fire this time.

"Down!" Kate yelled, throwing herself to the ground.

"Where the hell is that coming from?" Alaina shouted over the noise of the gunfire as she landed on the ground next to Kate.

"The lights of the house behind us mean they can see us, but we can't see them!" Kate shouted back.

She could hear the bullets wildly spraying around her in the darkness, fizzing through the air above her head.

"He's going to need to reload soon," Alaina said, handing the AK-47 to her. "When he does, start firing this at him. I'm going back to the house."

"You're leaving me out here alone?"

"No! Well, sort of—but I won't be long. I'm going back to get supplies. I know how to stop this guy, but I need you to entertain him for a minute or two while I go back and get them."

"Entertain him?" Kate asked, with a hint of concern in her voice. "I'm not sure how I am supposed to do that without getting killed. Just don't leave me out here by myself for too long!"

"Don't worry. I'll be back as quick as I can."

A few moments later, the bullets stopped. Just as Alaina had predicted. Taking her window of opportunity, Alaina leapt to her feet and sprinted back to the house as fast as her legs would take her.

Kate continued lying on the ground and fired the AK-47 into the darkness, spraying bullets across the landscape to distract the shooter and cover Alaina.

Fifteen seconds later, her rifle stopped firing.

She pulled the trigger several more times, hoping for a few extra rounds, but the magazine was empty. All she heard was a metallic—*click*.

"Fuck."

The gunshots from the darkness immediately returned. Kate ducked her head, glancing over her shoulder to see if Alaina had made it back to the house, and saw her disappearing through the fence.

She'd made it.

Kate was stuck in the middle of an airfield, with no further way of protecting herself, and if she stood up, would surely be killed. She hoped whatever Alaina had gone back to the house for was going to work.

As she waited for Alaina to return, she made herself as flat as possible amongst the grass as the gunshots got louder—and then they started to get *closer*.

Was this person coming towards her?

She raised her head slowly and saw the small, black figure standing no more than twenty metres in front of her and closing. The rifle muzzle flashes illuminated the shooter as they fired, pinpointing her exact location—and Kate had no bullets left to fight back. It was now that she realised this person was not just a silhouette; they were also dressed entirely in black to blend in with the darkness.

Although she was well camouflaged amongst the long grass, it would only be a matter of time before the shooter would be standing on top of her.

Hurry up, Alaina.

The silhouette sprayed bullets haphazardly around the scenery, searching for her. They knew she was there *somewhere*.

Kate lay as still as she could, desperately hoping the shooter wouldn't find her amongst the grass. For a moment, she was grateful someone had not mowed the airfield recently. Right now, it was the only thing keeping her alive.

The shooter kept advancing towards her—

BOOM!

A thunderous shot came from somewhere behind her, and the gunfire in front of her stopped instantly.

There was an eerie silence as everything went quiet, and Kate slowly raised her head.

The all-in black figure stood motionless in front of her, just five metres away, as the rifle fell from their hands, clattering as it hit the ground. A second later, the figure collapsed on top of it.

"ALL CLEAR, KATE!" Alaina bellowed from somewhere behind her.

Kate slowly got to her feet, brushed herself off and turned her head to see Alaina sprinting across the airfield towards her.

"Are you okay?" Alaina asked as she ran up to her.

"Yeah, I'm fine," Kate replied. "Any longer, though, and I wouldn't have been."

Kate saw the massive weapon strapped to Alaina's back. "What's that?"

Alaina swung the rifle around to her front and stroked the long, black barrel lovingly. "*This* is a Russian Dragunov SVD Sniper rifle. One of the best sniper rifles ever made, in my opinion. It may be a relic, but it is still one of the best."

"How did you even see this guy in the dark?"

Alaina tapped the scope on top of the rifle. "Thermal scope," she said proudly. "Lights up anything with a heat signature."

Alaina was a highly trained sniper. The best of the best. She had trained with some of the world's most elite snipers—and it showed. The Major had once taught Kate the art of sniper spotting to help Alaina, forcing them to work together as a team. It was a partnership that had proved its worth.

"Where the hell are these weapons coming from?" Kate asked.

Alaina waved the question away. "I'll show you later. Right now, we need to search that body. Maybe it holds more information."

"Yes. I'm afraid we do."

They looked down at the body in front of them. It was covered head-to-toe in black neoprene, similar to that of a diving suit. It was a small body, maybe only five feet tall and very thin. The only exposed parts were the now vacant, dark eyes staring towards the sky and a hole in the head from Alaina's bullet.

Kate patted her hand over the zipped pockets of the suit as Alaina pulled back the hood of the suit.

It was a woman of Asian descent.

"Shit. Didn't expect that," Alaina said, as she picked the rifle up off the ground next to the body. "I guess she won't be needing this," she said, slinging the rifle over her shoulder.

Kate's search of the body was yielding nothing, which didn't surprise her. The man who she'd searched earlier also had nothing on it. That was until she placed a hand over a pocket on the woman's leg and felt something solid and square. She unzipped the pocket and pulled out a small, black plastic case—no bigger than a deck of playing cards.

"What's that?" Alaina asked.

Kate shrugged and opened the case. Inside was a small vial of a clear liquid and a single syringe.

"What do we have here?" Alaina asked, looking over Kate's shoulder.

"I don't know," Kate said. "But I'd put money on this person not having a medical condition."

Kate closed the case and tucked it into her pocket.

"Let's get back to the house. It looks like the eagles have another meal."

"There's going to be some awfully fat eagles around here," Alaina said.

They walked back across the airfield, through the broken fence, and into the house. They found Sue had moved Matt onto the couch and continued to hold the bloodied piece of Alaina's shirt on his wound as he groaned in pain.

"Is he okay?" Alaina asked, cautiously stepping through the shattered remains of the back door, crunching through the glass.

"He's okay," Sue replied. "But he's lost a bit of blood. I'm not entirely sure it's as bad as he's making out, though."

Kate went over to Matt and pulled away Sue's hand to inspect the wound. "He'll be fine. The bullet passed through. I'll patch him up in a minute."

Kate turned to Alex and handed him the small black plastic case with the vial of liquid in it. "I don't suppose you know what this is, do you?" she asked.

Alex took the case from her and opened it. He stared at the contents for a moment. "Where did you get this?" he asked.

"The person who just tried to kill you had it on them. In fact, apart from a rifle, it was the *only* thing they had on them."

Alex went a ghostly shade of pale. "Oh no," he said, shaking his head. "No, no, no. This is bad, Kate. Very bad."

"Why? What is it?"

Alex ignored the question and continued to stare at the vial in the case. "I can't believe they've done it."

"Done what, Alex?"

"They always talked about it, but I never thought they would *actually* do it."

Kate snapped the case shut in his hands and snatched it away from him, breaking his focus. "Do *what*, Alex?"

"A long time ago, there were discussions about deploying biological weapons if Viribus were ever to get the upper hand on White Cloud." He nodded at the case. "If that is what I think it is, it seems someone is not too happy about what you did in Peru."

Kate held the case up. "Are you telling me this is a biological weapon?"

Alex nodded. "Why else would this person be carrying it? I think you also didn't find anything on the guy who tried to kidnap the twins, no?"

Kate shook her head. "No, I didn't."

"I thought as much. White Cloud personnel carry nothing that isn't essential to their mission, and to be honest with you, I'm afraid to find out the reason this person had this with them."

Kate stared at the case in her hand. "We have to stop them."

Alex nodded vigorously. "Yes. We do."

Kate looked over at Matt as Sue dabbed his forehead with a cloth. "We're going to need backup. Which means I will need him fully functioning as soon as possible."

Kate carefully put the small case containing the vial down on the kitchen bench and opened up a drawer. She pulled out a first aid kit, and within minutes, Matt's wound was cleaned, his shoulder professionally bandaged, and two painkillers were shoved into his mouth. He looked drowsy, but he was semi-coherent.

Kate handed him a glass of water to wash the painkillers down with. "Are you okay, mate?" she asked.

Matt took a large gulp of the water and nodded slowly. "Yeah, I think so. My shoulder stings like a bastard, though."

Kate smiled and was somewhat impressed with Matt's adoption of the Australian vernacular. "Yeah, it'll be painful for a while, but you'll be fine. Those painkillers will help. Hey, I need your help if you feel up to it."

Matt nodded as he slowly opened his eyes. "Of course."

"I need you to get in contact with as many Viribus operatives as you can and inform them about White Cloud's battleship stationed in the Pacific Ocean off the east coast of Australia. Tell them White Cloud appears to be planning another global attack, which is potentially biological, so I need everyone to stand up, be alert, and send any snippet of information they can muster to you."

Matt nodded and stretched out his good arm. "Hand me my laptop."

Kate picked up his laptop from the coffee table and put it on his lap. He opened it and went to work.

She then turned to Alaina. "Now, show me where these weapons are coming from," she said.

Alaina led her out to the garage and opened the back of the van. Inside were two large, green, military-style metal trunks.

"Jesus, Mary, and Joseph. Where in God's name did these come from?"

Alex appeared behind them in the garage. "I have had these stashed at your mother's house for a long time," he said. "I do not need them anymore."

Alaina excitedly got into the van and opened one of the trunks. "Wait until you see what's inside them!"

Inside the trunks were Kalashnikovs, AK-47s, shotguns, knives, pistols of various calibres and even a container full of hand grenades. It was a typical Russian spy's toolbox.

"I suppose I don't ask where these come from either?" Kate asked.

"It's probably best you don't," Alex said. "Although you are welcome to use whatever you need."

Kate hoped she wouldn't need any of it, but better to have it and not need it, than to need it and not have it.

"Thank you, Alex."

"Not a problem."

Alaina closed the trunks.

"We only have a few hours before the sun rises," Kate said. "I need to make a phone call first thing in the morning, and then we're going after Mike Royle to find out what he knows."

Shoalwater Bay, Queensland, Australia
10th February 2021
4:10 am Australian Eastern Standard Time

As dawn broke over Shoalwater Bay, Kate stormed into the Major's office, sat down at his desk, and dialled a number from memory using the secure line.

"Allied Maintenance, Hangar One," an over-enthusiastic female voice answered.

"I need to speak with Barry, please."

"Yes, of course. I will see if he's available. Who may I say is calling?"

"Tell him it's Kate. He'll know who I am."

"Okay. Please hold."

The receptionist flicked a switch and put the call on hold, as joyful melodic music blared through the phone. It sounded like the music you would hear in a supermarket or an elevator and certainly didn't feel appropriate for the moment.

A few seconds later, the music clicked off, and a familiar voice interrupted.

"Kate?"

"Hey, Baz," Kate replied.

"I haven't heard from you since... well, all that shit happened."

Barry, or Baz, as he was more affectionately called, used to be Sol's supervisor when Sol had worked at the aircraft maintenance hangar. Over the years they had worked together, Baz and Sol became good friends. There had been several occasions when Baz and his wife would come to their house for a barbeque and a few beers on the weekend, which meant Kate had got to know Baz just as well as Sol.

"Unfortunately, a *lot* has happened since then," Kate said. "Look, sorry to spring this on you, but I need some information."

"Of course, happy to help if I can. What's wrong?"

"Does Mike Royle still work there?"

"No. He left about eighteen months ago. Why do you ask?"

Kate ignored the question. "Do you know where he went?"

There was a brief pause. "I'm sorry, Kate. I can't give you that information. It would be a breach of the company's privacy policy. I could get in serious trouble if someone were to find out I gave you that."

Kate took a deep breath.

"Okay. Well, excuse me for being a little blunt here, Baz, but I need to explain a few things. Now, I am *extremely* pushed on time, so I will only give you the highlights of my current situation. Three years ago, Mike was manipulated by an international extremist group called *White Cloud,* who used him to get to Sol."

"What did they want with Sol?"

"Do you recall the aircraft that fell out of the sky?"

"Yes, of course I do."

"White Cloud required Sol to program those aircraft to do the things they did. They brainwashed him, used me as bait, and made him do things he wouldn't normally do."

There was another pause on the line while she let Baz do the computations in his head. "You're saying Sol was responsible for those aircraft coming down?"

"Unfortunately, yes. It was me who stopped him and White Cloud from killing thousands more."

"Jesus Christ, Kate. I'm so sorry. I knew none of this. We were told Sol and Jane had died in the LA incident. We didn't know the two things were related."

Jane was Sol's apprentice and also fell under Baz's line of supervision. She heard him swallow hard and sniff, choking back tears.

"I didn't expect you to know that. They don't want anyone to know the facts. The A380 incident in LA where Sol and Jane were supposedly *killed* was set up by White Cloud. They crashed that aircraft to get to Sol."

"Sol *wasn't* on the aircraft?"

"No. He got off the aircraft somehow. I don't know how, but I can only assume they took him off."

"But Jane *was* on it?"

"Yes. I'm afraid she was. Baz, the reason I am calling you is that White Cloud has resurfaced, and I've been informed that it is entirely possible Mike Royle is now a key member within the group. So I hope you can now appreciate why I'm in a rush. I will ask you once more—where is Mike?"

Baz sniffed. "He moved to Longreach."

"*Longreach?* What's he doing there?"

"I don't know. He handed in his resignation and moved out there. Happened real quick too, said something about working on vintage aircraft, and then he just vanished."

"Do you think he might still be there?"

"I *know* he's still there. If he's trying to hide, he's doing a terrible job of it. He puts posts on Facebook, tagging his location as *Longreach*."

"What an idiot."

"Yeah."

"All right. I have to go. Take care, Baz."

"You too."

She hung up the phone.

"Get anything?" the Major asked as she walked out of the office.

"Yeah, do you know where Longreach is?"

"Middle of Queensland somewhere," the Major replied. "Dust-bowl town with one pub and a petrol station. About a nine-hour drive west of here. You'd be there in under an hour in Moose."

"Excellent. Then that's where we're heading."

"Why? What's in Longreach?"

"A man called Mike Royle. Leader of the Oceania sector of White Cloud. The fat dirtbag is bound to know something about all of this, and if he doesn't, we'll use him as bait. How's the security situation?"

"I've doubled security and stationed checkpoints all over the base," the Major said. "No one is getting in or out of here unnoticed."

"Very good. Keep it that way. We have to get moving. I'll see you later, Major."

"Take care, Kate."

Kate left the hangar and walked back to the house. She found Alex and Sue fast asleep in the lounge chairs while Alaina sat with Liam and Kane, watching Shrek for the one-millionth time. Matt sat on the couch and was busy tapping the keys of his laptop.

Kate smiled at him. "Glad to see you're feeling better, soldier! Feel like a road trip?"

Matt smiled at her and pushed his glasses up his nose. "Give me some more of those drugs, and I will."

Kate threw the painkillers across the room at him and nodded at the laptop on his knees. "Have you made any contact?"

"I sure did. We have Viribus Operatives in Russia, Hong Kong, the UK, and the States," Matt said without looking away from the laptop screen.

"You've put them all on high alert?"

"Sure have."

"Good work. While you're there, could you also see if there's an airfield at a place called Longreach for me? It's in the middle of Queensland somewhere."

Matt looked up at her quizzically before tapping on the laptop again and staring at the screen for a moment.

"Yep, Longreach has an airfield," he said. "Although I'm not too sure if we'll be able to get Moose in there—"

"Wanna bet on that?" Alaina said, without taking her eyes off Shrek. "I'll get that plane in anywhere."

Kate sat on the floor next to the boys in front of the television and hugged them. "Grandad and Grandma are going to look after you for a bit while mummy goes and finds some bad people, okay?"

Both of the boys nodded.

"I'll be back as soon as I can. I promise. Uncle Richard and Auntie Sarah are just across the road and will come and check on you all the time, okay?"

The boys nodded again and stood up to hug her.

Kate went over to her mum and Alex, tapping them both on the shoulder. Sue roused from her slumber. "Kate? What are you doing, dear?"

"I have to go, Mum. I need you and Alex to take care of the twins for me."

"Of course, dear. We're happy to help. Those buggers will have to get through granny and grandad before they hurt anyone in *our* family."

Kate smiled. "Thanks, Mum. I feel better already. Alex, the Major is putting base security on high alert, so I don't expect anyone to be troubling us here anymore. However, as a precaution, I'd like you to stay alert and look after mum and the twins while we're gone."

"Got it," Alex said.

"And stay away from the windows. We don't need you getting shot at again."

Alex smiled a little. "Understood."

Sue stared up at her for a moment before leaning forward in her chair. *"Are we in danger, dear?"* she whispered, quiet enough so the boys didn't hear.

"That's what I'm going to find out, Mum."

Kate left the lounge and went upstairs to change into the tactical and tech-laden outfit Matt had made for her when they'd first met in Dubai.

She was surprised it still fit her after having the twins, even if it was a little more *snug* now.

She went downstairs and took the little black case containing the virus off the kitchen bench and tucked it into a pocket on her suit.

She saw Alex looking at her. "You never know," she said. "I might just need that."

He smiled.

QUEBEC

Broad Key, Florida, United States
27th August 2015
5:35 pm Eastern Standard Time

Ezekiel *Zeke* Horowitz stood atop the majestic, marble-lined staircase in the mansion of his Florida estate, looking out over the crowd of people in the great hall below.

Zeke was the CEO of a hugely successful pharmaceutical company and would often entertain influential people from all over the globe. His lavish dinner functions had become renowned for their opulence and extravagance, and tonight was going to be no exception.

He stood waiting for his only son and heir, Roman, who was tediously late to every function his father demanded he attend, much to Zeke's frustration.

Roman knew Zeke was grooming him to be his successor, but wasn't at all interested in the responsibility of running the business in the event of his father's absence. However, now that he had reached his early twenties, he'd become *extremely* interested in one particular product of the business—the money.

Despite Roman's obvious opposition towards leading the company, Zeke persevered. Demanding Roman's attendance at key strategic business meetings and the occasional dinner function, hoping that when the time came, he would have been subjected to enough of the lifestyle and the business strategy to, at the very least, keep the company within the family.

Zeke had invited several high-level guests from his pharmaceutical empire's Chinese contingent for tonight's event and had again insisted on Roman's attendance. The Chinese sector of his business was currently performing incredibly well, and Zeke wanted Roman to meet the people responsible for keeping him in nice clothes and fancy cars.

Roman eventually appeared at his father's side, dressed in jeans and a t-shirt. He looked out over the tuxedo-wearing guests below and leaned towards his father's ear. "Father, was it you who instructed everyone to dress like a penguin?"

Zeke shot him a dismissive glance and looked him up and down. "Yes, it was. If I hadn't, I risked everyone turning up looking like you," he scoffed, before descending the staircase towards his guests, denying Roman any chance to argue. Roman shoved his hands into his pockets and nonchalantly strolled down the staircase behind his father, who was already ten strides ahead of him.

The great hall of the mansion in Zeke's Florida estate was vast and comfortably accommodated the 500 invited guests. In the centre of the hall, a giant ice sculpture carved into the shape of an ornamental Chinese Dragon dominated the room in honour of the attending Asian contingent. This exceptional work of art created a prominent focal point among the guests—many of them stopping to have their picture taken next to the exquisite sculpture.

Floor to ceiling windows lined the perimeter of the expansive hall, and huge ornate crystal chandeliers hung from the ceiling. Beyond the oversized windows were gold-trimmed balconies that looked out over a private floodlit golf course surrounding the property.

Zeke smiled as he approached a small group of guests. "Welcome! It's wonderful to meet you all," he said as he began working his way around the group, shaking their hands and bowing to each person individually.

Roman caught up to Zeke and stood behind him.

"Allow me to introduce my ever-punctual son, Roman," Zeke said, forcing a smile.

Roman shook their hands but didn't bow to them like his father had. Instead, he let the Chinese businessmen bow to him.

Zeke sensed their disapproval. "Roman, it's polite to return the bow," he snapped through clenched teeth.

"Why should I?" Roman snapped back at his father. "It's not my culture."

The Chinese men scoffed in disbelief at Roman's insolence. Zeke needed to recover quickly.

"Get us some drinks," he ordered, waving his hand at Roman.

"Get them yourself!" Roman retorted. "I'm not your butler."

Zeke grabbed Roman by the arm and hastily spun him away from the gathering of businessmen. "If you *ever* talk to me like that again, I will cut the cord. Do you understand me? You are talking yourself out of an empire, Roman."

Zeke tightened his grip around Roman's bicep and saw a tear well in Roman's eye. He immediately released Roman's arm and huffed as he straightened his tuxedo.

Roman had pushed him too far this time. As Roman also gathered himself together and wiped the tear from his eye, a Chinese businessman appeared between him and his father.

"I'm sorry to interrupt, Mr Horowitz," the man said with his hands together as if in prayer. "But, if I may be so bold, I would like to offer some *friendly* advice to your son."

Zeke shot a glance at Roman. "Of course! Be my guest. But I think you're wasting your time."

The middle-aged Chinese businessman turned to Roman and smiled. He introduced himself again, even though they had met less than a minute before.

"Master Horowitz, my name is Tao Huang. I am a good friend of your father. You need to be mindful that this entire estate, along with your father's empire, will one day be completely under your control."

Tao put an arm around Roman's shoulder and turned him around to face the other Chinese businessmen behind him. "It would serve you well to allow your father to educate you and learn the business you will one day inherit. By bringing you to events like this, your father is trying to show you how to conduct yourself professionally in front of those who support your business."

Roman looked at the group of men staring at him.

"You must know your associates just as well as you know yourself," Tao said. "Respect them, and they will respect you. In Chinese culture, bowing upon greeting someone is a sign of respect. The deeper the bow, the more respect you are showing."

Roman looked at Tao and then at his father.

"Let's start again, shall we?" Tao said, patting Roman on the chest.

Roman moved towards the first Chinese businessman, who held out his hand for him to shake.

Roman shook the man's hand and bowed.

As Roman was facing the floor, mid-bow, the ice sculpture in the middle of the room violently exploded. Shards of ice flew through the air, scattering across the room and pelting the guests as they ducked for cover.

Roman quickly stood upright and saw the group of guests in front of him staring slack-jawed in horror at something behind him. He spun around to see what they were looking at and saw his father clutching at a gaping hole in his neck as blood gushed down his arm and dripped onto the floor.

Zeke then collapsed to the ground, and Roman instinctively leapt to his side as chaos erupted around them.

Guests began screaming and scrambling for the exits as Roman held his father's lifeless body in his arms and began sobbing.

Tao grabbed Roman by the forearm. "We need to get out of here. Come with me. Now!"

Roman shook Tao's hand from his arm and held his father while staring into his vacant eyes, oblivious to the terror surrounding him.

Tao shook Roman's arm again. "Roman! You will be the next to die if you don't move right now! Come with me!"

Roman didn't move.

Tao wrenched Roman to his feet by the arm, pulling him away from his father. "You run with me now!" Tao screamed at him.

Roman reluctantly ran alongside Tao, pushing their way through the crowd of guests towards what seemed to be the same exit everyone else had decided to use to escape.

Tao sensed the danger. They could not stop. Roman would be killed if they stayed still for too long. He needed an alternative escape plan.

He looked around the great hall at the floor to ceiling windows and saw the window on the southern wall had a perfect hole in it, nearly halfway up its length. The sniper's silent bullet must have made the hole, but it hadn't shattered the glass completely. However, the hole gave him an indication of where the shooter might be located.

Tao headed in the opposite direction, heading for the northern window while dragging Roman behind him. As he ran towards the tall window in front of him, he reached down to the ground and picked up a tennis ball-sized block of ice that had separated from the shattered sculpture in the centre of the room, and hurled it as hard as he could at the window pane in front of him.

The glass cracked but didn't break.

A thunderous shot fired from somewhere behind them. This one wasn't silenced. Tao and Roman ducked as they ran, waiting for the impact. A group of guests behind them shrieked in horror. Tao looked over his shoulder, only to see a male guest fall to the floor with a large hole in his face where his eye used to be.

Tao and Roman continued running as fast as they could towards the window the block of ice had cracked. As they closed in on it, Tao wrapped his arms around Roman and leapt into the air, spinning around in flight, and smashing through the glass backwards. They landed on the balcony floor with a thud as a shower of glass rained down around them.

The window they had crashed through was enormous, and they had only broken a small portion of it as they had gone through it. Tao looked up as he lay on his back with Roman face-down on top of him, watching the cracks from the lower section of the window fracture upwards.

"Run! Now!" Tao screamed, recognising the impending danger.

Roman got off Tao as several more fractures raced up the pane of glass, spreading out like an ever-growing spiderweb and emitting loud cracking sounds that could be heard over the commotion inside the hall.

The glass soon gave way, and the entire window came crashing down onto the balcony as Tao and Roman leapt over the gold-trimmed railing, falling onto the soft, green grass of the golf course below. Tao and Roman were now in the open and totally exposed.

Broad Key, Florida, United States
27ᵗʰ August 2015
6:12 pm Eastern Standard Time

Tao sprinted towards the shadows to escape the floodlights of the golf course and get as far away from the mansion as possible. "Roman! Stay close!" he shouted.

Roman desperately tried to keep up.

Tao knew the danger was still present. They had revealed their position by shattering the glass of the mansion window and creating commotion outside. There were sure to be more people lurking around in the darkness somewhere. Although he didn't know where they might be, what weapons they might have, or their motives for this attack. He had to get Roman to safety.

What he hadn't taken into consideration during his escape plan was Roman's fitness. After only a hundred metres, Roman had to stop and bent over with his hands on his knees, gasping for air.

"Roman! Run, or you die!" Tao shouted back at him.

Roman forced himself to keep running and followed Tao towards a patch of darkness between the floodlights.

They pushed their way through some dense vegetation and reached the golf course boundary. Tao crouched down, taking a moment to calculate his options, and giving Roman time to catch up and recover.

Roman arrived a few moments later and crouched next to him, panting.

"Lesson number one," Tao whispered. *"Always be one step ahead of your enemy. Stay as close to me as you can, and do exactly as I do, okay?"*

Roman nodded as he panted.

Tao and Roman breached the vegetation line and ran across the estate's vast, floodlit helipad. Several expensive looking, highly polished helicopters surrounded it, waiting for their owners to return.

Zeke's estate was situated on an island off the coast of Florida, and so, getting there was only by boat or, for the very high rollers, a helicopter.

Darting between the aircraft and using the shadows to maintain their cover, they made their way across the apron of the helipad towards a matte-black Airbus H160 VIP helicopter.

Tao opened the door and climbed inside.

Roman stayed close, as Tao had instructed him to do, and sat in the seat next to him. "Whose helicopter is this?" he asked.

"Mine," Tao said as he quickly flicked a dozen switches and toggled a few levers. The engine whirred in the compartment above them, and the rotor blades began rotating.

As Tao went through a very rapid pre-flight check, Roman stared out of the window and saw a woman with spiky blonde hair striding towards them across the helipad with a weapon raised to her shoulder.

"Oh shit," Roman said.

The woman then opened fire, showering the helicopter with bullets as Roman recoiled in his seat in fear, but Tao didn't flinch. He knew the aircraft was bulletproof.

The bullets skipped off the windows as the woman unloaded her rifle into the helicopter.

Tao quickly raised the collective control, a large handbrake-looking lever on the right of his seat, and the helicopter responded proportionally, ascending into the night sky vertically. Bullets continued to bounce off the aircraft as Tao tilted the aircraft forward and banked away from the helipad.

Tao looked out of his window and saw the blades of another helicopter beginning to rotate on the helipad. "Oh shit," he said. "I think we're about to have some company."

He directed the helicopter towards the ocean. Tao knew that flying close to the surface of the water would make them less detectable. The blackness of the helicopter would help to camouflage them—or so he hoped.

"Keep looking up," Tao said. "If we stay low, they can only attack from above."

Roman craned his head forward, looking up into the blackness of the night sky above them—as a missile came hurtling past his face.

"Holy shit, Tao! They're firing missiles at us!"

"I can see that!" Tao yelled, yanking at the cyclic control stick poking out of the floor and throwing the aircraft sideways.

As the aircraft banked hard to the right, Tao glanced behind them to see where the missile had come from. An enormous helicopter gunship stared back at him as a second missile fired from its pylon-mounted missile silo.

Tao aggressively nosed the aircraft upwards using spectacular evasion tactics as another missile flew past his window, missing them by only a few feet and leaving a trailing plume of white smoke behind it.

Tao levelled off and banked the helicopter hard to the right once more, heading towards a gorge in the coastline.

The gunship followed.

"Hold on to your stomach!" Tao yelled, before slamming the collective forwards and sending the helicopter into a rapid descent towards the opening of the gorge.

Roman felt his stomach leap into his throat as the aircraft quickly plunged from the sky and entered the high-walled crack in the coastline. Once safely concealed within the walls of the gorge, Tao levelled off, allowing Roman's stomach to settle into its correct position.

The rapid descent and dramatic loss of airspeed meant the pursuing gunship had flown over them as they had entered the gorge—and it was now right above them.

Tao positioned the helicopter under the gunship and took a breath. "They can't see us," he said. "Roman, go into the back and get the emergency evac kits. Now."

Roman undid his harness, got out of his seat, and went into the passenger compartment. He rummaged around in several containers and drawers until he found a bright yellow bag under a seat with the words *evacuation kit* embossed on the front. He returned to the cockpit with the bag and sat in his seat.

"Put the life vest on," Tao said.

Roman opened up the bag and pulled out a bright yellow vest. He searched for another. "There's only one vest in here."

"Yes. I know. Put it on. Grab the flare gun from under your seat and be prepared to jump when I tell you to."

"Jump? Are you joking?"

"Do as I say, and you'll survive this. I just hope to God that you can swim."

Roman put the vest over his head and grabbed the flare gun from under his seat.

Tao swooped to the bottom of the gorge, leaving the gunship above them. He then reached across Roman and threw open the door.

"Jump."

"No way!" Roman said, shaking his head.

"Do it, Roman! Or that gunship is going to blow us into pieces!"

Roman sucked in a big breath, closed his eyes, and leapt out of the helicopter, plunging into the ravine below.

He took a gasping breath as he surfaced and looked up towards the noise of the two helicopters beating blades above him. Against the moonlit sky, he witnessed the silhouette of Tao's helicopter heading straight at the gunship like a controlled missile.

Roman watched the helicopter spear into the underside of the gunship. The rotor blades of the two aircraft tangled, causing both aircraft to violently convulse in mid-air. The ensuing explosion lit up the night sky with a blinding orange glow as the tangled helicopter carcasses tumbled into the water below.

Burning pieces of helicopter rained down around Roman as he floated on the surface of the water, watching the wrecks of the two helicopters fall from the sky and splash into the ocean.

Roman bobbed around in the water, his life jacket keeping his head above water, and stared at the two aircraft float on the surface for a few moments, before they slowly disappeared beneath the surface.

Everything was suddenly calm except for the sound of burning fuel and the occasional splash of another piece of helicopter hitting the water. Roman knew no-one could have survived the crash, but listened in hope of any signs of life.

There were no screams of pain, no cries for help. Only the crackle of the burning spot fires and the water lapping at his side.

"Tao!" he shouted.

No response.

"TAO!" he shouted louder.

Still nothing.

He swam towards the spot where the helicopters had sunk. "Tao?" he said, as fear began overriding his feelings of panic. He was alone.

Tao suddenly burst out of the water, coughing and spluttering as he gasped for air.

"Tao!" Roman yelled, paddling towards him as quick as he could and grabbing him by the arm. "Hold on to my vest!"

Tao grabbed him around the neck as he coughed up water. "Roman…" he spluttered. "Do you… do you still… do you still have the flare gun?" he asked wearily.

Roman nodded. "Yeah, it's inside my lifejacket. But it's wet. Will it still work?"

"Yes… fire it."

Roman reached inside his life jacket and pulled out the big barrelled, gun-looking flare cannon. He pointed it at the sky and pulled the trigger.

The flare shot up into the darkness, illuminating them as they floated amongst the floating remains of the helicopter wreckage and pinpointing their location.

"Why did I do that? Who's coming for us?"

"Just wait," Tao said.

A few minutes later, Roman heard the familiar sound of a helicopter getting closer.

Tao smiled. "Lesson number two, Roman. *Always* have a backup plan."

A sleek, black helicopter, similar to Tao's, was soon hovering above them. A rope ladder was thrown out of its side door, unfurling as it dropped towards the water. Roman and Tao swam over to the ladder and held onto it as the helicopter climbed and turned away, heading east.

Shanghai, China
19ᵗʰ January 2018
8:05 pm China Standard Time

Over the next couple of years, Tao assisted Roman with the operational requirements of the empire he had inherited from Zeke, mentoring him to become the business executive his best friend had once desired.

Two and a half years after the Florida ambush, Roman constructed a tower block of his own in Shanghai and handed Tao the keys to a penthouse apartment within the building. The only thing Roman asked in return was for Tao to discover who was responsible for the assassination of his father.

Tao agreed but didn't inform Roman he already knew who had murdered his father. He chose to say nothing, as he felt the young man wasn't ready to handle such volatile information. The boy had power, money, and a desire for revenge—a lethal combination of traits that could only ever end badly.

However, the day eventually came when Tao decided it was time to tell Roman the truth about everything.

Tao entered the neighbouring penthouse and found Roman sitting on his enormous leather couch, dressed in only a bathrobe, watching American Football on a giant projector screen.

"Roman, I need to talk to you," Tao said.

"Hello, Tao. How are you?" Roman said sarcastically, without taking his eyes away from the screen.

"Turn it off, Roman."

Reluctantly, Roman reached for the remote and muted the volume, but didn't turn around.

"I'm listening," he said.

Tao took a deep breath. "It was an organisation called Viribus," he said.

"What the hell are you talking about, old man?"

"The people who killed your father."

Roman turned around and glared at him.

"Your father's killers were part of an organisation called Viribus," Tao repeated.

"And how do you know that?"

Tao walked across the room and sat next to Roman on the couch. Reaching for the remote control, he turned off the football on the projection screen. "Tell me, Roman, did your father ever mention anything about *how* he became so incredibly wealthy?"

Roman thought for a moment and then shook his head. "No, not really. He told me he was a self-made billionaire but never really alluded to how he had achieved that."

"Your father was a CIA agent during the Cold War. Did you know that?"

Roman shook his head again. "No, I didn't."

"Well, he was. A very good one too. He successfully completed countless missions during his career, although there was one particular mission he never completed. They once tasked Zeke to track down a Russian named Nikolai Zagrev, who the CIA had on their radar as a person of interest. Your father was the only one who had the guts to take on the mission and went deep undercover to track Nikolai down to provide intel back to the CIA."

"And what happened?" Roman asked, his eyes flaring with intrigue.

"Well, your father's true identity was uncovered by Nikolai and his two brothers, Alexei and Dmitri, but instead of killing him, they enticed him into joining their organisation with the promise of unfathomable wealth."

"And that's how my father made his money?"

Tao nodded. "Most of it, yes. These Russians and your father were the founding members of an organisation they called *White Cloud.* Over time, the organisation grew into a monster, and now controls the world's governments, banks, and political forces. With such control comes great wealth, and with great wealth comes great power."

Roman stared at him for a moment, unsure if what he was being told was fact or fiction.

"And how do you know all of this?" he asked.

Tao smiled bashfully and looked down at the ground.

"Like your father, I am also a member of White Cloud. In fact, I am the leader of their Chinese sector."

Roman shook his head in confusion. "Wait a minute. What? You're telling me you and my father are some sort of international gangsters?"

"I wouldn't call us *gangsters* exactly, but yes, to some degree, I suppose you are right," Tao said.

"Why have you never told me this before?"

"Your father was a very good friend of mine—more like a brother. In fact, I promised him that if anything should ever happen to him, I would make sure you were taken care of. I believe I have now delivered on that promise, and it is time for you to choose your own path."

"What do you mean by that?"

"You have reached an age where you can make your own decisions, Roman. But to make the right ones, you must first be armed with the truth."

"I'm all ears," Roman said.

"White Cloud are planning an attack of immense proportion. Many people around the globe will die, but I want you to help me ensure their attack fails."

Roman looked at him quizzically. "Huh? Why would you want it to fail?"

"Nikolai has transformed from the man I once knew. He has become psychotic and unpredictable with the power he bears. He talks of using aircraft like controllable missiles and flying them into the ground, killing millions upon millions of people."

Tao shook his head at the thought. "I don't want to do things that way. I want to do them my way. But to do that, I first need to split away from White Cloud, which is why I need you. They will kill me and all of my family if I walk away."

"And what makes you think I can help?"

"You are young, you have the capital, and you have your father's network."

"I'm not sure I understand."

"You will if you choose to help me."

Roman stared at him for a moment. This was a lot to take in. "How do these *Viribus* people fit into all of this?" he asked.

"Viribus is a vigilante group trying to stop White Cloud from operating, but they will not stop them—or Nikolai. He is far too powerful and has plenty of supporters. Viribus will fail."

"How can you be so sure?"

"Because I intend to make *everyone* fail. White Cloud intends to offer you the position of American sector leader, and I want you to say yes."

"I've only just found out who they are! Why would I accept their offer?"

"White Cloud is aware you are Zeke's son, Roman. They recognise your wealth, and your organisation, which they feel could be useful to them. If you were to take the position, we could destroy White Cloud from the inside, along with Viribus. If we wipe out both organisations, we can create a new organisation. *Our* organisation."

"What if they find out what you have planned?"

"I intend to fake both of our deaths amidst the attacks that Nikolai has planned. Once they think we are dead, we will go deep into hiding and wait for things to settle down."

"What happens after that?"

Tao sat back on the couch. "Then we clean up and take everything for ourselves."

"You wily old bastard," Roman said with a broad, toothy grin. "I like the sound of that. Let's do it."

A few weeks later, Tao escorted Roman to meet privately with Nikolai, the man at the head of White Cloud, who welcomed him like a prodigal son. Nikolai spoke fondly of Roman's father, telling him what a great man he was and how Zeke had defected from the CIA to join them, confirming Tao's version of events.

Nikolai informed Roman of his radical plan to kidnap an avionics and aircraft software engineer, using him to hijack civilian airliners remotely and turn them into missiles.

Roman sat politely, listening to Nikolai, safe in the knowledge he would play no part in his plan. He and Tao had a different agenda. However, when the position of

American sector leader was officially offered to him by Nikolai, he stuck to the plan and graciously accepted it.

Soon after, Nikolai issued him with his first task. Roman was to apprehend the captain of a ship docked in Los Angeles, capturing a vessel White Cloud had chosen for their secondary plan.

Tao advised Roman to do exactly what Nikolai asked and, once it was done, to head for Guam and wait for him there.

Roman carried out the job in LA, capturing the vessel along with its captain, and then moved to White Cloud's safe house in Guam to wait for Tao.

While Roman hid on the remote island, he was ambushed and confronted by the Viribus leader—Liam Miller. Roman retaliated, and along with his security detail, killed as many Viribus members as he could, including Liam.

Upon hearing of the events in Guam, Tao ordered him to move to Shanghai as quick as he could and lie low. They could use the Viribus ambush as a perfect excuse for him not being in Peru. From this point on, White Cloud deemed Roman as deceased.

While in Peru, Tao met with a man called Solomon, who Nikolai had appointed as the Oceania sector leader.

This was the man Nikolai had hired to assist with turning the aircraft into missiles. Tao also spoke with his long-time friend, Alexei, who agreed to assist him with escaping from White Cloud once the attacks began.

From the safety of his penthouse suite, Roman looked out over the twilight cityscape of Shanghai as Nikolai's attacks began and aircraft began plunging from the sky—nose first—into the ground below.

It ended a matter of minutes after it had begun. The aircraft suddenly stopped dropping out of the sky. Roman sat up in his seat. This was not part of the plan.

His phone rang, startling him.

"Roman, are you safe?" Tao asked.

"Yes, I'm fine. Where are you?"

"On a jet bound for Shanghai. I'll be with you tomorrow."

"What happened? Why did the attack stop?"

As he spoke, Tao sounded out of breath, "Viribus destroyed White Cloud's headquarters, Roman. Everyone is dead. Everything went exactly to plan. We are free."

ROMEO

The remote Western Queensland town of Longreach is home to approximately three and a half thousand people and is arguably best known for being the founding centre of Qantas, the world's third oldest airline.

The town's airfield boasts the first ever operational Qantas hangar, and over the years, the hangar, along with the decommissioned Boeing 707 and 747-200 aircraft moored at the Qantas Founders Museum, has become a much-loved tourist attraction.

The matte black C-17 touched down on the Longreach runway as the sun appeared on the horizon. It used the entire length of the dusty runway to wash off its speed before taxiing to a vacant piece of concrete opposite the hangar where the old 747 and 707 were moored and came to a stop.

Kate's crew disembarked into the dry heat, and although the sun wasn't all the way up yet, it was already swelteringly hot.

"I've found an operative in the area who is willing to help us while we're here," Matt said as he unhitched the van from the floor of Moose.

"A Viribus operative? Here?" Kate asked.

Matt nodded with a surprised look on his face. "I know. Who would have—"

The sound of a car backfiring interrupted him, causing them to duck instinctively.

Matt smirked. "Don't worry. That wasn't a gunshot. That'll be our man."

Kate walked down the loading ramp of the aircraft and looked across the apron towards the source of the noise. Through the heat haze emanating off the concrete, a billowing cloud of black smoke trailed behind a candy-apple-red, Holden HZ panel van heading towards them.

In the 1970s, the panel van utility vehicle, affectionately known as the *Sandman* by car enthusiasts, was widely popular within the surf culture. It was essentially a utility vehicle with a roof over the rear tray in which surfboards could be easily transported. However, the roof over the tray also meant the owner could utilise the space in the back to sleep in… or perhaps other, more private, pastimes.

"Who the hell is this guy?" Kate asked.

The Sandman spluttered to a halt next to Moose and a tall skinny man with spiky brown hair on top of his head, and long hair at the back—a hairstyle more commonly known as a *mullet*—got out of the vehicle. He wore a flannelette red shirt and disturbingly short blue shorts, which were drastically in danger of exposing much more than *anyone* needed to see. On his feet, he wore flip-flops— or *thongs,* as the Australians call them—and he reeked of cigarette smoke.

"How ya garn?" the man said, with a strong Australian accent—colloquially known as an ocker accent.

"Oi'm Daz," he said, plucking the mirrored aviator sunglasses from off his face. "Oi believe you blokes need some help?"

Kate was stunned by Daz's appearance and his smell was quite confronting, to say the least. "Um, yes. Perhaps we do," she politely replied.

Daz strode over to her and shook her hand enthusiastically. "Well, oi'm happy to help yuz. How may oi be of assistance?"

"Wait a second," Kate said, holding her hand up to stop him. "Before we go any further, are you *really* with Viribus?"

"Sure am!" Daz said proudly, with a smug grin on his face. "Been monitoring these White Cloud faks for fifteen years now. Caught a few of the nasty buggers, too."

Kate stared at him in awe. She was lost for words. He made chasing White Cloud sound like fishing.

"So, what can oi do ya for?" he asked.

"We're looking for a man by the name of Mike Royle. Have you heard of him?" Alaina asked.

"Moike Royle…" Daz said, stroking the stubble on his chin. "Can't say oi have, but that's not to say he isn't 'ere somewhere. It's a small place, ya know. Look in the roight places, ask the roight questions, and you moight get a result." He pointed to the Sandman. "Get in."

"Ah… no, it's okay," Kate said, reluctant to have Daz escort them anywhere in the beat-up old panel van. "We have our own vehicle, thanks. It will be best if we keep a low profile."

Daz peered into the back of Moose at the van still strapped to the floor and spluttered with laughter.

"You must be fakking joking!" he snorted. "You fly into Longreach in this monster of a plane and expect nobody to notice yuz droiving around town in ya shiny black van? The whole bloody state knows someone from out-of-town is 'ere now!" He shook his head as he returned the aviators to his face. "Youse are gonna stand out like dog's balls in that thing—not that yuz don't already. Now, come on, before Channel 7 turns up and shoves a bunch of cameras in yuz faces."

Daz spun on his heels and headed towards the Sandman, ending the conversation.

Kate hated to admit it, but he had a point. They did stand out. She turned to Matt with her eyebrows raised.

"Really? This is the best you could do?"

"Hey, he wanted to help!" Matt replied with a shrug and a smirk. "And we can't turn down good help, can we?"

"The jury is out on him being *good* help, Matt."

Kate reluctantly followed Daz to the Sandman and creaked open the door. Pieces of yellow foam poked from out of the seat, and the imitation leather was torn in multiple places. The stench of stale cigarettes wafted out of the cabin, hitting her in the face and causing her to recoil slightly. Still, she remained polite and got into the Sandman, slamming the door shut behind her.

Matt and Alaina followed and got into the back of the Sandman, carrying two duffle bags full of weapons they had grabbed on their way out of Moose.

Daz started up the van, and it spluttered into life. "Sorry about the wheels, mate," he said, lighting up a cigarette. "The old girl's getting on a bit, ya know?"

Kate began coughing, not only from the cloud of smoke from Daz's freshly lit cigarette, but also from the billowing cloud of exhaust fumes now enveloping the car. She went to wind down the window, but the handle came away in her hand.

Daz looked at her sheepishly. "Oh, er, sorry about that, darl."

Kate dropped the handle on the floor and wafted the smoke away from her face. "Where are we going?"

Daz put the car into gear and released the handbrake. "We'll try the pub first. If youse want to find anyone in this town, chances are, they'll be there. There's nowhere else to be." He wound down his window to let the smoke out and flashed a grin. "It's a bloody honour to finally meet ya, Kate. Bloody marvellous job youse guys did in Peru."

"Thanks… I think," she said, waving her hand in front of her face and coughing.

Twenty minutes later, Daz stopped the Sandman in front of The Commercial Hotel in the centre of Longreach.

Most bars in Australia call themselves *hotels,* even though many are not *actually* hotels bearing any accommodation. However, The Commercial Hotel was an exception to this. It was one of the very few hotels with actual rooms to accommodate the weary traveller, but it was certainly no Hilton, and looked in desperate need of a repaint.

Daz led them into the typical country Australian bar attached to the side of the hotel. The stench of stale beer filled the air, and the customers, all dressed similarly to Daz, looked like they could do with a good wash.

A bald, heavy-set, tattooed barman was busy cleaning the beer taps, preparing them for the day's trading. It was still early in the morning, but customers were already circling like vultures, waiting for the magical ten o'clock to arrive and the hotel's liquor licence restrictions were lifted, so they could get their fix.

"G'day, Steve," Daz said, approaching the bar. "Oi've got some people 'ere looking for a man called Moike Royle. You heard of 'im?"

Steve looked at the group of people standing in front of him on the other side of the bar. "Who's asking?" he asked defensively.

Daz turned to Kate.

Kate took over. "We're looking for Mike as a matter of national and international interest," she said. "He's wanted for information about his involvement with a terrorist group."

Steve bellowed out a laugh. "What? That's the funniest fakking thing oi've heard all week! Moike? An international terrorist? You've got to be kidding me, lady!" He turned back to Daz as he laughed. "That's a good one, mate!"

Kate stared at Steve with a plain expression, allowing him to laugh and waiting for him to finish.

Steve saw her glaring at him and calmed his laughing down quickly.

"Jesus Chroist. Youse are fakking serious, aren't ya?" he said, scratching the back of his head.

All of them nodded in unison.

"Shit. Yeah, he rents a room upstairs. Drinks in 'ere every noight."

"Well, fak me," Daz said, turning to face Kate with a smile on his face. "You can always rely on the pub as a bloody gold moine of information. First place we look, and fakking bingo."

"Very good," Kate replied dryly. "Alaina, Matt, unload the bags."

Longreach, Queensland, Australia
10th February 2021
5:41 am Australian Eastern Standard Time

Alaina and Matt went outside to the Sandman and retrieved the duffle bags full of weapons from the rear of the vehicle. They then returned inside the pub, marching through the bar as Steve pointed to the staircase leading to the hotel's accommodation.

"Room seven," he said.

Kate could feel her feet sticking to the carpeted floor of the bar as she moved across it. The countless years of spilled beer and other unknown fluids were highly evident.

Matt and Alaina followed her up the creaky timber staircase and stopped at the room with a gold-plated number seven attached to it.

"Daz, knock on the door," Kate whispered.

"Why me?" Daz asked. *"Oi'm only 'ere to watch the show."*

"If Mike sees us, he will run. He knows our faces. He doesn't know yours. Knock on the door."

Daz shook his head and stood in front of the door as Kate, Alaina, and Matt moved out of sight, arming themselves with pistols fitted with silencers from the bags.

"Ready?" Daz asked.

All three of them nodded back at him.

Daz knocked.

A female voice responded from inside the room.

"Hello?" the voice asked without opening the door.

"Ah, yes. G'day," Daz said, speaking into the door nervously, "Oi'm sorry to bother you, love, but oi'm looking for a bloke by the name of Moike Royle."

"Never heard of 'im, fak off."

"Oi was told he might be staying in this room. Are you *sure* you haven't seen 'im?"

"Oi'm certain! Get fakked!"

"Roight, you are love. Thanks for your help, darl."

Daz shrugged at Kate, Alaina, and Matt, who watched him intently from the top of the stairs.

The door of the room then violently swung open, and Mike Royle, holding a bedsheet wrapped around himself, ran through it, pushing Daz out of the way as he headed for the stairs.

Mike's eyes widened as he ran around the corner and into Kate, Alaina and Matt standing at the top of the stairs, aiming their pistols at his head.

He came to an abrupt halt. "Shit. What are you doing here?" he asked.

"I need some information," Kate said. "And you're going to give it to me."

"Who says?"

Kate marched towards him and jammed the barrel of her pistol into his forehead. "I *fucking* say."

She pushed him backwards into his hotel room.

Inside, the room was small, dimly lit and smelled of mould. A metal-framed double bed was in the corner of the room where the woman who had answered Daz lay perfectly naked.

Kate looked at the young, slim, attractive woman.

"Jeez, girl. What are you doing with this loser?"

"I hang out with a lot of losers," the woman replied as she casually got off the bed, totally unphased by the sight of Kate holding Mike at gunpoint. "It kinda comes with the job," she said, picking her clothes up off the floor and putting them on.

Kate waited for the woman to get dressed as she continued to hold the pistol in Mike's temple. Once the woman was sufficiently clothed, Kate said, "Now, get out of here."

The woman held her hand out.

Kate realised she was asking for money and kicked Mike in the leg. "Where's your wallet, weasel?"

Mike didn't say anything.

Kate shoved him onto the bed and bent down to check his jeans on the floor. In one of the back pockets, she found his wallet and fished out a wad of fifty-dollar notes. She handed them to the woman, who snatched them from her hand and walked out of the room.

"I guess she got what she came for, hey, Mike?" Kate said. "Now you need to give me what I want, but I guarantee you, it will be nowhere near as much fun as what you were having with her."

Daz slammed the door shut as the woman left the room.

"Jeez, she was a bloody hottie, mate!"

"Daz, get out," Kate snapped. "Wait in the car."

"Roight you'ar darl. Oi'm out." Daz opened the door he'd just closed and left the room.

Mike sat on the bed, clutching at the bedsheet around his midriff as Kate glared at him.

Matt and Alaina stood behind her, pointing their pistols at his head.

"Okay, Mike," Kate began as she sat on a chair. "I want to know *everything* you know, but a friendly word of warning. If at any time I think you're lying, I'm going to punch you in the head until that nose I have broken once before is spread even further across your stupid, fat face. Is that clear?"

Mike nodded.

"Excellent. Start talking. I'm all ears."

Mike glanced at Matt and Alaina, holding pistols at him, before shifting his gaze to Kate, sitting cross-legged on a chair, waiting patiently for his response.

"How the hell did you find me?" he asked.

"That doesn't matter. Come on, tell me a story. I'm waiting."

Mike stared at her some more. The look on her face showed she wasn't messing around.

He took a big breath in and let it out. "Not long after you guys paid me a visit at my home and broke my ribs,

White Cloud contacted me. They asked me to become their Oceania sector leader to watch over you and monitor your movements. They recognised you had the potential to become a problem."

"White Cloud contacted you?"

Mike nodded.

"*Who* contacted you, exactly?"

"A man called Tao. He told me he was rebuilding White Cloud and wanted me to be a part of a new organisation. I initially refused, but then they began threatening me by saying they would kill my family if I didn't do what they wanted me to do. I couldn't say no."

Kate sighed. "Tao. I should have known… wait a minute. Did you just say *they?*"

Mike nodded. "Yes. There are only two of the original leaders left."

Kate glanced at Alaina and Matt, who seemed equally confused.

"*Two* leaders?" she asked.

"Yep. A man called Roman is at the head of White Cloud now. I think he's the son of one of the founders, or something."

Alaina jumped in. "Wait… Roman *Horowitz?*"

Mike nodded. "Yeah, that's him."

Kate turned to look at Alaina. "You know him?"

"Yes, Liam once tasked me with assassinating Ezekiel Horowitz, his father, in Florida."

"Florida?" Kate said, as some pieces began falling into place. She took a moment to put them together. "Holy shit, Alaina. Roman must be *the American*," Kate said.

It made sense. The American hadn't been in Peru when they had destroyed the White Cloud headquarters. The last time she'd seen him was in Guam when his head was in her sniper rifle scope right before he assassinated Liam, the Viribus leader.

Tao and Roman are resurrecting White Cloud by themselves, she said to herself.

"And they're planning something *way* bigger than Nikolai's aircraft attacks," Mike added. "This one will wipe out humanity."

"Go on," Kate said.

"They now have a virus," Mike said.

The words made her spine chill. She remembered the vial of liquid she had discovered on the body of the woman who tried to kill Alex in her backyard.

Alex was right.

"Are there more leaders, Mike?" she asked.

Mike didn't respond.

"Tell me who else is involved," she demanded.

"I don't know of anyone else."

Kate stood up, swapped the pistol to her left hand, and punched him square in the face with her right. Mike's head flung backwards, emitting a fountain of blood into the air from his nose. He brought his head forward and spat a couple of teeth onto the floor before wiping the blood from his face with the corner of the sheet he held around himself.

"I warned you what would happen if I thought you were lying," Kate said.

"I'm not *fucking* lying," Mike spluttered.

Kate lurched forward and grabbed him by the throat, drawing her arm back to strike him again.

"Okay, okay!" Mike yelled, holding a hand up as the other remained clutched at the sheet around his midriff. "I'll tell you!"

Kate lowered her fist but kept hold of his throat.

"Gianfranco Ragonesi is the European sector leader, but he's hiding in an underground bunker somewhere in the Wudang Mountains."

"The Wudang Mountains?" she asked. "Where are they?"

"China," he said.

Kate stared at him as she held him by the throat.

"Keep going."

"Dmitri Zagrev is now the Russian sector leader, and a woman called Min Huang takes care of Asia—and that's all I know, Kate. I promise."

"Where are Dmitri and Min?"

"I don't know. The only one I know the location of is Gianfranco."

"I don't believe you," she said, squeezing his throat with one hand and raising her fist again.

"Wait!" Mike gurgled through his crushed windpipe as he clutched at Kate's hand around his throat, allowing the sheet to drop onto his lap.

She released her grip slightly.

"All right! I'll tell you!" Mike said, "But as long as you're aware that by telling you all of this, I am signing my death warrant."

"I know," Kate said. "But these guys are going to kill you anyway, Mike. It's only a matter of time. You know that."

He looked at her as tears began running down his face. "Yes, I know," he said.

"Then tell me everything. If we can stop them from killing everybody on the planet, we might just also stop them from killing you."

Mike didn't say anything for a long moment. Kate gave him the time to sob. Then he said, "Dmitri is in Moscow. Min is in Shanghai. They are positioning themselves in their respective sectors to coordinate the release of the virus. That's why I'm here."

"What about Roman and Tao?" Kate asked. "Where are they?"

"I don't know where they are."

Kate squeezed his throat again.

"You have to believe me, Kate!" he said, choking. "That's all I know, I promise!"

Kate squeezed until Mike began turning purple, and then she let go.

He coughed and spluttered, gasping for air while rubbing at his throat. "I have something of yours that I think you'll want," he said.

"You couldn't possibly have anything I want," Kate snarled at him.

Mike shuffled along the bed to the bedside table and opened the drawer.

Matt and Alaina raised their weapons, as did Kate.

Mike threw his hands into the air again.

"What's in there, Mike?" Kate asked, staring down the sights of the pistol at him.

"Look for yourself," he said.

Kate walked towards the bedside table and slid out the drawer Mike had intended to open. Her body went numb as tears instantly welled in her eyes. One of them escaped, rolling down her cheek and dropping onto the top of the bedside table.

Then, in one fluid movement and without hesitation, she aimed her pistol at Mike's head and pulled the trigger, shooting him point blank in the face.

Longreach, Queensland, Australia
10th February 2021
7:15 am Australian Eastern Standard Time

"Holy shit!" Matt and Alaina screamed in unison.

"What the bloody hell are you doing?" Alaina screamed.

Mike's body slumped up against the blood-spattered wall behind him with a perfect hole in his forehead.

Kate ignored her startled colleagues and focused on the contents of the bedside table drawer. She reached inside it and pulled out a necklace—the necklace Sol had given her for their first wedding anniversary. White Cloud had used this necklace to manipulate Sol. Unbeknown to him, they had loaded the pendant with explosives and ensured Sol purchased it so she would wear it. By her wearing the necklace, it had given White Cloud all the control they needed to blackmail Sol into doing what they needed him to do.

Mike helped to set that situation up. He had also told her he'd detonated the explosives in his backyard after Alaina sent the necklace back to him in the mail, hoping to blow *him* up.

Mike had lied to her again, and it had now cost him his life.

Kate kissed the necklace before tucking it into a pocket on the front of her suit.

"What's going on?" Alaina asked, wiping the blood splatter from her face with her sleeve.

Kate shrugged. "I don't like liars," she said. "And if what Mike told us is correct, he was going to be killed by White Cloud, anyway. He knew he was a dead man walking, and besides, we got what we needed, right?"

"Well, yeah, I suppose so," Alaina said. "But it would have been nice to have had a little more warning. Now we're covered in this prick's blood!"

"Mike is the first name to be checked off a very long list, Alaina."

"List? What list?"

"The list I just wrote in my head. A list containing the names of all the old and new White Cloud leaders. They will not get to my children, or anyone else's for that matter. It's up to us to wipe them out. We have the people to do it."

Kate left the room, walked down the stairs, and strolled through the bar to the exit. She walked out into the searing heat and peered through the window of the Sandman, only to find Daz asleep in the driver's seat.

She banged a fist on the side of the door to wake him up. He woke with a start.

"I need a clean up," she said through the window.

Daz looked at her, blinked a few times and sprung into life. "Hell yeah! Oi'll get the tarp."

Kate was a little surprised at his enthusiasm. She watched him open the rear door of the Sandman, pull out a red tarp along with a roll of duct tape, and then run inside the hotel. She followed him upstairs and entered the hotel room, where they found Matt and Alaina standing in the middle of the room, wiping blood off themselves with anything they could find.

"Need a hand?" Daz asked casually.

"Um… yes?" a perplexed-looking Matt said.

"Alright, oi'll wrap the body, but oi'll need one of yuz to help me get it in the van."

Alaina looked at Matt. She knew he couldn't do it because of his injured shoulder. "It's okay, Matt. I got this," she said.

Daz and Alaina dragged Mike's body off the bed by the feet and dropped it onto the tarp they'd laid out on the floor. They threw the blood-soaked bedsheets on top of it and began wrapping the tarp around it before securing it with duct tape.

Within minutes, the body was ready to move.

Matt peered out the door and scanned the hallway.

"All clear," he said.

Daz and Alaina picked the body up and carried it down the stairs. Mike was a large man, and as they carried him, he sagged in the middle, causing his behind to scrape on the floor.

They shuffled through the bar in front of several agitated looking customers, eagerly awaiting ten o'clock to come around. They were seemingly unfazed by the group of military-looking people carrying a body-sized object wrapped in a tarp through the bar in front of them.

Steve glared at Kate from behind the counter. He was clearly annoyed. "What state did yuz leave that room in?" he snorted. "And where can oi send the cleaning bill?"

She slapped Mike's wallet onto the bar. "Take it out of this. He won't be needing it anymore."

Steve picked up the wallet and thumbed through it.

"Oi didn't see a thing," he said with a smile, tucking the wallet into his shirt pocket.

Daz and Alaina shuffled out the hotel door and hauled the body into the back of the Sandman. Kate got in the front with Daz, while Matt and Alaina got in the back with the body. A few moments later, Daz sped away from the hotel, leaving plumes of black smoke behind him.

"What now?" Alaina asked from the back of the Sandman, mopping her brow with her sleeve.

"Now we lose this body and get youse outta here," Daz said. "That's what happens now!"

Daz drove for almost 30 minutes into what seemed like the middle of nowhere before pulling up outside an old derelict farmhouse.

"What are we doing here?" Kate asked.

Daz glanced into the back of the Sandman.

"Dropping 'im off," he said, opening his door and getting out.

Alaina helped Daz to drag the body out the back of the Sandman, dropping it unceremoniously into the dirt as Matt and Kate watched them.

Daz then shut the rear door of the Sandman. "Roight, that'll do. Let's get yuz out of here," he said.

"Is that it?" Kate asked. "You're just going to leave it like that? Out in the open?"

"Yeah, mate! We're in a rush, aren't we? Oi'll come back after dropping yuz off, and oi'll dig the bloke a top-notch grave if that's what you're worried about. It'll be real emotional."

"What if someone sees him?" Alaina asked.

Daz chuckled. "Don't you worry your pretty little head about that, mate. No one is going to find 'im. Nobody ever comes out here. With any luck, the dingoes will get to him first."

They returned to the Sandman, and Daz drove them back to the airport at speed.

"So, did yuz get what you came 'ere for?" he asked with one hand on the wheel, the other holding a cigarette to his lips.

Kate nodded. "He gave us the information we needed, yes. Whether it was the truth or not remains to be seen. I hadn't planned on killing him, but the man was scum. He's just another problem dealt with."

"So where will yuz go now?" Daz asked, puffing a lungful of smoke out of the window.

Kate glanced at Matt and Alaina in the back.

"Going off what Mike said, I think the logical place would be China."

"Choina?" Daz said with surprise. "Whoy Choina?"

"It seems like it is the focal point for White Cloud," she said. "Mike told us Min Huang and Gianfranco Ragonesi were there. If we can find them, it may just cause Tao and Roman to show themselves."

They soon arrived at the airport, and Daz stopped the Sandman next to Moose. "Well, this is where oi'll be leaving yuz," he said. "If yuz need me for anything else, just call me. I hope everything goes well from 'ere because, by the sounds of it, we're *all* screwed if you don't get them!"

Kate smiled. "Thanks, Daz. We appreciate it "

"Nah worries, mate!" he said with a grin.

Kate, Matt, and Alaina exited the Sandman and walked towards Moose as Daz drove away, leaving a signature black plume of smoke behind it.

SIERRA

The Wudang Mountain Range in the Hubei Province sits almost one thousand kilometres west of Shanghai. It is home to an ancient Taoist temple complex that is weaved amongst the peaks and troughs of the mountains and consists of a network of monasteries and buildings tracing back to the early Tang Dynasty of the seventh century.

This complex is renowned for being the birthplace of the popular martial art form, Tai Chi, and in 1994, the ancient buildings were listed under the heritage listing protection of the United Nations Educational, Scientific and Cultural Organisation.

One of these ancient buildings, the Purple Cloud Monastery, finished construction in 1126 and still stands today. It was here, above this monastery, that White Cloud constructed their top-secret cryopreservation facility, carved deep into the mountainside.

Cryopreservation, or cryonics, is the process of freezing organisms at temperatures below -140°C to preserve them for future survival. This differs from *cryogenics,* which is specifically the scientific study of such extreme temperatures.

Gianfranco Ragonesi had studied cryopreservation at the Cryonics Institute in Michigan for several years, and because of this, he was the perfect candidate to run and manage White Cloud's brand-new human cryopreservation facility.

The Wudang facility was a fortress. Its entrances were camouflaged to hide the facility amongst the mountainous terrain, making it entirely possible to walk past it and not even know it was there. The walls were constructed out of four-foot-thick steel, so no one could get in or out of it unless they possessed an ID card in conjunction with a unique biometric ID.

Inside, the frozen bodies were stored in rows upon rows of large metal drawers, like a giant filing cabinet system for humans, and the current head count was large. 456 people were stored in the mountainside facility, and it was almost at capacity, closing in on Gianfranco's target of 500—250 female and 250 male. The intent of this facility was for it to become a modern-day *ark* controlled explicitly by White Cloud.

Over the years, Gianfranco had gathered some of the most intelligent and special people in the facility, including scientists, engineers, architects, and musicians. People who, after White Cloud's virus was released, would create a new breed of human—a *superhuman* breed.

Amongst these numbers were two of Gianfranco's most prized additions. As part of the clean-up team who had arrived in Peru shortly after the White Cloud headquarters was reduced to rubble by Viribus, Gianfranco had extracted the White Cloud leader, Nikolai, from the wreckage of a helicopter—along with another body— Solomon Barrett.

Nikolai and Sol were both clinically dead when Gianfranco had scraped them out of the helicopter, and both were so severely burned, and so badly disfigured, that he had needed to use dental records to confirm their identities.

To assist Gianfranco with the upkeep of the facility and the bodies within it, White Cloud had appointed Natasha Miller to help him.

Natasha was a petite woman with a broad northern English accent and a beautiful Middle Eastern complexion. The long, straight black hair running down her back together with her big brown eyes and petite figure made her extremely attractive.

It was Natasha who was once tasked with attaching the wristband to Sol's arm in Los Angeles, allowing White Cloud to have complete control over him.

Natasha sat next to Gianfranco at his desk as he pondered over an email he had received from Roman. "So, when are we doing it?" she asked excitedly.

"I'm not so sure I *want* to do it," Gianfranco replied, staring at the screen.

"But Roman has *ordered* you to do it."

"That means nothing, Natasha. It is *my* decision to wake someone up, not Roman's. I manage these people and therefore I am responsible for their lives."

"Yes, but this one is a *special* one," Natasha said, smiling at a drawer on the other side of the room.

"Just because one leader is dead does not mean I should wake another."

"I agree, but Roman needs another Oceania sector leader in place so he can distribute the virus."

"I'm well aware of this, Natasha. Thank you," Gianfranco said, staring down at the file in front of him entitled *Solomon Barrett*. "What concerns me is that if I wake this man up, it has the potential to start something Roman has not taken into consideration."

Shiyan Wudangshan Airport, China
10th February 2021
2:06 pm China Standard Time

Alaina set Moose down onto the runway at China's Shiyan Wudangshan Airport—one thousand kilometres west of Shanghai and the closest airfield to the Wudang Mountain Range.

Kate disembarked and looked towards the southeast horizon. In the distance, she could see the Wudang Mountain Range, the head of which was covered by cloud.

A blue Toyota Hiace van raced across the airfield and stopped in front of her. The driver stepped out of the van and bowed towards her, which she graciously reciprocated.

"This one is better already," Kate said, smiling at Matt.

"Ha ha, hilarious," Matt said dryly. "Don't you forget, Kate, it was Daz who helped to tidy up your mess."

Kate smiled. "I know, I know. Do we have any other intel on the area?"

"I've had several reports from Viribus operatives in the area who have seen a suspicious western-looking couple around the Wudang Mountain temples. They believe the man might be Gianfranco."

Matt nodded at the man standing in front of the van. "That's why this guy is here. He's agreed to escort us up the mountain. It's quite a treacherous stretch of road, apparently."

"This guy is Viribus?" Kate asked.

"He sure is."

Matt went to assist Alaina with unloading a couple of trunks from Moose and load them into the van. His shoulder was feeling much better now and the painkillers Kate continued to feed him were helping.

Alaina handed an earpiece to Matt and then gave one to Kate. "We might need these. Let's keep the comms up," she said.

They inserted their earpieces and got into the back of the van. Kate pointed at the mountains in the distance. The driver nodded his understanding and set off on the hour and a half journey to the top of the Wudang Mountains.

The driver didn't say a word.

Kate didn't know if this was because he couldn't speak English or if it was a choice. Either way, she was comfortable with the silence after riding with Daz in Longreach.

The single-lane mountain road was tight and weaved its way through the dense forest on either side of the road. Clouds hung low and heavy on the mountain, creating an eerie, tense, and claustrophobic atmosphere.

As the van chugged its way up the treacherous mountain road, Kate heard the sound of motorbike engines coming up behind them. She looked through the rear window and saw a dozen dirt bikes tearing up the mountain road; the riders dressed entirely in black.

"Matt, please tell me these guys are with us," she said.

"If they are, I don't know where they've come from," he replied.

Kate thought back to what Daz had said when they had arrived in Longreach. Their aircraft *was* big and attracted a lot of unwanted attention—mainly in remote areas.

Areas just like this one.

"Ready your weapons," Kate said. "If you see someone pointing a gun at you, do not hesitate to fire back."

Alaina and Matt began arming themselves with weapons from the trunks and stared out the windows at the rapidly approaching squad of dirt bikes closing in on the rear of the van. The noise of the bikes was deafening. They sounded like a swarm of amplified, angry, rabid mosquitoes.

Matt cocked his weapon but kept it low and out of sight.

The van then passed a clearing in the road, and the bikes quickly overtook them, speeding away up the hill in front of them, one after the other.

No weapons were fired.

A few minutes later, the van pulled off the road and stopped in front of the rock wall entrance to the temple complex.

"It seems like we're on foot from here," Kate said, as she tied her hair into a bun and got out of the van. She watched a tourist coach turn into the car park to the right of the gate with a load of tourists onboard and turned to the others. "We're going to need an interpreter. Chances are there is someone on that coach who can speak Mandarin *and* English."

Without hesitation, Kate jumped over the rock wall surrounding the car park and walked towards the coach as it came to a stop. Tourists began shuffling out of the door as she walked around the front of it.

"Does anyone speak English?" she asked as the tourists filed past her. Some of them smiled and nodded politely, but none of them understood what she was asking.

The tour guide was last in line, shepherding his flock of tourists out of the coach.

"English?" Kate asked as the skinny tour guide, wearing blue shorts and a white tee shirt underneath a dress jacket, stepped out of the coach and shoved a white bucket hat upon his head.

"Yes, I speak English," he said. "How can I help you?"

"I am looking for someone. I was wondering if you could help me find them?"

"Ah, okay, okay," the tour guide nodded. "Yes, of course. My name is Chen," he said with a broad grin. "I would be happy to help, but first, I must take these people on a tour of the mountain. Maybe I can help you after that?"

Kate picked him up by the lapels of his jacket and slammed him against the side of the coach, causing his hat to fall off his head. Chen's face quickly changed from that of a cheeky tour guide to one of terror.

"I don't have time to waste arguing with you," she said. "You're either going to help me now, or you will not leave this mountain alive. Is that clear?"

Chen nodded furiously. "O-o-okay, okay," he stammered.

"Good," Kate said, releasing his jacket and dropping him to the ground. "I am glad we could sort that out."

Chen stood up, straightened his jacket, and bent down to pick up his hat, dusting it off before returning it to his head.

"Come with me," Kate said, making her way back to the gate where the rest of the team was waiting for her.

Chen scurried behind her, trying to keep up. "Who are you looking for?" he asked.

"A man by the name of Gianfranco Ragonesi," Kate said as she walked.

Chen spun around and started to run back to the coach, but Kate caught him by the scruff of the neck. "Why are you running, Chen?"

"Gianfranco is an evil man," he said. "You shouldn't be chasing him. He will kill you… and me."

"And if you don't help me find him, I will kill you now," Kate said. "Your choice."

Chen stared at her for a moment, as if trying to determine if she was lying. "Okay. Sure. I will help you. But if I do this, you must promise to keep me safe."

"I promise," Kate said.

Kate and Chen returned to the van where the other Viribus members were waiting. Chen instinctively threw his hands in the air at the sight of Matt and Alaina, armed with rifles, pistols, knives, and hand grenades, staring back at him.

Alaina pulled his arms down to his side. "Relax, buddy. We're not here to hurt you. We're with her," she said, nodding at Kate.

Kate introduced Chen to the rest of her team. "Matt, Alaina, this is Chen. He has kindly agreed to help us find Gianfranco, haven't you?" she said, patting him on the back.

Chen nodded.

"Good. Let's get moving," Kate said.

The team moved into the temple complex with Chen behind them. As they approached the first of the buildings with people gathered outside it, Kate grabbed Chen by the arm and pulled him to the front of the group. "It's your time to shine. Start talking."

"But, Miss Kate, is someone coming with me?" Chen asked.

"No. I think you'll agree that we stand out a little. You are far less confronting. But we will be watching you, don't worry. Now go."

"Okay, okay."

Chen walked towards the courtyard of the first temple. He spoke to several people milling around outside before entering it and interrogating a few more inside.

The team watched him come out and shake his head at them, signalling he had nothing, and then he moved to the next temple.

Outside the Purple Cloud Monastery, the team watched Chen talk with an elderly man. Chen then rushed back and told Kate the old man had met someone called Gianfranco at a Tai Chi session earlier that morning.

"So, he is definitely here somewhere," Kate said.

"I think I already know where he is, Miss Kate," Chen added. "The old man said Gianfranco lives somewhere *above* the Purple Cloud temple."

They all looked up. There was nothing above the temple except for the mountainside and trees.

"*Above?*" Alaina asked. "Ah, damn. Please don't tell me we're climbing that mountain."

"No. We're not," Kate replied. "At least, not yet."

Alaina breathed a sigh of relief.

"If we hang around here long enough, Gianfranco will surely turn up sooner or later."

"Although it's highly likely he already knows we're here," Matt said.

"May I get back to my tour now, Miss Kate?" Chen asked. "Have I done everything you needed me to do?"

Kate nodded. "Yes, you have, Chen. Thank you for your help."

He smiled back at her. "Thank you, Miss Kate. Best of luck."

Chen began scurrying away across the monastery's courtyard when a shot fired from somewhere high above them. The skinny tour guide's bucket hat flew into the air as his body fell face-first onto the ground.

Chen was dead.

Wudang Mountains, Hubei Province, China
10th February 2021
3:34 pm China Standard Time

Kate and Alaina looked at each other.

"Sniper," Alaina said.

"Get behind something! Now!" Kate yelled.

The team ran towards the closest courtyard wall as another shot fired, hitting the cobblestones in front of Matt. They dived behind a wall and lay flat on the ground.

Kate looked at where the shot had come from. "I know where it is," she said to Alaina. "Follow me."

They slipped through the vegetation and dense foliage surrounding the Purple Cloud Monastery, climbing the hill towards where Kate had seen the sniper's muzzle flash.

Halfway up the mountainside, they found a small trail leading up the mountain and began following it upwards. After several minutes of creeping along the trail, Alaina stopped and pointed at some bushes.

Kate stared at where she was pointing. Twenty metres down the mountainside, she could make out the outline of a person wearing a *ghillie* suit—a sniper's primary choice of camouflage. The ghillie suit could make a sniper look like a bush or a shrub, allowing them to blend in easily with their surroundings. Alaina's highly trained eye had spotted it, and there, lying on the ground between a clump of bushes facing the monastery courtyard, was their attacker.

Kate quietly took her pistol from its holster and crept down the mountainside towards the sniper, trying to not make a sound. Matt and Alaina followed in single file behind her and drew their weapons.

CRACK!

Kate spun her head towards the noise behind her and saw Matt staring back at her, wincing as he froze like a statue with a broken stick under its boot. The sniper also heard the sound and leapt to their feet, sprinting along the trail in the opposite direction to Kate and her team.

Kate pulled the trigger of her pistol and fired several rounds, one of them hitting the fleeing sniper in the back of the leg. The sniper fell to the ground, screaming in pain. Kate recognised the screams as female. She moved towards the incapacitated sniper with her pistol raised and stood over the writhing bush-like body for a moment, letting it suffer. She then leaned down and pulled back the hood of the ghillie suit, revealing a woman with long black hair and beautiful, big brown eyes.

The sniper had fallen dangerously close to the edge of a sheer cliff side drop. Kate resisted the urge to kick her off it. "Who are you?" she asked.

The woman didn't reply.

"WHO ARE YOU?" Kate yelled, pushing her pistol into the woman's face.

The sniper put her hands in the air. "Natasha! My name is Natasha."

"How did you know we were here, *Natasha*?"

"Just as you have your intel, *Kate*, we have ours."

"How do you know my name and who sent you?"

Natasha slowly held up her bloodied hand and extended her middle finger. "Fuck… you."

Kate pointed the pistol at the back of her other leg and fired.

Natasha screamed in pain again and clutched at the back of both of her legs, blood streaming from the wounds and spilling over the trail.

Kate knew she would bleed out fast and stood over her again. "Tell me who you're working for, or your kneecaps are next."

A beeping noise suddenly began emitting from Natasha as a smile formed on her face. Kate looked around, trying to locate where the beeping was coming from. Natasha's smile then became a hysterical laugh as the beeping increased in volume. Then the beeping, along with Natasha's deranged laughter, stopped abruptly.

Natasha stared up at Kate and smiled. "Bad luck, bitch. It looks like they're done with me."

BANG!

Natasha's neck violently exploded, severing her head clean off her body as a fountain of blood ejected from her neck. Kate watched Natasha's head sail out over the edge of the cliff, bouncing off the rocks and surrounding trees as it fell into the ravine below.

A blood-spattered Kate looked at Matt and Alaina, who stared back at her, wide-eyed and confused. "What the hell was that?" she asked, wiping Natasha's blood from her face.

"I have no idea," Alaina said. "But maybe we had better get rid of the body before it decides to explode as well."

"Yeah, I suppose we had," Kate replied. "Let me see if she was carrying anything we can use first."

Matt turned and vomited in the bushes. "What's with all the body parts, man?"

Kate crouched next to Natasha and began searching the headless body, but all she could find was a small, white plastic card—like a credit card—with no markings on it, in one of her ghillie suit pockets.

"This is all she has," Kate said, shoving the card into her pocket. "Now, where do you suppose she was running to?" She asked as she looked along the trail to her right, which ended in a leaf-covered rock face. "Why would she be running into a dead-end?"

Kate got up and walked along the trail towards the rock wall at the end of the path while Matt and Alaina waited behind Natasha's body sprawled across the trail.

Upon reaching the wall, she parted some vines and brushed away some leaves from the front of it and discovered the wall *wasn't* rock.

It was concrete.

She began tearing at the vines and branches, exposing a large, solid concrete wall. She turned to Matt and Alaina.

"Hey! I think I've found something!" she shouted back at them. Matt and Alaina slowly stepped over Natasha's body and walked along the trail to see what Kate had discovered. They stood behind her, staring at the wall.

"What *is* this?" Matt asked.

Kate shook her head. "I don't know, but whatever it is, it was designed to *not* be found."

"You think this is where Gianfranco is?" he asked.

Kate nodded. "Quite possibly. Why else would Natasha be running towards it? There must be some kind of way through it," she said, pushing on the wall. A few seconds later, a small red light, buried deep inside the concrete, lit up and blinked in front of her.

"Woah," she said, pulling her hand away. "What's that?"

"Maybe this is what the card is for," Alaina said.

Kate took the card out of her pocket and placed it flat on the concrete wall. The small red light stopped blinking, and some words appeared above it—

Biometric Required

Kate looked at Natasha's body behind them. "Well, I hope it's her hand and not her eyes," she said, turning around and walking back to the headless body lying across the trail.

Matt realised her intent. "Ah, shit. Really, Kate? More body parts?"

"I promise to not cut anything off if you help me drag her body to the wall," Kate replied.

"But it's got no head!"

"Toughen up, Matt."

Kate picked up one arm of the body as Matt swallowed his fears and grabbed the other. Together, they dragged the headless body along the trail towards the wall.

Kate held up Natasha's hand to the area below the blinking light, holding it onto the wall while Alaina placed the card in the spot where she had before. This time, the light went green, and the words now read—

Access Granted

Whatever this building was, they were in.

Kate shoved Natasha's body over the edge of the cliff like a piece of garbage. "Thanks, bitch," she said, as she watched the body bounce down the side of the mountain.

The concrete wall moved inwards with a loud, rock-on-rock sound, exposing a dark corridor leading deep inside the mountainside behind it. Kate entered the corridor, but no sooner had she crossed the threshold, the door began to close. "Everybody in, quick!" she shouted.

But the door was moving much quicker than it had opened, and in an instant, the door slammed shut with a thud, isolating Kate from her team, and in impenetrable darkness.

She banged her fists on the door from the inside.

"Alaina! Matt!" she shouted through the door.

"We're here, Kate! We're going to get you out of there! Don't worry!"

Kate realised their earpieces were no longer transmitting since she'd entered the corridor.

Her heart was beating fast.

As her eyes adjusted to the darkness, she could see a fluorescent light illuminating a room at the end of the long corridor in front of her. She started to walk along the dark, narrow corridor towards the light.

As she neared the end of the corridor, she could hear a man's voice coming from the room in front of her. She stopped with her back to the wall and glanced around the corner. It was a large room and perfectly square. The walls were lined with enormous steel drawers from floor to ceiling, and it felt clinical, almost as if it were a morgue. A grand oak desk sat in the middle of the room, behind which a man sat with his back to her, holding a phone to his ear.

"Yes, sir. Viribus is here," he said. "Yes, I will, sir. Not a problem. I can do that... I had to kill her, sir... She compromised our position—"

He cut himself off and turned his head slightly over his shoulder. "I have to go. I have company."

The man slammed the phone down and keyed a code into a security pad attached to his desk, causing a cascade of red laser beams to shoot up out of the floor, surrounding him entirely like a rat in a red, laser-walled cage.

"Mrs Barrett," the man said, his voice echoing around the room as the lasers hummed. "How nice of you to pay me a visit."

Wudang Mountains, Hubei Province, China
10th February 2021
4:15 pm China Standard Time

Kate's eyes widened, and her heart beat faster. She lifted her pistol and stepped out of the dark corridor, into the bright fluorescent light of the room.

"Gianfranco Ragonesi, I assume?" she said, pacing slowly towards the red laser wall surrounding him.

The man spun around in the chair to face her. "Correct," he said, smiling as he raised himself out of his chair.

"Be careful of this laser wall in front of you, Mrs Barrett. It can cut metal. God only knows what it can do to a human…and don't try to shoot me. Your weapon will not penetrate it."

Kate ignored his warning and fired her pistol at Gianfranco's head, but the bullets disintegrated as they hit the laser wall.

"So, you didn't believe me?" Gianfranco asked as he approached the wall, stopping a few feet from Kate on the other side.

She could smell the gel in his slick-backed hair and his cheap Italian aftershave.

"Now, why are you here, Mrs Barrett?"

Kate lowered her pistol. "I came for you."

"You came all the way here for me?"

"Not just for you," Kate replied, staring at him through the wall. "You and the rest of your godforsaken terrorist organisation. I'm going to take you all down."

Gianfranco chuckled. "My word, that is quite ambitious. You will need one hell of an army to kill us all. We have people all over the world."

He clasped his hands together behind his back as he paced along the length of the red laser wall. "I do not recall ever harming you, Mrs Barrett. Why would you want to kill me? To be quite frank, I think you should be thanking me."

"*Thanking* you?"

Gianfranco stopped pacing and stared at her. "Yes. I think once you find out what we have planned, you will be pleasantly surprised."

"You're delusional," Kate said.

"No, I am simply going about my business and trying to do what is right for planet Earth."

"You think wiping out the human race is *helping*?"

Gianfranco's eyebrows raised. "Ah!" he said. "You are already aware of our plans?"

"I know you intend to release a virus into the world that will wipe out humanity, yes."

Gianfranco smiled. "But that's where you are wrong. We do not intend to wipe out *all* of humanity, Mrs Barrett," he said, nodding his head at the metal drawers.

Kate looked around the room and realised what he was alluding to. "You have *people* in here?"

Gianfranco nodded his head. "Each one of these drawers contains a cryonically frozen body. All of which were once dead, but now, every single one of them is perfectly alive, thanks to me."

She stared at the drawers on the walls in stunned silence—oblivious to the fact her husband, whom she had decided to kill for the sake of humanity three years ago, lay inside one of them—barely metres away from her.

Frozen but *alive*.

"You're collecting people..." she said to herself quietly, in a moment of realisation.

Gianfranco heard her. "The best people!" he bellowed excitedly, opening his arms wide towards the drawers. "These people will breed generations of intelligence back into the human gene pool, dragging humanity out of the dark ages and propelling us forward for the next thousand years."

Kate turned back to face him. "Yes, well, hopefully these *super-people* will also be able to design top-secret facilities that are secure enough to keep unwanted people out, hey?" she said.

Gianfranco lowered his arms as the smile on his face faded. He returned to the desk and sat in the chair, glaring at her.

"Did you think we did not know you were coming here, Mrs Barrett?" he asked with a calm tone in his voice. "Did you not realise we would be watching you from the moment you killed Mike?"

"It doesn't make any difference," Kate replied. "You're all going to end up dead."

Gianfranco laughed. "Is that right? Did it also not occur to you that maybe you were led here for a reason?"

Kate looked at him, confused.

"Mrs Barrett, while you are here wasting time with me, your colleagues waiting for you outside are under attack."

Gianfranco turned a monitor around on his desk so she could see it. On the screen, a gunfight was occurring between Alaina, Matt, and many other people dressed in combat clothing. She saw them firing their weapons at their attackers across the courtyard of the monastery outside, desperately trying to defend themselves.

"You are all trapped, Mrs Barrett. Like little tiny flies in a massive spider's web. Soon, your friends will be dead, and you will no longer have anyone to help you."

Kate raised her pistol as several doors behind Gianfranco flung open and a group of heavily armed Chinese soldiers piled into the room with rifles aimed at her.

"Checkmate, Mrs Barrett," Gianfranco said.

A massive explosion emanated from somewhere behind her, rocking the mountain beneath her feet and causing the fluorescent lights above her to flicker.

It was the perfect distraction.

Kate turned and ran for the corridor. It was the only way out.

Gianfranco immediately deactivated the laser wall as Kate disappeared into the blackness of the corridor.

"After her!" he ordered.

The soldiers leapt into action, firing their weapons as they ran, showering the corridor with bullets.

Kate ran as fast as her legs could take her, ducking and dodging the bullets being fired at her from behind.

A second explosion rocked the ground again. This one destroyed the door at the end of the corridor in front of her, filling it with a billowing cloud of concrete dust and smoke.

Kate ran straight into it—using the airborne debris as a smokescreen. She could hear the bullets ricocheting off the concrete walls around her as she ran with one hand touching the wall, hoping it would lead her to freedom.

She burst out of the dirt cloud and into the daylight, only to find chaos had erupted outside.

As she ran, she looked down at Alaina and Matt crouching behind a wall below her, shooting at people on the opposite side of the courtyard of the monastery.

They were trapped. They couldn't go up, and they couldn't go down.

Kate sprinted along the mountainside trail they had walked up earlier, making her way down the mountain towards her team below. "ALAINA!" she screamed into her earpiece, hoping it would work again now she was outside the facility.

"Kate?" Alaina replied in her earpiece.

"I'm behind you! Look up!"

Alaina and Matt glanced up to see Kate hurtling down the mountain trail towards them. They then saw the Chinese soldiers emerge from the dust cloud behind her, firing their rifles in her direction.

Alaina turned and took aim and fired, picking the pursuing soldiers off the trail above her one by one. The soldiers fell off the cliff edge as they were shot, their bodies tumbling down the side of the mountain and vanishing into the dense foliage below.

Kate quickly reunited with Matt and Alaina behind the courtyard wall and began firing at wave after wave of advancing Chinese soldiers coming up the mountain.

"There's too many of them!" Matt shouted.

"Just keep shooting!" Alaina yelled as she stood up and lobbed a hand grenade into the courtyard. The grenade exploded, launching several attacking soldiers high into the air.

Suddenly, the ground lit up with several tremendous explosions, ripping the Chinese soldiers into pieces and throwing them into the air. Bombs fell from the sky, turning the mountain into nothing but flames and dust.

Kate, Matt, and Alaina ducked behind the wall, shielding their eyes from the flying debris and body parts.

Once the wave of explosions had passed. Kate looked out at the devastation in front of her. "Where *the shit* did that come from?" She looked skywards through a small gap in the dust cloud and saw a fighter aircraft banking away into the distance.

"Who the hell is in that?" she asked.

"A friend," Alaina said, standing up and reloading her weapon. "I don't have time to explain, Kate. We need to get out of here."

"Agreed," Kate said, "But who is *he*?"

The bombs from the fighter had annihilated the Chinese Army. Dismembered bodies and body parts lay strewn over the ground as Kate and her team ran down the mountain towards the complex gates, passing by the ancient temples they had walked past earlier. All of them were now nothing but smouldering piles of rubble.

As Kate ran past one of the old temples, she noticed several dirt bikes laying mangled amongst the rubble. They were the same as those that had overtaken them on the way up. It made sense now—they must have been Gianfranco's reinforcements, racing up the mountain to get to Gianfranco before Kate and her team could find him.

They soon reached the complex's front gate and returned to the van they had used to get up the mountain. They found the driver slumped forward on the steering wheel with blood streaming out of a circular wound on his forehead. He'd been murdered.

Matt reached through the window of the van and turned the key. The engine started.

"All right, get in," he said, opening the door and dragging the driver's body out of the van.

Alaina and Kate quickly got into the back and shut the door. As Matt was about to drive off, he looked out of his side window at a four-wheel-drive vehicle with a monstrous bull-bar attached to the front of it, heading straight at him.

"Ah, shit," he said.

The four-wheel drive ploughed into the side of the van, barging it off the road and sending it tumbling down a small embankment. The van came to rest upside-down on its roof, with its occupants lying completely motionless inside.

A few minutes later, Kate woke, only to find herself being hauled up the embankment the van had rolled down by her arms. She looked up at the man dragging her, but the hood of his sweatshirt cast a shadow over his face, concealing his identity.

"GET OFF ME!" she screamed, thrashing her body around wildly to get free.

The man responded by violently jerking his knee into the back of her head, causing her to black out once more. He then dragged her limp body to the rear of a waiting sedan, where another man wearing a black hooded sweatshirt emerged from the vehicle, and together, they lifted her into the trunk.

One of the men shoved a gag into her mouth and secured a blindfold around her head, while the other cable tied her hands together and shut the trunk lid. A few moments later, the black sedan took off down the mountain at speed.

Gianfranco smiled as he watched the vehicle disappear from his monitor and dialled a number.

"Sir, she's on the way," he said before putting the phone down again and turning to face the drawers full of human bodies.

"Okay, Mr Barrett," he said, rubbing his hands together. "I think it's time you were woken up."

TANGO

After the entrance to the facility was destroyed, Gianfranco hit a button on his desk to initiate the building's emergency lockdown system. As metal walls slid into place, sealing him from the outside world, he donned a pair of blue rubber surgical gloves and walked over to the drawer containing Sol.

He picked up a large syringe from a nearby surgical tray and began carefully injecting its dark blue contents into a machine above the drawer, causing it to hiss and gurgle. As soon as the syringe was empty, he turned a small dial on the front of the machine, flicked a few toggle switches, and watched some parameters change on the small display.

A few seconds later, he pushed a large green button on a keypad, and the door to the wall-mounted drawer hissed open.

The drawer slid out automatically and slowly, revealing a body that had transformed dramatically. Its chest bore a large vertical scar stretching from the collarbone to the pelvis. The face was severely disfigured by scarring, and there wasn't a single hair on its head.

The drawer stopped, and the body of Solomon Barrett, dressed in a white hospital gown with wires and tubes running out from under it, lay lifeless on the cold metal shelf.

Sol slowly opened his eyes and frowned at the harsh fluorescent light in the room.

"Welcome back, Mr Barrett," Gianfranco said, smiling as he helped Sol to sit upright. "We have a lot to catch up on."

Sol blinked his eyes as he tried to focus on his surroundings.

"Where am I?" he asked, rubbing his face.

"You are in my cryonic laboratory. Welcome back."

Sol ran a hand over his face, touching the strange bumps and ridges from the scarring and multiple skin grafts. He quickly snatched it away.

"What's wrong with my face? Why am I here? Why don't I remember anything?"

"Just relax. Your memory will return in due course. Your brain is in a fragmented state at the moment. Some things you will remember, some you won't."

"Has my face always been like this?"

Gianfranco ignored the question. "I understand you are going to have many questions, Mr Barrett, but you are not yet ready to hear all the answers."

Sol looked down at his body and traced a finger along the scar on his chest. "How do *you* know I'm not ready for the answers? Give me something here."

Gianfranco stared at him for a moment. "I pulled you out of a burning helicopter in Peru," he said. "You were clinically dead. But I have repaired you the best I can with the tools I have." Gianfranco nodded at Sol's chest. "Hence the not-so-pretty scar. I'm no surgeon. I apologise for the quality of my stitching."

Still groggy from his three-year hiatus, Sol frowned and asked, "What the hell are you talking about? I... I was dead?"

Gianfranco nodded. "Yes."

"Why have you kept me alive?"

"I didn't *keep* you alive. I brought you *back* to life. You were, for all intents and purposes, deceased. All of your questions will be answered in due course," Gianfranco said as he turned and walked away. "But right now, you need to rest."

Sol sat up on the tray and grimaced as he attempted to move his legs. "I... I... I can't move my legs."

"Your motor skills will also return," Gianfranco replied as he continued towards a door at the back of the laboratory. "But for now, please lie down, and I will get you something to eat. Your organs have been dormant for quite some time. They will soon begin operating normally, and you will be ravenous."

"How long have I been here?" Sol called after him.

Gianfranco opened the door and glanced back at him over his shoulder. "Three years," he said before exiting the room.

Sol laid back down on the tray, trying to gather himself and his thoughts. He couldn't remember anything other than the last few minutes.

He realised his last name must be *Barrett* because the man kept calling him that. However, he had not used his first name.

Straining to sit upright again, Sol looked around at the other metal drawers in the room. He leaned the upper half of his body in front of the neighbouring drawer to look at his reflection in the polished metal—the image he saw looking back at him made him feel sick.

He could see scarring had ravaged his face. *I'm a monster,* he thought as he turned away and laid back down on the drawer, staring at the ceiling.

Gianfranco returned to the laboratory, walking across the room carrying a plate of food and handing it to him. "Here, eat this."

Sol sat up again, took the plate from Gianfranco, and began feverishly devouring the food. "So, what now?" he asked with a mouthful of food.

"Now we try to get you back to normal as quick as we can. I'll start giving you some physio shortly to get those legs moving and fill you in with what your objectives are."

"Objectives?"

"Yes. *Objectives.* You are now going to repay the debt you owe me. I did not bring you back from the dead without a good reason."

"What's the reason?" Sol asked, shovelling the food into his mouth.

Gianfranco smiled. "All in good time, Mr Barrett."

"Well, can you at least tell me what my name is?"

"Your name is Solomon Barrett."

Sol stopped chewing for a second.

"Solomon Barrett," he repeated, pausing for a moment to say his own name as if trying to recall something. "Call me Sol," he said, resuming his chewing.

"Okay, *Sol*, finish your food and then we can concentrate on getting your motor skills back to normal."

Sol cleaned the plate off and set it down to one side.

Gianfranco stood next to him. "Okay. First of all, I want you to concentrate on wiggling your toes."

Sol stared at his feet and tried to wiggle his toes, but they wouldn't budge. Nothing was happening.

"This is the first hurdle," Gianfranco said. "Your brain has not used this function for some time. It is going to need some re-training. You keep trying, and eventually, they will wiggle. Let me know when that happens."

Gianfranco headed to his desk, leaving Sol to plead with his toes to move.

An hour later, Sol's little toe finally twitched. "It moved!" he shouted in excitement.

Gianfranco's head spun around. "Really? Already? Are you sure?"

"Yes. Watch," Sol said, staring at his toes again.

Gianfranco watched as Sol's little toe twitched again. "This is quite miraculous," he said. "Most people take days to make this kind of progress. I'm now beginning to understand why they wanted to keep you alive."

"They? Who are *they*?"

"White Cloud, Sol. Your new employers."

"White Cloud?" Sol asked with a perplexed look, which slowly transformed into a smile as he giggled. "What a stupid name."

Gianfranco ignored him. "Okay, so now that we have some toes moving, let's get to work on your legs." He picked one of Sol's legs up by the ankle and began moving it around in a circular, bicycle kick-type fashion.

"So, what do I do for these White Cloud people?" Sol asked as Gianfranco cycled his legs alternately.

"You are a leader."

"A leader? A leader of who?"

"The entire Oceania sector."

"And what does this *sector* do?"

Gianfranco, growing tired of the questions, decided enough was enough. He explained to Sol who White Cloud was, what they stood for, his role in the organisation, the

Viribus attacks three years ago, and who their enemies were.

"Wait a minute," Sol said. "You mean these Viribus people blew up our headquarters and then killed the boss, as well as me?"

Gianfranco nodded. "Correct, and they will be back for more. Our latest mission will no doubt attract their attention once again, and they will return to try and stop us again."

"Well, who is their boss? Can't we just kill him?"

"*Her*, Sol. The leader of Viribus is a woman."

Sol stopped for a second. "Okay, so can't we just kill *her* then? What's her name?"

"Kate… Kate *Fabianski*," Gianfranco said. "An Australian who lives in your sector—and we cannot just kill her, Sol. There will always be someone else to fill in the gap. No, we need to destroy them all."

"How are we going to do that?"

Gianfranco smiled. "I think you need to speak with our leader about that plan. I have arranged for you to meet with him tomorrow."

"What's his name?"

"Roman Horowitz."

Sol recalled the disfigured image looking back at him from the metal drawer next to him. He didn't want anyone to see him like this, let alone the leader of the organisation he now worked for; he would terrify everyone he encountered.

"Is there anything you can do about my appearance?" he asked.

Gianfranco looked at him and paused for a long moment. Sol pointed to the drawer next to him. "I saw myself in the metal."

"Ah, I see."

"What did I look like before?"

Gianfranco shrugged. "I don't know. But I can tell you that you look a lot better than what I scraped out of the fire."

Sol hung his head. "I can't be seen like this."

"I suspected your appearance might be a concern, so I have had our tech cell construct a personalised mask for you."

"A mask?" Sol said, chuckling to himself. "You're joking, right? What's next? A cape?"

Gianfranco smiled. "It's your choice, Sol. If you want to remain hidden inside this lab for the rest of your life, be my guest. Or you can wear the mask."

Sol thought for a moment.

"Would you like to see it?" Gianfranco asked.

"Okay," Sol said, nodding.

Gianfranco turned to leave the room.

Sol grabbed his arm to stop him. "Wait. I don't know your name."

"My name is Gianfranco, but you may call me Frank."

Frank left the room and returned a few minutes later carrying a hard industrial black case. He placed it next to Sol on the metal drawer where he was sitting.

"Here you go. This is yours."

Sol flicked up the latches on the case and opened it.

Inside was a silver and white mask with a single elongated red visor on the front, just wide enough to see through.

"It's a full-face mask," Frank said, removing the mask from the case and handing it to Sol. "You can put your entire head inside so that it's covered."

Sol took the mask from Frank and, with a bit of help, wriggled the mask over his head.

"Does it fit?" Frank asked.

Sol moved his head around in a circular motion.

"Yeah, it's very comfortable," he said, his voice deep and robot-like. "Shit! What happened to my voice?"

"Oh, yes. Sorry, I should have warned you. I had the mask fitted with some additional features. It has a digital voice amplifier inside it, which, admittedly, makes you sound a little like a robot, but I thought it would be for the best if we *changed* your voice somewhat."

Sol stared at Frank. "Why?"

"To keep your identity hidden."

"Yes, I get *that*, but *why* would you want to do that?"

"Think about it, Sol. Viribus has already tried to kill you once. There is every chance they will try to do it again."

Frank reached over. "So, if we just push this…" he said, pressing a button on the side of the mask.

Inside it, Sol could see all kinds of displays and parameters pop up in his field of view. "Woah, what the hell just happened?"

"Those displays you can see are infrared and thermal images. You can toggle through whatever image you wish to use."

Sol began pressing the buttons on the side of the mask, switching between infrared for night vision and thermal for heat-seeking.

As he played with the mask, he asked, "Where is my family? Surely I had one once?"

Frank cleared his throat. "Yes, you did."

"Where are they?"

Frank fidgeted with his hands awkwardly and said nothing, as if searching for words.

"Frank?"

"Viribus killed all of them as well."

Sol stopped playing with the mask and took it off his head. He stared at Frank in disbelief.

Before he could ask any further questions, Frank jumped in. "I have given you a second chance at life, Sol. This is an opportunity for you to seek revenge on those who killed you and your family. Very few people get that opportunity. You should embrace it."

Sol reflected on this for a few seconds.

"You know what?" he said. "You're right. These people are going to pay for what they have done. Get me to Roman tonight. We need to talk."

"You are not ready to go anywhere yet. Your legs are not yet working."

"You leave that part to me," Sol replied. "Organise the meeting for tonight."

Somewhere in China
10th February 2021
5:30 pm China Standard Time

Kate opened her eyes in the darkness of the trunk as panic instantly grabbed her. She could feel her hands bound behind her back and could taste the plastic of the ball gag in her mouth. Something was tied around her head, covering her eyes, and the smell of musty old carpet combined with the oppressive heat inside the trunk stifled the air.

She closed her eyes again and took three deep lung-filling breaths to slow her heart rate down. As the Major had once told her, panicking achieves nothing. It only clouds your decisions further.

Her legs were tucked up to her chest, leaving little room for movement, which only added to her battle with instinctive fear. She would not usually enter small, enclosed spaces with any enthusiasm.

She needed her eyes. Without them, she was surely going to be killed. She began rubbing the side of her head on the carpeted trunk floor and, after a few awkward attempts, she dislodged the blindfold from over her eyes.

Kate saw streetlights flashing past what looked like a bullet hole in the lid of the trunk.

The air was stale, and her mouth was getting increasingly dry. The hole in the trunk lid was her only source of fresh air, and it was hot. *Incredibly* hot. Like being in a small, dark sauna.

With her hands bound behind her back, she felt around for something to break the cable ties and get her hands free. With limited space to move, she wriggled around, exploring as much of her surroundings as possible until her fingers touched something hard and metallic.

Something that was a different texture to the carpeted floor of the trunk.

Her fingers had found a small hole in the trunk lining, exposing the metal of the car chassis. And as she scratched around inside the hole in the carpet, her fingers touched the head of what felt like a bolt head. Kate rubbed the plastic cable ties across it to weaken her restraints—she knew it could take a while, but it was all she had, so it was worth a shot.

Eventually, the cable ties snapped in two, and her hands were free. She quickly searched around for a latch on the trunk lid to see if she could open it from the inside, but there was nothing. She tried pushing on the lid with her shoulder, but this also did nothing.

With no obvious way out, she searched around in the darkness to see what else was in the trunk. Her reach was much better now that she was free from the restraints and could use her arms more effectively.

Her hands touched something that felt and sounded like a plastic bag. She put her hand inside it to explore its contents. With her hand, she could make out the shape of an aerosol can—and better yet—there were two of them.

Kate knew *exactly* what to do.

She shook both of the cans, rattling the metal agitator ball inside them, and turned to lie on her back with her legs skewed to one side.

The need for fresh air soon became unbearable, so Kate craned her head towards the bullet hole, putting her mouth over it and drawing in large breaths of revitalising fresh air from outside. She could hear aircraft taking off and the familiar sounds of an airport as the car stopped and switched its engine off.

Her heart rate quickened.

She listened intently as she heard the driver get out of the car and slam the door shut behind him. She listened for more doors shutting, trying to determine how many people might be outside.

Only one door slammed. That meant only one man.

Kate readied the aerosol cans, one in each hand, her fingers poised on the nozzles—and then, the trunk lid unlatched in front of her.

Her heart rate shifted a gear.

The trunk lid lifted, and Kate leapt up, pushing down on the nozzles of the aerosols as hard as she could to spray her attacker in the face. The hooded man recoiled backwards, shielding his face with his hands—but then he realised nothing was happening.

Kate looked curiously at the misfiring aerosols in her hands. They were both empty.

"Ah, fuck," she said.

The man punched her square in the face, knocking her out cold and causing her to fall back into the trunk. The man grabbed her arm, slung her over his shoulder, and carried her across the airfield apron towards a waiting helicopter.

Somewhere in China
10th February 2021
6:22 pm China Standard Time

Kate's eyes slowly opened and looked around at her new surroundings. She was sitting on a chair in the middle of a room with a highly polished concrete floor and eight large black timber doors embedded into its stone walls—two doors on each wall. Candles flickered in candelabras mounted to the walls illuminating the room and creating a dungeon-like atmosphere.

Kate noticed her high-tech outfit had been replaced by a plain white t-shirt and a pair of ill-fitting jeans, and the gag had been returned to her mouth. She looked down at her wrists and found they were shackled and secured to the floor on either side of the chair by a thick wrought-iron chain.

As she gave the chains a hopeful tug, all eight doors around the room swung open simultaneously, and eight Chinese men wearing dark sunglasses and expensive looking suits took a single step into the room.

The doors shut behind them with a thud, and the men stood perfectly still with their arms behind their backs, staring straight ahead.

Kate looked around the room, wondering which one was going to make the first move. She saw they all had the same tribal tattoo running up their neck that reached the side of their faces.

These guys were the Chinese Mafia—Triads.

A door in front of her swung open, and a man dressed all in black with a mane of blonde wavy hair entered the room. He marched towards her confidently. "Mrs Barrett," he said. "How nice of you to finally join us. I trust your trip was… enjoyable?" he asked with a grin.

Kate didn't answer.

"My name is Roman Horowitz," he said as he spun a chair around to sit on it backwards and lean on the backrest. "I think we need to have a little chat. Don't you?"

Kate didn't move a muscle. She stared at him intensely, playing out all the horrible things she would like to do to this man in her head.

"Oh, my apologies. It's a little difficult to talk with that thing in your mouth. Let me get that for you." He leaned towards her and removed the gag from her mouth.

"What do you want with me, you fuck?" Kate spat the second she could speak again.

"Mrs Barrett," Roman said, acting shocked. "I have been nothing but polite with you. I see no reason why you shouldn't reciprocate the gesture. I am happy to talk, but let's keep it civil, shall we?"

Kate paused as she stared into his face. "*Okay*, what do you want with me, *pretty please?*"

"That, my dear, is a damn good question," he said, getting off the chair and sitting on the floor in front of her with his legs crossed like a young child would before a teacher.

"What do I want with you?" he asked himself, pondering the question like he didn't know the answer. "Quite frankly, the only reason you are not already dead is that I am using you as bait."

"Bait?" she asked. "Bait for who?"

"For the rest of your friends who are, right now, on their way here to rescue you, are they not?"

"How would I know?" Kate replied. "You had me kidnapped, remember?"

Roman laughed, shaking his head. "Don't tell me you haven't worked this out yet! I already know the suit you wear contains a GPS transmitter—hence the reason you are no longer wearing it. That GPS signal will bring them straight to me like flies into a spider's web." Roman nodded towards the Triads standing around the room. "My assassins here have orders to kill them all on sight."

Kate glared at him. *"Assassins?"* she asked. "These guys are Triads."

"They are indeed," Roman said. "However, we have struck a deal with the Triads, and they graciously agreed to help us. Tell me, do you remember the hooded man who tried to take your twins in Shoalwater Bay?"

Kate nodded. "Yes. Of course, I do."

"What about the woman who tried to kill your father in your backyard?"

"Where are you going with this, Roman?"

"Those were our assassins, or Triads, if you prefer. Each of our sector leaders has at least one assassin allocated to them. Our leaders have far more important things to take care of than to go around kidnapping children…"

Kate launched herself out of the chair to attack him—but the chains held her back. "I'll fucking kill you!" she screamed.

The Triads all took a step forward. Roman held up a hand, and they stopped, before retreating to their original positions in front of the doors.

Kate sat back down in the chair, her gaze unwavering and fixed solely on Roman while she panted like an attack dog.

Roman stood up and paced around the room in front of her. "Mrs Barrett, you have no idea who you are dealing with, do you? I am in charge of the biggest and most powerful organisation in the history of mankind. We have the capacity and resources to act on our own volition."

"I know you have a virus," she said.

Roman stopped pacing and stared at her. He reached into his jacket pocket and pulled out a small black plastic case—the same black case she had taken from the woman's body in her backyard. Roman waved it in front of her face.

"Oh yes. I meant to ask, where did you get this from?"

"We killed your *assassin* and took it."

"How incredibly sloppy of them," Roman said, staring at the case. "Okay, yes. You are correct. I have a virus."

"And you're going to use it on the world, aren't you?"

"Yes, that is my intention."

"And you're storing bodies in the Wudang Mountains."

"Yes. My word, aren't you clever? However, you are stealing *all* of my thunder, Mrs Barrett. Except there is one particular fact you could not possibly know, and that is *when* I intend to unleash it—that's the best part."

"No. I don't know that, but I'm guessing you are about to tell me."

"The virus shall be released when the sun rises on Chinese New Year."

"But… that's the day after tomorrow."

"Correct! And as we speak, our leaders are positioning themselves in anticipation of what will be the most monumental event since the extinction of the dinosaurs." Roman said as he paced in front of her, smiling like an excited little boy on Christmas Eve as he spoke.

"Would you like to know what the virus does to its victims?" he asked.

Kate shook her head. "Not really. But again, I have a feeling you're going to tell me, even if I don't want to hear it."

"The virus attacks the human respiratory system by embedding itself deep into the lungs. Within a matter of hours, your lungs will fill with fluid, and you will suffocate."

Kate looked up at him. "Why? Why go to all this trouble?"

He stopped pacing and leaned close to her face. "People are filth!" he spat. "That's *why*, Mrs Barrett. Humans have ravaged this planet with greed and a never-ending quest for more power, more wealth, more of everything. Enough is enough. The Earth needs to reset with a new breed of supreme, clean, intelligent, and most importantly, *kind* people."

"So that's the reason behind the human depository?"

"Exactly. We have gathered the most knowledgeable and remarkable people from all walks of life and assembled them there. Those people are the future and will produce a better race of human for generations to come."

Kate nodded. "Gianfranco said something very similar. But what makes you think these *new* people won't just make the Earth exactly the same as it is now?"

"Gianfranco isn't just storing bodies in Wudang. He has been tasked with giving us the ability to alter the brain patterns of every one of those people. We can now program them to do whatever we want them to do."

"You're creating human robots?"

Roman thought about this for a second.

"For the want of a better term… yes, I suppose so. If we can control 500 people to raise a generation of exquisite humans who do not believe in money or power, then why not?"

"How ironic," Kate said. "So, you're creating people to *not* be you. You're insane."

Roman laughed. "Am I, Kate? Or am I simply facilitating the Earth to rid itself of its own virus? *My* virus is so highly contagious that we only need to release it into a single human in each quadrant of the globe, and within a week, it will have spread around the Earth like wildfire, cleansing the world of its disease. Once that stage is complete, we can begin creating a superhuman version of our species."

"You *are* insane," Kate said. "And we will stop you."

Roman ignored her and leaned in close to her face again. "The *very* best part of this plan is that geographically, the virus is going to be released in your country first."

"What do you mean?" Kate asked, with a quiver of fear in her voice.

"Australia will be amongst the first countries to see the sun on the morning of the 12th of February, meaning the virus will kill your family first. A new world is about to be born, and there is *nothing* you can do about it."

"Watch me," she snarled back at him.

Shiyan Wudangshan Airport, China
10th February 2021
7:05 pm China Standard Time

At Shiyan Wudangshan Airport, a Russian-built, Chinese Air Force operated Sukhoi SU-35 multi-role fighter jet stopped next to Moose, and the canopy raised.

Jesse had arrived at the Wudang Temple Complex at precisely the right time. Dialling into the team's earpiece frequency, he'd heard Kate get isolated from the rest of the team and instructed Alaina to mark their location using a flare. When the flare went up, Jesse fired at the corridor entrance with a missile from the aircraft and peppered the ground with bombs—clearing a path for Kate and her team to escape.

Jesse waited next to Moose, watching the smoking mountain he had recently destroyed in the distance, while he waited for the team to return to the aircraft. But when they didn't, he got worried and decided to go back to the mountain to find them.

He scanned the airfield for something he could use as transport. His eyes came to rest on a rusty, weathered-looking ground support vehicle. Jesse went over to the car and quickly hot-wired it, driving it out of the airport and towards the mountain at speed.

An hour after departing the airport, he reached the temple complex gate and, to his left, saw a van resting on its roof. He stopped the car in front of the gate and went over to investigate.

Inside the van, he found Matt strapped into his seat, upside down and unconscious. He then looked into the back of the van and in the darkness, could see Alaina lying motionless on the roof of the van—but there was no sign of Kate.

Jesse leapt into action, checking both of their pulses and vital signs. They each had a heartbeat and were breathing, so he began quickly checking for any major injuries.

Satisfied neither of them were severely injured, Jesse sat Alaina up and patted her face, repeating her name over and over to get a response. She soon began groaning and moving her head, so Jesse turned his attention to Matt.

Crawling through the passenger side window, Jesse unclipped Matt's seatbelt and sat him upright. Matt wasn't responding to the pats on the face like Alaina, so Jesse slapped him harder and shouted his name to wake him up.

He still didn't respond.

Alaina opened her eyes and became coherent.

"Where's Kate?" she asked, looking around the van as she rubbed at her head and neck.

"I was going to ask you the same thing," Jesse replied. "Did the van get hit by the bombs or something?"

"No. We were on our way back to the airport… and the next thing I know, well… you're here in front of me."

"Well, at least you're alive," Jesse said. "Come on, help me get Matt into the car. He's got a pulse, but he isn't responding, and we still have to find Kate."

Alaina helped Jesse extract Matt from the van, pulling him through the driver's side window head first. As they carried him up the embankment, Alaina noticed a set of fresh tyre tracks leading towards the upturned van. They were *large* tyre tracks. They placed Matt in the back seat of the stolen ground support vehicle and got in the car.

"Any ideas where we start looking?" Jesse asked.

"Head to the airport," Alaina said. "We have to keep moving. She's been kidnapped."

"What? How do you know that?"

"Tyre tracks, Jesse. Someone drove into the van with an off-road vehicle. Take me back to Moose. I know how to find her."

They arrived at the airport an hour and a half later. Matt was muttering some indistinct words from the rear seat as they pulled up to Moose and opened his eyes as they stopped.

"So, what now?" Jesse asked.

"We track her," Alaina replied.

"Track her?"

Before she could explain, Matt opened his eyes again. "The suit," he said.

Alaina smiled at Jesse. "What he said. Kate is wearing a tailor-made, high-tech suit Matt made for her when we were in Dubai. This gurgling genius in the back put a GPS transponder inside it. We can track her using my laptop."

Alaina leapt out of the car and raced over to Moose. She grabbed her laptop from the cockpit and turned it on. Once it had booted up, she opened an application and saw a red blip hovering over a map of Shanghai—a 12-hour drive east.

She returned to the car and stuck her head through the window. "She's in Shanghai."

"Shanghai? How did she get there so quickly?" Jesse asked.

"I can only guess she flew there," Alaina said. "And we are going to do exactly the same. Come on."

"What about the Sukhoi?" Jesse asked.

Alaina looked over at the sleek-looking aircraft parked next to Moose and thought for a moment. "Leave it here. If we need it, we can come back for it."

Alaina and Jesse helped the unsteady Matt walk up the loading ramp of Moose and sat him down in the cargo area, strapping him to a seat.

A few minutes later, they were airborne and heading through the night sky towards Shanghai.

Jesse sat next to Alaina in the cockpit, thumbing through flight maps of China. "There are several airports in the Shanghai area," he said. "Which one do you want to land at?"

"We need to get as close to the blip on the laptop as possible," Alaina replied.

Jesse picked up the laptop with one hand, comparing it to the flight maps he held in the other. "Shanghai Longhua is the closest to Shanghai Central."

"Perfect, then that's where we're going."

"The only problem is that the runway is too short for this aircraft to land on," he said.

Alaina smiled across at him. "You've never flown with me before, have you? Radio in, tell Shanghai Longhua emergency services to be prepared for a hot brake stop on a C-17 cargo aircraft."

"What? There's no way you'll—"

Alaina held a hand up. "Jesse, with all due respect, shut up and call the airport."

Jesse keyed his radio, informing the airport of their imminent arrival and to be prepared for an emergency landing.

A couple of minutes later, a familiar voice came across the radio. *"Jesse? Is that you?"* the voice asked.

Jesse stared at Alaina.

She stared back. "Is that who I think it is?"

Jesse keyed the radio and spoke into it.

"Yes, it's me, Major. I got them."

"What's the situation?" the Major asked.

"Kate's been kidnapped and is somewhere in Shanghai. We're on our way to rescue her."

"Which airport are you landing at?"

"Shanghai Longhua, ETA 30 minutes."

There was a long pause.

"You're in Moose, right?" the Major asked.

Jesse nodded. "Ah, yep. Yes, we are."

"Alaina's flying?"

"She sure is."

"Godspeed, kid," the Major said. *"Make sure you strap in tight. I'll meet you there. Hopefully, you get there in one piece."*

"How did he get here so quick?" Alaina asked.

Jesse sighed. "I'll be honest with you, Alaina. The Major and I have been tracking Moose through the Flightradar app," he said. "We saw you guys depart Longreach and head towards China, so we figured you would eventually need some help. We left Shoalwater and headed straight for Shanghai. Once we got here, it was only a matter of tuning into your earpiece frequency and waiting for someone to say something. We soon heard you were in trouble and responded. It turns out the Major has friends in some very high places, and they let me use the Sukhoi to come and help you."

"I'm bloody glad you did," Alaina said. "They would have killed us all on that mountain."

Thirty minutes later, Alaina lined up the Shanghai Longhua runway and began sweating. The runway was *very* short. *Much* shorter than the one at Longreach. She quickly realised she would need to hit the runway as early as possible to pull the aircraft up without overshooting. She disengaged the autopilot and began guiding the aircraft down manually as Jesse tightened his seatbelts and held on to them tightly.

"Are you sure about this?" he asked.

"No runway has ever beaten me," Alaina replied. "But admittedly, this one is the shortest I have ever attempted."

"Aw, man. Don't say that!" Jesse said, looking up at the heavens.

"Just hold on and be ready to pull back on those reverse thrust levers," Alaina said as she focused on the aircraft's instruments in front of her.

The C-17 Globemaster is one of the few aircraft with the ability to deploy its thrust reversers in flight. This ability enables the aircraft to land on much shorter runways than it should—a manoeuvre more commonly known as a *tactical landing*.

Alaina knew her aircraft. Although she had never undertaken the manoeuvre herself. As the aircraft's altimeter dropped below 500 feet, she yelled, "Reverse thrust now!"

Jesse looked at her wide-eyed. "But we're not on the ground yet!" he shouted.

"Just do it!"

Jesse quickly yanked the levers up and was thrown violently forward in his seat as the aircraft rapidly decelerated. Alaina grunted as she wrestled to keep the nose of the aircraft pointing skyward as it began plummeting sharply towards the ground.

The instant Moose's main gear hit the beginning of the runway, Alaina slammed the nose down and stood on the brakes with everything she had.

Jesse closed his eyes and clenched his teeth as the other end of the runway came into view quickly.

Alaina deployed all her strength to press the brake pedals down, and as the end of the runway approached, the aircraft came to a sudden and complete stop. She looked across at Jesse and breathed an enormous sigh of relief before sinking back into her seat.

She released the brakes and engaged full reverse thrust again, utilising the C-17's other party trick—reversing under its own power.

Alaina reversed the aircraft along the runway until the first runway exit became visible, and then taxied forward, parking the aircraft on a remote apron.

On the eastern side of the airport, several helipads were lit up in the darkness. A fully armed helicopter gunship waited on one of them and a figure stood beside it.

"That's the Major," Jesse said.

"Yes, I can tell," Alaina said, getting out of her seat and heading into the rear of the aircraft. "Let's see what he has to say, shall we?"

Matt had woken up after the erratic landing and was already loading their van with weapons.

"Good morning, Princess," Alaina said, walking into the cargo bay. "Did you have a nice nap?"

"What happened?" Matt asked.

"I'm not sure, buddy, but we need to find Kate; she's here somewhere. The Major and Jesse have come to help. The Major is waiting outside and has a helicopter."

"Bloody hell," Matt replied, turning to Jesse. "How long was I out for?"

Jesse shrugged a response.

They put a selection of weapons into duffle bags and gathered their laptops before walking to the waiting gunship.

The helicopter was a Chinese Air Force Harbin Z-9, armed with an under-nose machine gun turret, and missiles mounted on the wing-like pylons attached to its side. It accommodated six people inside the cabin, not including the pilots.

"Your friends let you play with some very expensive toys, Major," Alaina said, staring up at the enormous helicopter behind him.

The Major smiled. "I figured we might need this if someone doesn't play nicely."

She gave him a friendly hug. "Let's hope it doesn't come to that."

"Yes, I hope so too—that was one hell of a landing, by the way."

"Thanks," Alaina said, glancing over at Jesse. "Although I'm not so sure he would agree with you."

Jesse still looked a little green from the rapid descent.

"So, where's Kate?" the Major asked.

Alaina opened up her laptop. "The GPS says she is still in downtown Shanghai. The signal hasn't moved. I suppose this doesn't tell me if she's dead or alive."

The Major turned, opening the door of the helicopter. "Well, let's go find out, shall we?"

UNIFORM

Gianfranco picked up the phone and dialled a number. He had a short, concise conversation with someone on the other end and put the phone down again before turning to Sol. "A helicopter will be here in an hour to pick you up. Are you sure you are going to be ready?"

Looking down at his legs as he crept around the laboratory, Sol said, "I'll make sure I am."

An hour later, Gianfranco and Sol entered an elevator, heading for the mountain top helicopter landing pad. Sol, dressed in a pristine White Cloud uniform sporting an Australian flag on the sleeve, looked a touch robotic with the mask over his head and his unsteady walk.

The sound of a helicopter's beating blades got louder as they walked out onto the helipad, and before long, a matte black, stealth-looking helicopter was landing in front of them. Its engine shut down, and the side door slid open.

Gianfranco turned to Sol. "This is where I must leave you," he said.

"You're not coming with me?"

"No. I'm sorry. I can't," Gianfranco said. "I have some business I must attend to in Italy. But I wish you all the best, and I hope you can assist Roman to get White Cloud off its knees."

He held his hand out for Sol to shake.

Sol stared down at the open hand. His memory not recalling this social convention.

"It's a gesture of friendship," Gianfranco explained. "You put your hand in mine, and you shake it."

Sol put his hand into Gianfranco's but left the act of the actual shake to him. "I appreciate everything you have done for me," Sol said. "I will do my best to return the favour."

Gianfranco smiled at him. "Godspeed, Sol. Godspeed."

Sol walked slowly over to the helicopter and got in. Inside the rear section were three men, all dressed in black and wearing headsets. They acknowledged him with a simple nod, which Sol mimicked in return.

"Where are you taking me?" he asked.

None of the men answered him and stared straight ahead, unresponsive and cold.

"Good chat," Sol said sarcastically.

An hour later, the helicopter landed on top of a skyscraper high above a city. Sol could hear the blaring of car horns coming from somewhere below as frustrated drivers battled with city traffic and the wind howled across the top of the building. A well-groomed man in a suit strode towards him.

"Welcome, Mr Barrett," the man said, holding his hand out as Gianfranco had done. "My name is—" he paused for a moment, leaning forward to examine the mask on Sol's head, "—What the hell is that on your head?"

Sol shook the man's hand. "It's a mask."

"Yes, I can see that, but… why?"

"Because what is under this mask should not be seen by anyone, and you do not need to introduce yourself. I know who you are," Sol said. "Frank told me all about you."

"Frank?" Roman asked, standing up straight and blinking in confusion. "Who's Frank?"

"Gianfranco."

Roman smiled. "Ah, okay. *Frank*."

"So, what do you need me to do?" Sol asked.

"Let's go inside, shall we?" Roman said, placing a hand on Sol's shoulder and turning him around. "It's far too noisy to talk out here."

Roman led him inside the building. They entered a vast penthouse suite with Greek-style floor-to-ceiling columns all around, and the floor was made entirely of marble. Strange looking pieces of art and antiquities sat upon plinths positioned around the room, individually illuminated by a single, ceiling-mounted spotlight.

Roman opened a side door and ushered him into another room. This one looked like more like an office. Roman shut the door and walked over to a mini bar to pour himself a scotch. "Would you like one?" he asked, holding the bottle in the air.

Sol stared at him. He didn't know what Roman was offering. "One of what?" he asked.

"Never mind," Roman said, putting the bottle down. "Now, what is it you are here to help me do, exactly?"

"I want to assist White Cloud and take revenge on the people who killed my family... and me."

Roman sipped at his whiskey as he sat down. "Hmm, okay. Interesting. Well, maybe we can use you," he said, swilling the ice around in his glass and thinking. "You are aware who Viribus is?" he asked.

Sol nodded. "Yes. Frank told me."

"Well, that's a good start. It certainly saves me some time," Roman said, swilling his whiskey around some more as he gazed into it. He set the glass down on a side table. "What if I were to inform you that right now, I have the person responsible for killing your family tied up in a room on the other side of this apartment?"

Sol stared at him. "Is it the same person who did this to me?" he asked, pointing at his face.

Roman nodded and picked up the glass of whiskey as he stood up. "In fact, this person is someone you would be very familiar with. The leader of Viribus, Kate—"

"—Fabianski," Sol said, interrupting him. "Frank told me about her too, but I don't understand how you think I would know her."

Roman looked at him, confused. "Is that what Frank told you? The leader of Viribus is Kate *Fabianski?*"

Sol nodded.

"*Okay.* Well, I suppose we'll go with that," Roman said.

"Why do you think I know her?"

Roman waved away the question. "Never mind, forget I said anything."

Sol went to stand up, but Roman pushed him back down into the seat by his shoulder. "Where are you going?" he asked.

"I am going to kill her."

"No, you're not."

"Why? I'm the perfect man for the job. I'm dead already, remember? I'm practically a ghost."

"I know this, Mr Barrett. Which is why we must use this to its greatest potential."

"What do you mean?"

"How would you like the honour of being the first person to release my virus into the world?"

"Will it kill her?" Sol asked.

"Oh, absolutely—and her family. I want you to use her to release it! In doing so, we can eradicate Viribus at the same time—two birds, one stone."

"Sounds good."

"The men who travelled with you in the helicopter earlier will escort you and administer the virus on your behalf. All you need to do is go to Australia, get Kate to a place where the rest of Viribus can easily find her, and let your assistants do their thing. Do this for me, and you will have your revenge in the greatest way possible."

"Australia?" Sol asked. "Where's that?"

Roman smirked. "This is precisely why you will have their help. I realise you are not completely aware of your surroundings just yet, Sol. It's understandable when you have been on ice for three years. These people will assist you."

"If she is in this building right now, how can you be so sure she'll return to Australia?"

"Her colleagues are on the way here to rescue her, and I intend to let them do just that. Once they have successfully rescued her and escaped, she will naturally return to Australia to protect her children." Roman shrugged. "If she doesn't, we can always force the issue."

"How will you know where she is?"

"Ah, yes," Roman said, opening the cabinet drawer behind him and taking out a device that looked like an e-reader.

"Take this with you," he said, handing him the device.

"What's this?"

"It's a tracking device. We have planted a GPS transmitter in the pendant of a necklace she carries with her." Roman paused to clear his throat. "Her deceased husband gave it to her as a gift, so it holds a lot of sentimental value to her. She will never let it leave her possession. Good for us."

Roman reached over and switched on the device as Sol held it in his hands. It booted up and displayed a map of the world with a blue dot pulsing over Shanghai.

"How am I going to get to Australia?" Sol asked.

Roman smiled. "Once Mrs Fabianski's friends arrive and carry out their daring rescue attempt, we will head to my ship that is waiting for us in the Pacific Ocean. The ship is loaded with everything you will need to carry out your mission. Jets, helicopters, missiles, explosives, tanks. You name it, it's on board. It is a fully functioning, floating warlord's toy box and will be entirely at your disposal. You can wait for Mrs Fabianski to make her move from there, and then you can make your way to Australia."

There was a knock at the door.

"Come in," Roman said.

A beautiful blonde, tall woman came into the room.

"Are you ready for me yet, sir?" she asked.

"Yes, I think we are, Samantha."

Samantha floated across the room like a supermodel, holding a silver tray she placed gently on the desk next to him.

Sol saw the syringe.

"Although, before you go anywhere, we must give you this," Roman said.

"What is that?"

"This is your immunity. When we unleash the virus, it will protect you from its effects."

Samantha loaded the gun-looking syringe with a small cartridge and approached him. He saw her staring at his mask as she rolled up the sleeve of his uniform.

He looked her dead in the eye. Her perfume was familiar. He had smelled it before…

Underneath the Australian flag on the arm of his uniform, Samantha injected him with the tiny capsule.

"Welcome to White Cloud, Solomon Barrett," Roman said cheerfully.

Sol rolled his sleeve down. "What do we do now?" he asked as Samantha picked up the silver tray and left the room.

Roman gulped down the remaining whiskey in his glass, slammed it down on the bar, and followed Samantha towards the door. "Now… we wait," he replied with a glint in his eye as he walked past him. "Stay here. I'll be back soon."

Shanghai City, China
10ᵗʰ February 2021
9:45 pm China Standard Time

As Kate sat in the dungeon-like room, shackled to the chair surrounded by the statuesque Triads, she heard the sound of a helicopter coming from outside. She listened intently to the helicopter's engine as it shut down, and then everything was quiet again. If Alaina and Matt were onboard the helicopter, they would surely not have been permitted to get this close without Roman having them killed. She listened for gunshots, shouting, explosions, anything that might signal that she was about to be rescued—but nothing happened.

Silence.

She then heard doors opening and closing beyond the walls of the room she was in and strained to listen for familiar voices, desperately hoping someone had arrived to help her get out of her prison.

An hour later, Roman burst into the room and stood over her, his face radiating with a sinister smile as he stared down at her shackled to the chair.

"I cannot wait to see the look on your face," he said.

Kate caught a waft of alcohol. "What?" she asked.

"I have a *wonderful* surprise for you. I wonder if you will thank me," he said, staring at her like a maniac.

"I strongly doubt that," she replied, looking up at him suspiciously. Roman's character had shifted since he was last in the room. Maybe it was the alcohol, maybe it wasn't, but now he was making her feel *very* uncomfortable—he seemed completely unhinged.

Roman snapped out of his trance-like state and began pacing in front of her again. "You need to understand that this plan has been in motion for over two years now, Mrs Barrett, and you and your friends will not be permitted to get in the way of its execution. Once your friends arrive, I will kill all of you, ending Viribus forever and eradicating you from the face of the Earth."

Kate looked up at him with a smirk. "Tao controls you like a puppet, doesn't he?"

Roman stopped pacing and leaned over at the waist, staring her in the face. "You think you're so *fucking* smart, don't you?" he said. "I don't answer to Tao. This is *my* plan and *my* organisation."

Kate saw her window of opportunity open as Roman was bent over in front of her, putting his head exactly where she knew she could reach him. She launched herself at him, latching her teeth around his nose and biting down as hard as she could.

Roman howled in pain as blood began pouring from his nose and gushing out of Kate's mouth.

The Triads leapt into action, raising their knives, pistols, and knuckle-dusters into striking positions as they ran towards her.

"WAIT!" Roman screamed.

Kate let go of his nose and he stumbled backwards onto the floor, clasping a hand over his blood-soaked face to hold the blood in while throwing his other hand into the air.

"Stop!" he shouted at the onrushing Triads.

The Triads stopped and stared at him.

"We need the others to arrive before we kill her," he said.

Kate spat out a mouthful of Roman's blood as he slowly gathered himself up off the floor and stumbled towards the door while still clutching at his nose.

"Get back to your posts!" he yelled at the Triads before exiting the room.

The Triads did as they were ordered—all except one of them.

Kate could feel the Triad's presence behind her. She turned around as far as her shackles would allow her, and in the corner of her eye, could see a large Triad member standing behind her.

"There is a way you can stop him," the Triad said.

The other gang members turned their heads, staring at the one who had dared to defy Roman's orders.

Kate looked at the other Triads, uncertain if she should respond or not.

"How do I stop him?" she whispered.

"Each of the five leaders has a chip containing a code implanted in their bodies."

The other Triads turned around and began walking towards the one who was speaking out. The Triad behind her barked something in Chinese, making the others stop immediately. He then shouted some more words and the gang members retreated to their posts.

Kate, wide-eyed and covered in blood, meekly continued her questioning.

"Like a chip you put in a dog?" she asked.

"Yes. The same."

"And what do these chips do?"

"Each contain a piece of a unique code. Combining all five codes creates a formula. This formula will eliminate the virus."

"Why are you telling me this? Why haven't you just killed him yourselves?"

"Killing *him* is not the answer, Mrs Barrett. If he dies, there is no hope. The implanted chips monitor their host's heartbeat, which means if any of the leaders are killed before the code is extracted, you cannot create the formula. To retrieve all the codes will require much more than a small group of Triads. You and your global organisation are the best option humanity has right now."

The Triad cut the cable ties on her wrists and unshackled her from the floor. *"If he comes back in, act as though you are tied up,"* he whispered.

Kate nodded. *"I need weapons,"* she whispered back.

The Triad hurried across the room and disappeared behind one of the doors.

While he was gone, Kate quickly felt around in the jeans pockets for anything she might use to escape. They had taken everything; her earpiece, the vial containing the virus, and the necklace she had retrieved from Mike's possession.

The Triad returned to the room, walked over to her, and held out a fist. Kate held out her hand, and the Triad dropped her earpiece into it.

"It's the best I can do right now," he said, before quickly returning to his post.

She shoved the grommet-like earpiece into her ear.

"Can anyone hear me?" she whispered.

Shanghai City, China
10th February 2021
10:15 pm China Standard Time

In the night sky above Shanghai, the Major flew the Russian gunship with the Viribus members onboard towards Kate's GPS signal.

Alaina stared at her laptop as the helicopter headed towards the lights of the city. "It looks as though she is in that massive high-rise up ahead," she said, pointing out of the window. "Is there anywhere you can set the helicopter down?"

"No. There's a helicopter already on the helipad of that building, and there's not enough space anywhere on the ground," he said, looking out of the window at the ground below. "The closest landing area would be that park over there, but it would mean we have to walk the rest of the way."

"That will have to do," Alaina replied, as she heard a voice crackle through the static in her earpiece.

"Can anyone hear me?"

"Kate?" Alaina said. "Holy shit. You don't know how good it is to hear your voice. Thank God you're alive."

"I am for the moment. Where are you?"

"In a helicopter over Shanghai coming towards you. We tracked your suit's GPS signal. Are you in a skyscraper or something?"

"I'm not sure where I am, Alaina. Although, wherever it is, it's a trap. They are waiting for you to rescue me, and then they're going to kill us all."

"I'd like to see them try," Alaina said. "Sit tight, babe. We're on our way. Just hold on."

Sit tight, Kate thought. *If only she knew the irony of that statement right now.*

"Alaina?"

"Yes, Kate?"

"I love you, man."

"I love you too, babe."

"I gotta go."

Kate removed the earpiece from her ear, tucked it into a pocket, and put her wrists together behind her back, imitating them still being tied together.

A few seconds later, Roman entered the room. "I cannot wait to kill you," he said with a bandage over his face. "I now understand why Tao wants you dead."

Kate said nothing.

In the distance, she heard the thumping sound of helicopter blades getting louder.

Roman heard it too. A smile appeared under the bandage strapped across his face. "Oh! I wonder if this is your friends now?" He said as he turned around to exit the room.

Kate saw her opportunity.

She leapt off the chair and charged at him. Using the element of surprise to her advantage, she ploughed into him shoulder-first, crash-tackling him to the floor and straddling his chest before he could right himself. Kate slammed a fist into the middle of his bandaged face, causing blood to spurt out from underneath the bandage— and then she hit him twice more.

Roman jerked his body upwards like a professional wrestler, ejecting her off him like a wild bull would eject its cowboy.

Kate got to her feet and ran for the open door behind Roman, closely followed by the seven Triads. The one who had freed her did not move from his post.

Kate sprinted through the door and into the vast penthouse apartment on the other side, jamming the earpiece back into her ear as she ran.

The Triads continued to chase.

She picked up various ornaments and artefacts as she ran past them, hurling the objects at the apartment windows to break them—but they didn't crack, and she was running out of apartment space quickly. It was an enormous suite, but not large enough to stay in front of seven Triads.

She had to think fast…

The lights!

Kate ran for the nearest light switch and began flicking it up and down as many times as she could before the advancing gang of Triads could reach her.

"Alaina! Do you see the lights?" she yelled into her earpiece.

In the helicopter hovering outside the skyscraper, Jesse was the first to spot the apartment with lights flickering on and off inside it.

"Over there," he said, pointing out the helicopter's window.

"We got you!" Alaina replied as the Major manoeuvred the helicopter to face the apartment.

Kate watched the aircraft loom into view, as did the Triads, who stopped to stare at the gunship hovering outside the window.

"Is that thing armed?" Kate asked.

"Yes," Alaina replied. "Heavily!"

"Then shoot the fucking windows!"

"Okay! Get down!"

Alaina turned to the Major. "Shoot the windows!" she screamed.

"Are you serious?" the Major replied.

"Just do it!"

The Major slammed his finger on the trigger of his control stick and opened fire, shattering the windows and causing glass to shower down the face of the building towards the ground below.

Kate threw herself to the floor of the apartment to avoid the volley of bullets coming into the apartment from outside.

The Triads were mown down and killed instantly, the hefty rounds tearing them apart as Kate hid in the corner of the room, flat to the floor.

The Major stopped firing. "Was that enough?" he asked.

"Kate? Are you okay?" Alaina asked.

"Get me some weapons!" Kate screamed over the howling wind that was now fiercely whipping around inside the apartment, carrying dust, debris, and pieces of paper with it.

"No problem! Get ready!" Alaina yelled back.

Kate noticed Roman hadn't yet emerged from the room where she had broken his nose. She got to her feet and went over to where the windows used to be as the Major flew the helicopter as close as possible to the side of the building.

Matt threw out a rope to her, which she deftly caught and tied to a nearby pillar. Matt then fed the other end of the rope through the handles of a duffle bag and pushed it out of the helicopter. The Major elevated the helicopter slightly, causing the bag to slide down the rope and into Kate's hands.

She untied the rope from the pillar, armed herself with weapons out of the bag, and moved towards the room where she had been held hostage by Roman.

She kicked open the door of the room, expecting to find Roman on the ground inside, but there was no sign of him. Nothing except a small puddle of blood on the floor.

One of the doors where the Triads once stood was now slightly ajar—it was the same door the helpful Triad had entered earlier to retrieve her earpiece. She pushed it open with her foot, and inside the room was a table with nothing on it except for her necklace. She snatched it from the table and shoved it into her pocket.

"Kate, we have movement on the roof!" Alaina yelled through her earpiece.

Kate spun around and ran out into the apartment.

"I need you to pick me up," she yelled over the noise of the helicopter hovering outside the building.

"But we can't land anywhere!" Alaina said.

Kate saw the rope they had used to send the bag of weapons down, still dangling underneath the helicopter.

"Who said anything about landing? Bring it in as close as you can and leave that rope where it is."

Alaina realised what Kate was about to do. *"Oh, hell no,"* she said.

"Just fucking do it, Alaina!"

Alaina turned to the Major. "Put the rope in front of the window! Kate is about to jump out of the building!"

"She's what now?"

"Just do it, Major!"

The Major manoeuvred the helicopter into position, as Kate ran over to a fire alarm panel on the apartment's wall and pushed the button. Fire alarms began ringing inside the building as the sprinkler system initiated. Kate took a breath as the sprinklers drenched her and then turned towards the helicopter hovering outside, sprinting towards it.

She leapt out of the building and sailed through the night sky towards the rope. She caught it with both hands but slid down it due to her hands being wet from the sprinklers inside the building. The rope tore the skin on her hands as she desperately grappled with it to slow herself down. She then quickly whipped a leg around the rope to arrest her descent and stop herself from sliding off the end.

It worked. She took a moment to catch her breath and then climbed the rope towards the helicopter. Grimacing in pain with every inch she ascended.

As she reached the top, Matt and Alaina grabbed her arms and heaved her inside the helicopter.

"Hey," Kate said as she lay on the floor, panting as her team stared at her with their mouths open.

"Hey, *Jane McClane*," Matt said with a smile.

"You are one badass bitch. I'll give you that," Alaina said. "All right! Let's go, Major!" she yelled towards the cockpit. "We got her!"

Kate looked at Alaina and then towards the cockpit.

"Did you say, *Major?*"

Alaina nodded.

"How did he get here?"

"Rooftop!" Matt said, pointing at the skyscraper.

On the roof, a United States Marine Corp V-22 Tilt Rotor Osprey was taking to the air. The Major aimed the helicopter's cannon at it and put his finger over the trigger.

"No! Don't shoot!" Kate screamed, realising what was about to happen.

"Why the hell not?" The Major yelled back from the cockpit.

"I'll tell you later. Just DO NOT FIRE!"

The Major moved his finger away from the control stick's trigger and pouted like a scolded child.

"Major?"

"Yes, Kate?"

"You can destroy that building, though!"

The Major smiled a little. "What about the people inside it?"

"Look down!" she yelled back.

The Major peered through his window at the ground below where swarms of people were already evacuating the building.

"I set off the fire alarm before I jumped," she said. "Everyone should be out by now."

The Major turned the helicopter to face the building and launched a missile at it.

The missile hissed away from the helicopter, ploughing into the side of the building and causing a massive fireball to erupt. As the night was illuminated by the fireball, the Major looked down at the ground and saw the crowds of people running further away. He gave them a few more minutes to scramble to safety before unleashing several more missiles on the building.

The building soon began to creak and moan until, eventually, it could take no more and imploded, crashing to the ground under a cloud of dust, concrete, and metal.

Shanghai City, China

10th February 2021

10:35 pm China Standard Time

From inside the retreating helicopter, Kate watched Roman's Shanghai skyscraper collapse to the ground into a pile of dust and rubble. She gathered herself for a moment. She had information she urgently needed to relay to her team and an ever-decreasing amount of time.

A red tactical light illuminated the helicopter's cabin, creating an eerie and tense atmosphere.

Matt sat next to her, watching the building fall with her. "Nice outfit," he said, looking at her jeans. "What happened to the suit?"

Kate nodded at the crumbling building. "It's in there somewhere. Roman took it and used it to lure you here. Sorry."

Matt waved her apology away. "Don't worry about it. I can make you another," he replied. "What happened in there?"

She ignored the question, leaning forward in her chair to address the team. "I need all of you to listen to me carefully."

Alaina adjusted herself in her seat to get comfortable. "Ooh, go on," she said, evidently quite excited by what Kate had to say.

"It appears we have grossly underestimated Roman," Kate began. "He is a massive problem, and our mission here is going to have to change proportionally."

"You found him?" Alaina asked.

Kate shook her head. "No. He found me. It was Roman who had me kidnapped from Wudang and brought here to Shanghai. That was his building we just levelled."

"Oh, dang," Alaina said. "Was he in the Osprey?"

Kate nodded.

"What did he want with you?" Jesse asked.

"He was using me as bait, waiting for you guys to turn up so he could get us all out of the way."

"Out of the way? Out of the way of what?" Alaina asked.

"Mike was right, Alaina. Roman and Tao *are* resurrecting White Cloud. But what Mike didn't tell us was that Roman isn't just the leader of the American sector— he's in charge of the *entire* operation and has some horrifying plans."

"Well, we know he has a virus—"

"Yes, but that's not all, Alaina. Roman told me precisely *when* he plans on releasing it."

"Go on," Matt said.

"He intends to release it as dawn breaks around the world for Chinese New Year, starting with Australia—oh, shit!" Kate said, holding her hands over her face. "I totally forgot! What time is it in Australia now?"

"Australia is two hours behind Shanghai, so it's 9.00 pm on the 10th there right now," Matt said.

"And what time is dawn in Australia?"

"Around 6.30 am."

Alaina did the math quickly and gasped. "Chinese New Year starts on the 12th—holy shit, Kate! That only gives us 33 hours to stop them!"

Kate sat back in her seat and looked up at the ceiling.

"I don't get it," Matt said. "Why did you stop the Major from shooting down the Osprey? If we kill Roman; we kill the problem, right?"

Kate shook her head. "Wrong. Roman has been very smart about this, Matt. He's implanted the five leaders with unique chips that carry some kind of scientific code for a formula which will stop the virus."

"Then we kill the leaders, dig out the chips and hand the codes over to a scientist."

"You think we can do all that in 33 hours?" Kate asked. "No, we can't do that either, Matt. The chips are programmed to erase the code if it detects the host's heart stops beating."

Matt looked impressed. "Wow. That *is* smart. A heart sensor. Although it begs the question; why go to all the trouble of making a virus that can end humanity and then create a way to make a formula that can erase it?"

"Yeah," Alaina agreed, nodding her head. "Good point! That does seem kinda dumb."

"I suspect the formula code was set up for two reasons. One, to protect themselves from the effects of the virus should they ever need it, and two, so no one kills them on sight. Roman knows we will try to get the code for the formula—I guess that's why he made sure I knew everything about his plan. We are now aware of what we can't do."

Matt nodded his head. "That makes more sense; spreading the code between the leaders and installing the heart sensor on the chip protects *them* from *us*."

Alaina chimed in. "And Roman needed to create the antidote to look after himself, but couldn't risk a single point of failure. If it was only him that knew the code—as you said before—we kill him, we kill the problem. This way, there is no point to us just killing him."

"That's right," Kate said. "And in addition to the code being split into five pieces, the leaders are also spreading out all over the globe—"

"—Which makes it impossible for us to stop them," Matt said, finishing her sentence. "They will have five different entry points of the virus in five different areas of the world. There is no way we can gather enough people together to stop that."

Kate nodded. "I agree. It's going to make it extremely difficult, but it won't stop me from trying. We have to get that formula code for the sake of humanity."

"Hold on a second," Matt said, putting his hand up. "Did you just say—*get the code?* Why are we focusing on getting the code and not trying to destroy the virus before it's even released?"

"The virus isn't going to be released by the leaders, Matt. Roman informed me that each of the leaders has at least one assassin assigned to them—they will be the ones who release the virus."

"Assassins?" Alaina asked. "Like right-hand men?"

"Or women," Kate said. "You remember the shooter we chased over the fence back home?"

"Yeah," Alaina said.

"She was an assassin. The vial I pulled out of her pocket contained Roman's virus."

Alaina stared at her for a moment. "Holy crap. Were we really that close to it?"

Kate nodded.

"Well, why can't we just kill the assassins, then?" Matt asked.

"We don't know who they are or where they are going to be. If they can get into my backyard on a military base undetected, they can get anywhere. No, I think we stand more chance of finding the leaders, getting the five pieces of code, and releasing the formula into the community."

"In 33 hours," Matt said.

Kate nodded. "Yes, in 33 hours… I hope."

The Major began descending the helicopter towards Shanghai Longhua Airport and set it down on the helipad. The engine spooled down, and the team exited the aircraft.

Jesse and the Major walked behind Kate, Alaina, and Matt, who were already striding across the airfield towards Moose.

Kate spoke with Alaina and Matt as they walked on either side of her. "Roman said the leaders were getting into position in their respective sectors," she said. "And we already know Roman and Gianfranco are here in Asia somewhere. Although chances are, Gianfranco is now heading for Europe after we blew up his facility, as that is his sector. That means we only have the Russian, Asian, and Oceania sector leaders to find."

"Oceania leader?" Alaina asked. "But you killed Mike Royle already. What makes you think they have another?"

Kate dismissed the question quickly. "They're about to eliminate the population of the world, Alaina. They would have replaced Mike with someone else, for sure. Now, if you remember, Mike told us the Asian sector leader's name is Min Huang, and the Russian is a man called Dmitri Zagrev."

Alaina did a quick brain calculation. "So, we potentially have two of them in the vicinity right now, Roman and Gianfranco—three, if we can find Min, who you would assume is also already here somewhere."

"Correct," Kate said, pointing her finger at Alaina. "Which means we need to, at the very least, begin tracking these clowns while we have the opportunity."

The Major stopped walking. "May I pitch in my two cents?" he asked behind them.

"Of course, Major," Kate said, turning to face him.

"From what I can see, your safest bet right now would be to head to their destinations."

Kate looked at him, somewhat confused.

"Before you say anything, let me explain," he said. "Yes, you can search for these people right now because, as Alaina has rightfully pointed out, most of them are potentially already here in Asia. It makes sense, right?"

"Right," they all agreed.

"But if you know where they are *going* to be, wouldn't it be better to go there and wait for them to come to you rather than waste time you don't have, searching for a handful of people in a grossly overpopulated area?"

Kate, Alaina, and Matt looked at each other.

"Needles in a haystack," Kate said. "I see your point, Major, and you're absolutely right. But all we know is that they are going to their respective sectors. We don't know exactly *where* they are going to be."

The Major smiled. "They are releasing a virus, Kate. They will want maximum impact, which means they will no doubt head for the largest cities in their sectors, and you are already aware of how they travel, aren't you?"

Kate nodded. "In private jets."

"Correct. So, do what Viribus does best."

"What's that?"

"Utilise the power of people."

"What do you mean?"

"Do what you have always done," the Major said, somewhat scoffing at the fact she didn't know. "Use your people to watch for their aircraft and follow them when they arrive in location. There are more Viribus members involved in this than what's standing in front of you right now. Am I right, Matt?"

Matt nodded as he looked at Kate. "We are global," he said. "We can use my database of operatives."

"There you go!" the Major said, smiling. "Now is your time to lead and delegate, Kate. You cannot be everywhere all at once. *Use your people*."

Kate closed her eyes and took a deep breath, letting it out slowly. The Major was right. She did need to use her people, and she needed to focus on the bigger picture. She took a minute to soak up the situation at hand and formulate a plan. The rest of the team stood around her, eagerly awaiting her decision.

Kate opened her eyes and looked at the Major. "Are you able to get me home?" she asked.

Alaina's head snapped around in shock. "What the fuck? What do you mean? We have Moose. I can take you home," she said, slightly panicked.

"Major?" Kate asked, ignoring Alaina.

The Major knew what she was planning and nodded.

"I can make some calls," he said.

"Kate? What are you doing?" Alaina asked desperately. "You're scaring me."

Kate turned to face her. "I have to go home, Alaina. I need you to stay here with Matt and Jesse to track Roman and find Min. If we split up, we can find them all quicker.

Matt and Alaina looked at each other, screwing up their faces.

"Don't do that," Kate said, scolding them. "Matt, I need you to scope out whoever you can, in and around as many airports as possible, in *every* sector in question.

Russia, America, Europe, and Asia. We need as much help as we can get. We have to find those White Cloud aircraft, and we have to find those leaders."

"You forgot Oceania," Jesse said.

"No, I didn't," Kate snapped. "The Major and I will try to locate him… or her."

Matt raised an eyebrow. "And what if we can't find the leaders before dawn in Australia?"

"We're going for the solution, Matt. Not the problem."

Matt raised the other eyebrow. "You mean we're going to let them release the virus, but we will have the code for the formula?"

Kate looked up to meet his stare. "Exactly."

Matt rubbed his face in disbelief. "Holy shit, Kate. But that means a lot of people are going to die."

"Not if I can help it. However, we need to focus on the bigger picture here. There may be collateral, yes, but we need to protect the *billions* of people who will be exposed to this virus if we do nothing to stop it."

Matt looked at her doubtfully.

Kate put a hand on his shoulder. "They are *expecting* us to go for their assassins to stop them from spreading the virus. That's *why* they are using them to distribute it. They will not be expecting us to pop up on their doorsteps shoving guns in their faces. The Major is right. We don't have the time to chase multiple assassins around the globe. But we *do* stand a much better chance of getting to the leaders."

Matt looked her dead in the eye. "My God, I hope you're right."

She gave him a tight-lipped smile. "So do I."

VICTOR

28.5 Hours Until Virus Release

Sol, Roman, and his assistant, Samantha, sat in the back of the Bell Boeing V-22 Tilt Rotor Osprey as it sped low over the surface of the North Pacific Ocean. As the aircraft rapidly approached the white container ship anchored in the middle of the ocean, the huge rotor blades at the end of each wingtip rotated upwards, transforming its flight profile from a large propellor-driven aircraft into a dual-rotor helicopter, allowing it to land vertically on the ship's deck.

Sol looked out of his window and saw this was no ordinary ship. Around the perimeter of the deck, twelve Mk-29 missile launchers, six on each flank, surrounded the deck's centrepiece—an enormous radar-guided Phalanx, anti-aircraft, anti-missile cannon.

245

As the aircraft touched down upon the deck, a large Polynesian-looking man with long, black, curly hair poking out from beneath a captain's hat approached them as they disembarked and shook Roman's hand. He looked Sol up and down with distaste. "Is everything going to plan, boss?" he asked, while glaring at Sol.

"Yes, Josiah. Everything is going exactly as planned," Roman replied. "However, I need you to get this ship heading east immediately."

"You got it. Who's this guy?" he asked, jutting his chin at Sol.

"This is our new Oceania sector leader, Solomon Barrett. He will be on his way to conduct a very important mission in Australia for us very soon."

Josiah's eyes widened a little at the name. "Did you say *Solomon Barrett?*" he asked. "The same Solomon Barrett who brought down all those air—"

"That's the one," Roman said, cutting him off.

"What's with the mask?" Josiah asked.

Roman pulled Josiah to one side. Sol watched Roman whisper something indistinct into Josiah's ear and then slap him on the shoulder. "Now, once this ship is moving," he said loud enough for Sol to hear him. "I'd like you to introduce Sol to his assassins and show him around the ship. He needs to prepare for his mission."

"No problem, boss," Josiah said, fixing his gaze upon Sol.

Roman, Samantha, and Josiah led Sol to the bridge of the ship. Roman and Samantha continued into a side room, leaving him alone with Josiah, who had already begun busying himself with preparing the vessel for launch.

As the anchor retracted and the ship began moving east, Josiah turned to him. "You don't remember me at all, do you?" he asked.

Sol shook his head and shrugged. "No. Should I?"

Josiah leaned on the ship's control panel and stared at him for a moment before slowly raising the sleeve of his jacket, revealing a shiny metallic wristband clamped around his wrist. "This doesn't ring any bells?" he asked.

Sol shook his head again. "No. I'm sorry, it doesn't. We really need to be getting on with this," he said impatiently. "We're running out of time."

Josiah dropped his sleeve. "Yes, of course. Come on, I'll show you below deck."

Josiah led Sol out of the bridge and down into the cavernous belly of the cargo ship, where three private business jets sat parked on one side of the hold. Several helicopters of various shapes, sizes, and differing applications were parked on the other. In the centre of the hold was a mountainous stack of large wooden crates reaching high into the air and behind them was a large, hydraulically operated aircraft lift, providing vehicular access to the deck above.

Tucked away behind the crates in a dark corner of the hold, Sol saw something resembling a built-in accommodation block.

"How long are you with us?" Josiah asked as he headed towards the accommodation block. The question sounding like a poor attempt at small talk to break the awkward silence.

"Once I know where my target is going, I shall be leaving," Sol replied. "Roman said I could use whatever, and *whoever*, I need from the ship."

"How do you know where your target is going to be?" Josiah asked. "Are you tracking them?"

Sol produced the small tablet from his pocket and waved it in the air. "Once this dot moves, we will know exactly where she is heading."

"*She?*"

Sol nodded. "Yes. Kate Fabianski, the leader of Viribus."

Josiah stopped and turned to him with a look of confusion. "Wait a second. Are you telling me your mission is to kill the leader of Viribus?"

Sol nodded. "Correct."

"Oh man," Josiah said, resuming walking. "I hope you know what you are getting yourself into, bro."

They reached the accommodation block and entered a makeshift briefing room. Inside, a large group of black-clad men were busily gearing up, loading and checking their weapons as they laughed and joked together. All of them fell silent as Josiah and Sol entered the room.

"Are you guys going somewhere?" Josiah asked.

"Roman is heading to Mexico," one of them replied. "We are going with him to release the virus into the Northern and Southern continents of the Americas."

"You will also be the last ones to see the sunrise," Josiah said. "And therefore, the last ones to release the virus."

The man nodded. "Correct."

Sol noticed all the men were of Asian descent, and every one of them sported tattoos that ran up the side of their necks and onto their faces.

Outside, a siren began blaring inside the ship's hold, accompanied by rotating, flashing amber lights. The men instantly reacted, gathering up their weapons and hurriedly running for the exit—all except for three of them.

"You aren't going with them?" Josiah asked the remaining men.

The older-looking one of the trio shook his head. "No. We have been assigned to him," he said, pointing at Sol.

The tablet tracking Kate's necklace buzzed in Sol's pocket, and he pulled it out to stare at the screen. "The target has just departed Shanghai and is moving south," he said.

One of the men laughed to himself inwardly. "Of course they are," he said. "They are trying to beat you to Australia."

Within the hour, Sol and his three assistants were inside an aircraft, ascending towards the ship's deck and runway on the vehicle lift, heading for Canberra.

Shanghai Longhua Airport, China
11th February 2021
12:05 am China Standard Time

27.5 Hours Until Virus Release

As Kate and the Major approached the Chinese Liberation Army Ilyushin 76-MD transport aircraft the Major had organised to get Kate home, a Chinese airman stepped out of a side door and shook the Major's hand.

Kate looked at him questioningly. "Is there anyone you don't know?" she asked.

He looked back at her and shrugged his shoulders before entering the aircraft and taking a seat inside. "It helps to have friends in high places," he said, strapping himself in. "You just never know when you might need them."

Fifteen minutes later, the Ilyushin aircraft took off out of Shanghai, heading south.

As soon as the aircraft levelled off and settled into the cruise stage of flight, Kate opened her laptop and connected to the aircraft's satellite internet. The Major, sitting next to her, nestled into his seat and closed his eyes.

After an hour of scouring Matt's database for suitable Viribus operatives, Kate came across a familiar name on the list—Yousef Shirazi. She curiously clicked on the profile and instantly recognised the face. This was the bartender from the hotel in Dubai where she had first met Alex.

Kate gasped. "What are the chances of that?" she said out loud and to no one but herself. She got up from her seat and approached the Chinese aircrew, who, she found out quickly, spoke minimal English. She made the internationally recognisable sign for a phone using her thumb and little finger extended on the side of her head, and they handed her a satellite phone.

Kate took the sat-phone back to her seat and called the number underneath Yousef's profile picture.

Shangri-La Hotel, Dubai, United Arab Emirates
10th February 2021
10:02 pm Gulf Standard Time

25.5 Hours Until Virus Release

Yousef Shirazi spoke with front-of-house staff members as they cleared tables after a busy dinner service. Yousef had been promoted from his position as a bartender serving drinks behind a poolside bar where he'd met Kate three years ago and was now the supervisor of the Shangri-La hotel restaurant.

His phone buzzed in his pocket, and he reached into his suit jacket to pull it out.

Private number flashed up on the screen.

He swiped the screen. "Yousef Shirazi," he said, answering the call.

"Marhaba, Yousef. It's Kate Barrett here."

Yousef froze at the sound of her voice and grabbed a chair from a nearby restaurant table to sit down.

"Marhaba, Mrs Barrett," he said. "Why are you calling me?"

"I came across your profile in a Viribus database. You didn't tell me you were a part of Viribus when I met you at the poolside bar."

Yousef shifted in his seat. "If I had told you that, you would not have known who they were, and besides, Viribus prefers to stay under the radar. I am sorry I did not help you when I had the opportunity. The Russian you met that day was a very bad man. I should have done more."

Kate chuckled. "Don't worry about it, Yousef. Funnily enough, that Russian turned out to be my father."

"Your father?"

"Yes, but never mind that right now. We have come a long way since then, and there are far more important things at hand. Which is precisely the reason I am calling you. I need your help."

"Of course. What can I do?"

"We are expecting the European sector leader of White Cloud, Gianfranco Ragonesi, to return to a location in Europe. As he is Italian by birth, we can only assume he could be heading for Italy. I would like you to co-ordinate the search and surveillance mission in the European sector on my behalf."

Yousef went silent.

"Hello? Yousef? Are you there?"

"That's a lot of ground to cover, Miss Kate."

"Yes, it is. But we have plenty of people in the area who can help you."

Yousef drew a breath of air in through his teeth. "I do not think I am the man for this kind of job, Miss Kate."

"Why not?"

"I am not capable of such things any more. Now, I am just a restaurant supervisor."

"Yousef, there was a time when I didn't think I was capable of what I have done, either. Sometimes, you just have to do it. I have faith in you. The brightest stars shine on the darkest nights, and you are a bright star, Yousef."

The line fell silent for several seconds.

"Yousef?"

"Okay. I will do it for you, Miss Kate. Send me what you have."

Kate smiled to herself, mostly out of relief. "I'll send you an email shortly, but I need you to muster as many Viribus people as you can and get them watching and reporting on any suspicious White Cloud movement, especially their aircraft. If we can find their aircraft, we can find them. I strongly suggest you start with the largest cities in Europe."

"For what reason?" Yousef asked.

"I will put everything in the email along with a database of people you can contact. Once you have located Gianfranco, we can focus on the next stage."

Yousef puffed up his chest. "Okay, Miss Kate. Leave it to me. I will do my best."

"Thank you, Yousef. Wait for my email."

She hung up the phone and punched the air. "Yes!" she shouted loudly, disturbing the sleeping Major sitting next to her. He shuffled in his seat and murmured a few indistinct words as he roused, before settling back to sleep.

As she quickly typed an email to Yousef, a notification appeared on her screen. It was a message from Jesse—

Roman's Osprey has landed on a ship heading east. We are beginning the search for Min Huang.

Kate replied—

Thank you, Jesse. Keep me up to date. Get some rest. Take care.

This confirmed to her that Roman was heading towards America to release the virus in his sector and he was taking what she could only assume was the ship she had seen off the coast of Shoalwater Bay with him. She needed someone on the ground in the States to meet him when he got there. She quickly finished the email to Yousef and scrolled through the database again, searching for an active Viribus operative in North America. She came to rest on a profile based in Los Angeles and quickly dialled the number.

Los Angeles International Airport, United States
10th February 2021
11:15 am Pacific Standard Time

25 Hours Until Virus Release

Chuck Walters strolled into his office from the hangar floor, wiping his hands on a rag before picking up the ringing phone.

"You fly 'em. We prime 'em," he said, shoving the phone into the crook of his neck and holding it with his head while continuing to wipe his hands on the rag.

"Hello? Is this Chuck Walters?" Kate asked.

"Yes, Ma'am. What can I do for ya?" he said with a southern drawl.

"My name is Kate Barrett—"

"Oh, shit," Chuck said, dropping the rag and snatching the phone from the nape of his neck. "What can I do for you?"

"Are you still an active member of Viribus?"

"I am, but Viribus has not tasked me with anything for some time now. If you want me to do something, I am happy to help."

"Good. White Cloud has returned, and its new leader, Roman Horowitz, appears to be heading in your direction. We need him tracked immediately."

"Tracked? Like... killed, tracked?" Chuck asked, pointing at his head with his finger and thumb in the shape of a gun, even though Kate couldn't see him.

"No. You cannot kill him. We need him alive."

Chuck shrugged. "Oh, okay. Yeah, no problem, leave it with me."

"We're not sure exactly where he will arrive. All we know is that he is heading towards you and bringing a warship with him. We need the *entire* West Coast of America monitored."

Chuck took his baseball cap off with his free hand and scratched the top of his head. "Woah. A *warship?* Really? And just how do you expect me to monitor the entire West Coast for this *warship?*"

"I am sending you an email with a link to a database. Please go through it and find as many people to help you as you can. Report back when you have him, or the ship, under surveillance."

"Jesus Christ. I've got four planes to paint here!"

"Chuck, read the email I'm about to send you, and once you have, you are welcome to call me back and let me know if you still give a shit about painting planes."

Kate ended the call, took a deep breath, and forwarded him the same email she had sent to Yousef.

Somewhere over the South China Sea
11th February 2021
3:27 am Pacific Standard Time

24.5 Hours Until Virus Release

After initiating Yousef and Chuck, Kate turned her attention to Russia. She delved into the Viribus database once again, but this time, her search proved fruitless. The Russian Viribus operatives seemed to have completely vanished from existence entirely.

Next to her, the Major stirred and stretched his arms above his head.

"How was your nap?" Kate asked, without taking her eyes off the laptop screen.

The Major shook his head to wake himself up. "Very good, thank you. How long was I asleep?" he asked.

"A couple of hours," she shrugged.

The Major saw the laptop perched on her lap.

"What are you doing?" he asked.

"Contacting Viribus operatives to get them tracking the sector leaders down. I already have people moving on the ground in America and Europe, but I'm struggling to find anyone in Russia."

The Major snorted and burst out laughing. "You can't be serious," he chuckled.

Kate stared at him as he laughed. "Yes. I am. Why is that so funny?"

The Major wiped away a tear of laughter with the back of his hand. "Ah, man. It must be the generation," he said to himself. "Your *father* is bloody Russian, Kate! Use him!"

Kate shook her head. "No. I can't do that. Alex wants no part of this."

"You're kidding me," he said. "Alexei is the best asset you have to fight these guys, and he *owes* you. If anyone can help you find the Russian sector leader, it will be him; he has all the inside knowledge. Why *wouldn't* you use him?"

Kate thought about this for a moment.

"Isn't it worth a try?" the Major pleaded.

"I suppose it wouldn't hurt to ask," she said.

"Who have you contacted so far?"

"I have Yousef Shirazi in Dubai taking care of Europe and Chuck Walters in LA. Chuck is working on getting people on the West Coast of the States."

"The *entire* West Coast?"

Kate nodded. "Alaina and Matt tracked Roman's Osprey to a ship in the middle of the Pacific that is heading east. It's highly likely it's the same ship I saw at sea in Shoalwater."

The Major sat back in his chair. "Let's hope not. If he's taking the ship, he's taking the trouble. Chuck will need some help. We need to get to Canberra."

"Canberra? Why? What's in Canberra?"

The Major stood up. "You leave that part to me. Contact Alexei and get him on a flight to Russia immediately," he said, striding away towards the cockpit.

Kate picked up the sat-phone and dialled Alex's number from memory.

"Kate? Where are you?" Alexei asked. It was now the early hours of the morning in Shoalwater Bay, and it sounded like she had woken him.

"We're on our way to Australia," she replied.

"You are coming home?"

"Not quite. I don't have time to explain, but I need your help."

"Of course. What can I do?"

"We are trying to locate the current Russian sector leader, a man by the name of Dmitri Zagrev. Would you know who he is?"

The line went quiet for a few seconds.

"Did you say, *Dmitri Zagrev?*"

"Yes."

Alex chuckled to himself. "Yes, Kate. I know Dmitri. I know Dmitri *very* well. You might say he was my *junior* when I was part of the organisation."

"Do you know where he might be now?"

"Dmitri is a… ah, how you say… *loose cannon,* if you know what I mean. If he is in position of power, he could be anywhere. He is very dangerous man. Kate, you need to be careful."

"I was sort of hoping you would help me find him."

The line went silent again. Kate quickly realised Alex did not want to do this and pleaded with him. "You know Russia better than any of us," she said. "And you would know the places where Dmitri *could* be. It would be in national, no… *inter*national interest, Alex. Please, please, please? I really need your help with this one."

Alex sighed. She had him on the ropes, and he knew it. After several seconds of silence, he sighed once more. "Okay. What is it you want me to do?" he asked.

Kate smiled. "All I am asking you to do is track Dmitri down and watch him. They are intending to release that virus on the dawn of Chinese New Year."

"But that is tomorrow morning."

"Yes, I know. Which is why I am trying to move this along quickly. If you have to go to Russia, I need you in the air as soon as possible.

"I will be in Moscow before dawn tomorrow," he said. "I will find him for you."

"Thank you, Alex. I will email you the details of everything that has happened so far. Let me know if you need anything else."

"Okay, Kate… I love you."

Kate hesitated and furrowed her brow. Alex had never said this to her before. "I love you too," she replied. "Give hugs to Mum and the boys for me. Are they okay?"

"Yes, they are fine. They miss you."

"Mum and Roxy?"

"Both okay."

She knew Alex was not very good at small talk, so she wished him well and hung up the phone.

The Major returned from the cockpit as she put the phone down. "Did you get hold of Alexei?" he asked.

Kate nodded. "Yes. He's on his way to Moscow."

The Major looked at her with an *I told you so* look on his face.

"Okay, okay, you don't need to say it," she said. "Why are we going to Canberra, anyway?" she asked.

"I have some more friends there that may prove very useful," he said.

"*More* friends," she said. "And who might these *friends* be, exactly?"

He waved away the question and patted the aircraft frame. "Let's just say friends with bigger and better toys than this one, and also ones who may have a vested interest in *all* of this."

Kate smiled. "You're a man full of surprises and mystery. I'll give you that."

He smiled. "Let's just hope your friends on the ground come through with finding these leaders."

"At the moment, Major, hope is all we have."

Leonardo da Vinci Airport, Rome
11th February 2021
1:27 am Central Europe Time

19 Hours Until Virus Release

Parked alongside the Leonardo da Vinci Airport runway in Rome, two men, dressed all in black, sat in a blue Pagani Zonda hypercar. The machine looked like it was going a hundred miles an hour sitting still, with its sleek, low-slung profile and large-rimmed alloy wheels.

As the men sat watching the airfield in front of them, a small white business jet swooped over the car and landed on the runway.

Fabrizio De Angelis reached for his phone and quickly dialled a number. "Yousef. One of their jets just landed in Rome," he said.

"Excellent work," Yousef replied. "Follow it and see where it goes."

Fabrizio tucked his phone away and tightened his racing-style seat belts. "Let's go, Luciano," he said in Italian.

The blue hypercar spun its tyres as it departed the side of the road under the runway flight path, leaving a cloud of smoke and dirt behind it. Fabrizio De Angelis and his brother, Luciano, sped to the other side of the airport, where they found the private jet parked in a remote corner of the airfield. A man in white disembarked the aircraft and entered one of three white limousines. As soon as he was inside, the limousines drove out of the airfield.

"That's him," Fabrizio said. "Follow them, Luciano."

The hypercar rapidly caught up to the limousines and began following them at a distance.

"You did not choose the most inconspicuous of cars for this mission, brother," Fabrizio said. "We may as well have a sign that says, *look-at-me-I'm-coming-to-kill-you* on the roof of this thing. Could you not have got a car that blended in a little better?"

Luciano shrugged a shoulder and didn't say a word. He hadn't said a single word in years.

The procession of limousines sped down the motorway towards Rome's residential and business district with the hot blue hypercar in pursuit. A few minutes later, the limousines suddenly fanned out in three different directions, each of them taking a different exit off the motorway.

"Shit! They've spotted us. Follow the middle one!" Fabrizio said, making the decision for Luciano.

Luciano did as he was told and followed the middle limousine, letting the other two escape on either side of him. He glanced at Fabrizio.

Fabrizio knew the look. "Yes, I know, brother. I hope it was the right decision as well."

The limousine in front of them sped up.

"Stay with him," Fabrizio said, grabbing the handrail above his head and tightening his seat belt.

Luciano weaved the hypercar through the early morning traffic of Rome in pursuit of the expertly driven limousine as a man emerged through a rear window brandishing a pistol. The man hung out of the window and fired.

Luciano took drastic and evasive action, swerving violently on the motorway to dodge the incoming bullets.

The gunfire then stopped as the gunman went to reload his weapon, and Luciano saw his opportunity. He dropped his car down a gear and launched it towards the limousine, spearing into the rear quarter panel of the stretched vehicle and causing it to fishtail wildly across the road.

The gunman was violently thrown around as he hung out of the window. The collision making him lose his grip on the weapon and sending it clattering down the road behind them.

Luciano lined the limousine up for another hit. From the passenger seat, Fabrizio realised what was about to happen and reached over Luciano, yanking the steering wheel to the right, directing the hypercar away from the limousine, and sending it into a spin. The car hit the motorway barriers, rear first.

There was a moment's silence as Luciano stared at Fabrizio with a look of anger in his eyes.

"We cannot kill him, Luciano," Fabrizio said. "We must only follow. Those are the orders."

Luciano got out of the damaged vehicle, angry at his brother for making him crash the expensive car, and snatched a pistol from his waistband as he walked out into the middle of the busy motorway. He held the weapon aloft, aiming it at the first oncoming vehicle.

A motorbike came to a shuddering halt in front of him. Luciano pointed his pistol at the rider, who immediately threw his hands in the air and kicked out the bike's stand before slowly getting off the motorbike.

Luciano graciously nodded at the rider and got onto the Ducati 1098 Panigale Superbike.

"I'm sorry for my brother's behaviour," Fabrizio said to the rider as he perched himself on the back of the bike behind Luciano. "He's a very compulsive person. Beautiful bike, by the way!"

The superbike launched after the white limousine and was far nimbler and quicker than the car. They easily weaved their way through the traffic and soon caught up to the target vehicle again. This time, Luciano kept his distance and followed it into the centre of Rome.

They watched the limousine turn into a lavish hotel driveway as Luciano stopped the bike on the other side of the road, about fifty feet away. Fabrizio looked up at the hotel's roof and saw *Valentino Moretti* emblazoned across the top in bright purple neon lights.

"Wow. Fancy place," he said, getting off the bike.

Luciano's eyes widened as he nodded his agreement.

Fabrizio pulled out his phone and made a call.

"Yousef, we have him," he said.

"Good work, Fabrizio. Keep your eyes on him."

Yousef ended the call and immediately sent a message to Kate.

WHISKEY

18 Hours Until Virus Release

Matt and Alaina had driven into Shanghai using the van from the cargo hold of Moose, leaving Jesse behind to carry out some much-needed maintenance on the aircraft. The extreme landing it had endured at the hands of Alaina meant the aircraft required some penalty inspections to be carried out, and Jesse was the most qualified to perform them.

Matt and Alaina had set up camp in a secluded alleyway behind a row of shops on a Shanghai beachfront while they waited for further instructions from Kate. They had already successfully tracked Roman's Osprey by intercepting satellite data transmissions—something Matt had learned from his old friend and colleague, Kane.

Nestled between a row of buildings facing the beachfront that formed part of the coast of China, the alleyway was dark and smelled of rotten fish, but it served a purpose.

They took the opportunity to rest, and slept in the van dressed in their full military fatigues, with various weapons hanging from the many loops and buckles on the front of their clothes—not very inconspicuous amongst the people of a sleepy Chinese fishing village on the outskirts of Shanghai. However, it was the perfect spot for lying low and staying away from prying eyes.

Matt had fallen asleep with his laptop on his chest and woke to a young Chinese boy standing over him, trying to pry it from his hands. He growled at the boy, who leapt out of the van and dissolved into the morning hustle and bustle at the other end of the alleyway.

Matt sat up and rubbed his eyes before reaching over and giving Alaina a gentle nudge.

"Hey. Get up."

Alaina stirred. "What time is it?"

"Well, the sun is coming up, so… morning, I guess."

"Has Kate been in contact?" she asked as she put her head back down on her makeshift pillow.

"Not yet, but we have to find Min," Matt said. "You need to get up."

Matt got out of the van, turned on his laptop, and waited for it to boot up, taking full advantage of the neighbouring restaurant's unsecured Wi-Fi.

Alaina got out of the van and stood next to him. "So, where do we start?" she asked.

There were no further updates from Kate, so Matt snapped his laptop shut. "I suppose we start by finding Viribus operatives in Asia and get them to help us scour the place. Surely someone knows something," he said, stuffing the laptop into its bag. "But first things first. Let's get some coffee. No day can start properly without it, and if this is going to be my last day on Earth, I am not going anywhere without it."

They walked into the neighbouring restaurant from whom they had been stealing the Wi-Fi as an old Chinese lady came rushing out of the kitchen, waving her arms in the air and smiling. "Sorry, sorry, sorry! We are closed!" she shouted.

Matt whipped out his pistol and pointed it at her. The lady stopped smiling immediately and froze with her hands straight above her head.

"I *need* a coffee," he said.

The lady nodded and retreated backwards into the kitchen with her arms in the air.

Alaina scowled at him. "Matt!" she said, elbowing him in the ribs. "There was no need for that."

"I have no time for negotiations, Alaina. We need a game plan. My laptop needs power, and I need coffee."

Removing the upside-down chairs the cleaners had placed on top of a table, they sat down, and Matt plugged a charger into his laptop.

Alaina could see he was already deep in thought.

"What are you thinking?" she asked.

"These codes for the formula…" he said, furrowing his brow. "They would have to be contained in some kind of implanted chip—an RFID-type setup would make sense. Although, then you would need a device to scan the chip and extract the information from it."

"Woah up, buddy," Alaina said. "Your brain is going a million miles an hour, and I can't keep up. RFID?"

"Radio Frequency Identification. It's mainly used in livestock, pets, and I suppose potentially… even humans. I mean, that's only a theory — we couldn't possibly know that's what they're using for sure, but I would put money on it being the most likely candidate."

"So, you think we're going to need some kind of device to extract the data from the chip?"

Matt nodded.

"Jesus," Alaina said. "This is getting more and more difficult as we go along. Oh, and don't forget, on top of all that, we also need to find Min."

Matt looked at her and thought for a long moment.

"Maybe if we can find Min, we can also work out how to extract the code from them," he said.

"You mean use her as a test subject?"

"Exactly."

"Good idea. But we still need to find her first."

"You would think Roman would position her where she can inflict the most damage… a city would be the most likely target."

Alaina nodded. "Okay, so let's get operatives moving into Asia's largest cities as soon as we can. The more eyes on the ground, the better. We are running out of time quickly. Get some operatives on the ground in Beijing, Tokyo, and Delhi. We can take care of Shanghai."

Matt opened his database and scrolled through the list of names, picking out those who were based in the major cities throughout Asia. The list was alarmingly small. There were barely any Viribus operatives left on the Asian continent—but there was one name that leapt out at him. A name based in Shanghai and one that was very familiar.

"Ah, Alaina?" Matt said, staring at his laptop in confusion. "What was Min's family name again?"

"*Huang*," Alaina said.

Matt spun the laptop around so she could see what he was looking at. "I have a *Min Huang* living in Shanghai and flagged as an active Viribus member."

Alaina stared at the laptop screen in disbelief.

"No way. It couldn't be the same person, could it? How could she be White Cloud *and* Viribus?"

Matt shrugged. "I don't know, but there aren't many other options. Maybe we should check it out."

"Damn straight, we should. Where does it say she's located?"

"Shanghai City, apparently. Half an hour west of here. I've got an address."

"Then we shouldn't be sitting here waiting for coffee," Alaina said. "Let's get moving."

Matt made a sad face. "But... coffee?"

"Pack your stuff up, princess. Let's go."

Matt reluctantly packed away his laptop and left the restaurant with Alaina just as the female restaurant owner appeared from the kitchen, holding a tray with two cups of coffee on it.

Matt quickly turned around and ran back into the restaurant, flashing her a smile as he snatched one of the cups off the tray and left again.

They got into the van parked in the alleyway and drove it towards Shanghai City.

Shanghai City, China
11ᵗʰ February 2021
9:57 am China Standard Time

17.5 Hours Until Virus Release

The Oriental Pearl Tower in Shanghai is an eccentric-looking building with large spherical structures positioned strategically amongst its trellis-like framework. The building's primary purpose was originally for television and radio broadcasting. However, as the years passed, it became an iconic landmark of the Shanghai cityscape and took on various other functions. Today, the building boasts exhibition facilities, a small shopping centre, a 20-room hotel, a glass deck that cantilevers out from the spherical structures, and a rotating restaurant on the top floor, all underneath an oversized helicopter pad on the roof.

"Are you sure this is the address?" Alaina asked, looking up at the weird-looking building as she stopped the van outside the tower.

"Yeah, that's what it says here," Matt said, pointing at his laptop.

"Something doesn't seem right. It's almost too obvious."

"Well, let's go find out, shall we?" Alaina said, opening the door and getting out of the van.

They entered the tower and stopped at the security checkpoint, which looked like that of an airport. There was a full body scanner, an x-ray machine for bags and belongings, and multiple guards stood around waiting for someone to come into the building.

The guards stopped and stared as Matt and Alaina, dressed all in black tactical clothing, walked through the door, armed to the teeth.

Several of them drew their weapons while a nervous-looking guard pointed to a sign displaying all the things they were prohibited from bringing into the building.

Matt leaned over to read the sign and chuckled as he began loading a little plastic tray with everything from his pockets. Alaina did the same behind him.

"You cannot bring these in here!" One guard shouted. "You leave now!" he said, wagging his finger in the air.

"Do you know who we are?" Matt asked.

The guard shook his head.

"We are Viribus. Do you know what that is?"

The guard froze, and after a brief pause, nodded his head slowly.

"Oh, you do. Well, what a surprise. Then we are coming into this building whether you like it or not."

Matt quickly reacted to some movement in his peripheral vision and turned to see a guard reaching under a desk to press a button.

"Woah! Woah! Woah! What are *you* doing?" he shouted as he marched over to the counter and grabbed the man behind the desk by the neck. He waited for the alarms to sound as the man gasped for air.

"Was that a *silent* alarm?" he asked the gasping guard in his hand.

The guard slowly nodded his head.

A few seconds later, the elevator on the opposite side of the security hall announced its arrival with a melodic and happy—*ding!* Everyone, even the security guard being choked in Matt's hand, turned to look at it.

The doors of the elevator opened, and a petite Asian woman dressed in a brilliant white uniform with a teal blue pinstripe down one side appeared into view, closely followed by three people dressed entirely in black.

Matt recognised the woman from his database.

This was Min Huang.

Alaina snatched a weapon from the plastic tray in front of the x-ray machine and aimed it at her. Min stopped walking and slowly raised her hands in the air. "There is no need for any violence," she said.

Matt dropped the security guard, who collapsed to the floor behind the desk and turned his attention to Min.

"We need to speak to you," he said.

Min stared back at him. "Are you Viribus?"

"Yes. We are," Matt replied.

She smiled. "Good. I was waiting for you to turn up. Come with me."

Min turned around and returned to the elevator, holding the door open for the Viribus members to follow.

Matt and Alaina quickly gathered their weaponry from the plastic trays and made their way into the elevator.

The elevator wasn't large, and it proved quite cosy with six people on board. Min pressed a button and music played as they ascended, which seemed extremely inappropriate for the situation. They were in the middle of an international crisis, face to face with one of the potential antagonists, and the elevator felt like such a happy, dreamy kind of venue.

The elevator stopped with another cheerful *ding* and they exited into the empty rotating restaurant at the top of the Oriental Pearl Tower.

Min led them over to a table and motioned for them to sit down.

Matt wasted no time. "We have reason to believe you might be a Viribus member. What's going on? Are you batting for both teams?"

Min looked at him with a questioning look on her face. "I beg your pardon?"

Matt, realising the cricket euphemism had been lost in translation, put it simpler. "Are you working for both organisations?"

"Yes. You could say that," Min said, pulling out a chair and sitting down.

"We're listening," Matt said.

Min cleared her throat. "As I'm sure you are aware by now, I am the leader of the Asian sector of White Cloud—but yes, I am also a member of Viribus."

"How can you do both?" he asked.

Min took a breath. "My birth parents were both murdered by White Cloud when I was very young. A man named Tao Huang took me in and raised me, but it was only when I grew into a woman did I discover Tao was also a part of White Cloud."

"So, you were raised by the people who killed your parents?" Alaina asked. "And you didn't seek revenge on the people who killed your family?"

Min shook her head. "No. Keep your friends close and your enemies closer, as they say."

"So why join Viribus as well?"

"Good question. I requested to join Viribus so I could safeguard myself. White Cloud is notorious for turning on their own, so I decided that if they should ever turn on me, I would be able to hurt them from a different angle. Your previous leader, Liam, asked no questions, so I never told him. Otherwise, he would never have let me join if he knew I was part of the very organisation they were hunting."

"Did you deliver intel between each party?" Alaina asked.

"No, I have always stayed loyal to White Cloud. My adoptive father and brother were both members of the organisation, and although I had my name down at Viribus, they never actually called on me for anything."

"Did you say, *brother?*" Alaina asked.

"Yes. Roman Horowitz is my adoptive brother."

"Woah," Matt said.

"Look, I don't agree with everything my father and brother have done or *are* doing," Min said. "But I go along with what they ask me to do to maintain the peace. Roman made me the leader of Asia, which means I get to say what happens here."

"Does that mean you intend to release his virus in China?" Matt asked.

Min shook her head. "No, that will *not* happen."

He smirked. "That is going to severely aggravate Roman. The other leaders are already getting into position."

She nodded. "I know, and I don't care. You need to understand that these are *my* people, and I will not let Roman hurt them for any amount of money, power, or greed."

"You may not have a choice if the virus infiltrates China's borders from elsewhere," Matt said.

"As soon as I know my brother has released his virus, all means of transport in and out of China will be stopped, forcing the country into lockdown. Every border will have armed guards patrolling it with strict orders to kill anyone who tries to enter China. That virus will not get in here, mark my words."

Alaina nodded at the men sitting behind Min, who were watching their every move. "I take it these are your assassins?" she asked.

Min smiled. "Yes, they are, and no, they will not give you the virus," she said, anticipating Alaina's follow-up question. "They won't even give it to me."

"So technically, the virus is already here," Alaina said. "These guys have it with them, right?"

"Yes, they do. But they too do not want to see China die. The virus will be safe in their hands. Trust me. They have their orders from Roman, but they also have orders from me. Besides, *you* are going to retrieve the formula code for me—I can only assume that is why you are here, no?"

Alaina glanced at Matt briefly and then looked back at Min. "Yes, it is. But why do you want it? Aren't you already protected from the virus?"

"I am, but China is not," Min said. "I want the code to create my own formula in the unlikely situation that the virus finds its way into China somehow. Roman is the only person who knows the complete code."

"I see," Alaina said. "So, you have a part of that code inside you right now?"

Min looked down at the Chinese flag on her shoulder. "Correct."

"Well, in order for us to help you get the formula, we need to know how to extract the code out of the leaders. Would you let us have yours?"

Min stared at her for a moment before turning around to the assassins sitting at the table behind her and muttering something in Chinese. One of them handed her a phone that Min touched on the Chinese flag on her right shoulder.

The phone beeped.

She then handed the phone to Matt. On the screen was a string of hexagons surrounded by different numbers and letters.

"What's this?" he asked.

"That is a piece of the chemical equation for the formula," Min said.

Matt and Alaina smiled in unison.

"Can I get this app?" Matt asked, pointing at the phone in his hand.

"Sure, we can give it to you, but you must first agree to give me the code once you have it. Together, we can end this war, but if you do not deliver me the formula code, I *will* find you and… well, I'm sure you can guess the rest."

Alaina shrugged. "And if you don't play nicely, you don't get what you want either."

Min clicked her fingers and one of the assassins appeared next to her with a laptop in his hand. He snatched Matt's phone from him, plugged it into the laptop, and began transferring a copy of the app onto his phone.

Matt leaned forward and rested his elbows on the table as he waited. "Our colleagues are currently on their way to Australia to locate the Oceania sector leader. Would you know who, and where, he might be?"

Min casually sipped at a cup of tea and smiled.

"Yes. Of course, I do."

"Would you perhaps be willing to share that information with us?"

Min thought about this for a second and glanced at the pair of them. "What if I don't?"

"We walk out the door, and China remains vulnerable to your brother's attacks."

She stared at Matt for a long, lingering moment, as if weighing up her options. She drew in a full breath of air. "White Cloud has a cryonic laboratory high in the Wudang Mountains. This lab is crucial to Roman's mission. He appointed Gianfranco Ragonesi to *collect* people from around the world and freeze them in the lab to use whenever he desires."

Matt nodded. "Yes, we know about the lab. We've been there," he said. "But what has that got to do with anything?"

"You've been to the lab?" Min said with a look of surprise.

"We didn't go inside it, but our colleague did. She met with Gianfranco Ragonesi."

"Interesting," Min said. "Very few people get to go inside, and even fewer people have spoken with Gianfranco."

"I wouldn't say she was *invited* exactly," Alaina said. "Anyway, how is Roman intending to use these frozen people?"

"If Roman ever requires a particular human to be developed for any specific purpose or mission, Gianfranco can create it for him using their DNA."

Alaina stared at her in disbelief. "You're harvesting the DNA of dead people to create *new* people?"

Min shrugged a shoulder. "You could say that. Although sometimes, *harvesting* isn't always necessary. Sometimes we already have exactly what we need—ready-made."

"I'm not sure I'm following," Matt said. "What's this got to do with us finding the Oceania sector leader?"

Min stood up and paced behind the table. "Three years ago, Gianfranco retrieved a body from a burning helicopter outside the old White Cloud headquarters—you know, the one you destroyed."

"Oh God," Alaina said, realising where this was going. "Please don't tell me you have resurrected Nikolai."

"Nikolai can rot in hell," Min spat. "No, Gianfranco collected this body from Peru and has had it on ice since those attacks. In fact, he only woke this person up last night to replace Mike Royle—oh, what was his name again... Solomon, *something,* I think."

Matt and Alaina stared at her, slack-jawed.

"You have got to be shitting me," Alaina said.

"This *Solomon* guy," Matt said. "Would he perhaps be the same Oceania sector leader that you guys had at the time of the aircraft attacks in Peru, by any chance?"

Min nodded. "Yes. He was the one who programmed the aircraft to crash into the ground. Do you know him?"

"You could say that," Alaina said. "He's Kate Barrett's husband."

Min chuckled a little. "Ah! Now I get it. *Now* it all makes sense!"

"What does?" Matt asked.

"Why they chose him for this mission."

"You're absolutely certain it's Sol they have brought back to life?"

"Oh yes, this plan was extremely well communicated—and they haven't just *brought him back to life,* more like, completely *rebooted* him."

"What does that mean?" Alaina asked.

"Solomon doesn't know who he is," Min said. "He has no idea where he came from, who he is related to, or what he used to be. Gianfranco has *reprogrammed* his brain to do exactly what White Cloud requires him to do."

Matt leaned back in his chair. "Christ. You're using him to get at Kate, aren't you?"

Min nodded.

Alaina turned to Matt. "I don't understand. What do you mean?" she asked.

"They're going to send Sol to kill Kate. That's why they wiped his memory. Kate won't kill him."

Alaina stared back at Min. "Is he right?"

Min nodded as she gently placed her cup down on its saucer. "I'm afraid so. Roman wanted Solomon brought back to life to kill the Viribus leader, removing her from the equation and enabling him to complete his mission freely. It's nothing personal, of course. It's more like a *statement*. He is trying to kill Viribus by removing someone he believes to be an extremely effective leader."

"He won't find her," Alaina said. "She'll be arriving in Australia in a few hours."

Min sighed. "Never underestimate the power of a man with a lot of determination and an endless supply of money," she said. "Roman has instructed Solomon to track Kate down using a GPS transmitter she carries in a necklace."

Alaina froze. *"Necklace?"* she asked. "What *fucking* necklace?"

"Mike Royle was ordered to ensure the safe return of a necklace into Kate's possession—at least he managed that before she murdered him, the useless son-of-a-bitch."

"Mike *fucking* Royle," Alaina said.

Matt stood up. "We're done here," he said. "We have everything we need. You'll get your code as long as Kate is alive. You might want to pass that on to your brother if you care about China so much."

Min nodded her understanding and handed Alaina a business card. "Here are my details. Contact me when you have the code."

Shanghai City, China
11ᵗʰ February 2021
11:29 am China Standard Time

16 Hours Until Virus Release

Jesse stood at the top of a ladder, pouring a can of oil into one of Moose's giant engines as the van sped across the airfield and drove straight up the rear loading ramp of the aircraft into the cargo hold.

Jesse got down off the ladder and followed it up the loading ramp. "Did you find Min?" he asked.

"Yeah, we did," Matt said, opening the door and getting out of the van. "And now we have bigger problems. Is this thing ready to fly?" he asked.

Jesse wiped his hands on a rag and nodded. "Yeah. Why? Where are we going? What's happened?"

"Sol's alive," Alaina said.

"What?" Jesse asked, with confusion all over his face. "But… didn't he die in Peru?"

"He did," Matt said, "but White Cloud picked up his body and *rebooted* him, as Min put it. They've messed around with his brain so he doesn't know who he is anymore, and they're using him to kill Kate."

Jesse stared at him, wide-eyed and slack-jawed.

Alaina nodded. "Min told us Sol was on ice at the Wudang facility when we were there. They have only just revived him. He is tracking Kate to Australia right now."

"Jesus," Jesse said. "Have you told her yet?"

Alaina shook her head. "No. We've tried, but it seems something is jamming our communications. Min said China was going into lockdown to protect itself against the virus, so maybe it has something to do with that."

"She's not releasing the virus?"

Matt shook his head. "No. It seems she loves her country way more than her brother."

"Brother?" Jesse asked, getting more and more confused.

Matt smiled and put a hand on Jesse's shoulder. "We have a lot to bring you up to speed on, but we can do that on the way. Right now, we need to get to Kate before Sol does.

He handed Jesse his phone. "On this, there is an app that extracts the code from the chips in the leader's arms, as well as an image of Min's piece of the code. I need you to extract both files and send them to Kate, along with a message telling her she is in danger."

"No problem," Jesse said, taking the phone from him.

"I need to hook into the GPS signal coming from Kate's necklace so we can locate her," Matt said, turning to Alaina. "Get Moose in the air. We have to move."

Canberra, Australian Capital Territory, Australia
11ᵗʰ February 2021
3:05 pm Australian Eastern Standard Time

15.5 Hours Until Virus Release

Canberra was selected as the capital of Australia because Sydney and Melbourne could not come to an agreement on which of them should be nominated as the capital. And so, to stop the bickering, they built Canberra, a brand-new city, right in the middle of the two quarrelsome cities.

As the monstrous Chinese military cargo aircraft with Kate and the Major onboard came into land at Canberra's International Airport, Kate gazed out of the window and saw a familiar white building perched on top of a hill in the distance—Australian Parliament House.

Kate and the Major were met by an Australian Government vehicle sent by the Major's friend, Dexter, and were rushed towards the parliamentary building. Through the window of the car, Kate watched the everyday people innocently going about their business. She remembered a time when her life was like theirs. Tears welled in her eyes as she thought about Sol and the boys. She missed her old life, and she missed them dearly.

The car screeched to a stop in front of Parliament House, and she wiped the tears from her eyes with her sleeve. "Why are we here, Major?" she asked.

"We need resources, people who can help us, and some shelter," he said, pointing towards the building in front of them. "This is where we'll get all of that."

They retrieved their bags from the trunk and walked towards the building. As they approached the front entrance, two security guards marched up to them.

"Kate Barrett?" One of them asked.

"Yes. Who's asking?" she replied.

"Major Barton?" the other asked.

"Yes," he answered.

"Come with us."

The guards ushered them towards a side entry void of body scanners and x-ray machines the public entry had.

Kate looked around in awe as they stepped inside the cavernous foyer of Parliament House, lined with dusky pink marble floors and columns spanning all the way to the ceiling high above them.

A natural skylight illuminated the room, and on the east and west wings of the building, two grand marble staircases reached up to a mezzanine level, where several small groups of important-looking people had gathered.

"As I live and breathe!" A voice bellowed, echoing down a hallway behind them. "Is that Major Richard Barton?"

Kate and the Major turned to see a man with slicked-back hair in a tailor-made black suit approaching them. His large, muscular frame looked set to tear the suit apart at any moment.

"Dex?" the Major asked.

"Yes!" Dex said with a broad grin, grabbing the Major's hand and shaking it vigorously. "How are you, mate?"

"Jesus Christ," the Major said, looking him up and down. "I never thought the day would come when Dexter *bloody* Wheatley would be seen in public wearing a suit."

They embraced each other vigorously, patting one another heavily on the back.

"Nice to see you, mate," Dex said.

"You too, pal. I just wish it was under better circumstances."

The Major turned to Kate. "Dexter, this is Kate. Kate, this is Dexter."

"Very pleased to meet you," Dexter said, taking her hand and gently kissing the back of it.

"Don't let him suck you in, Kate," the Major said. "This man is no gentleman."

She smiled and blushed a little. "How do you two know each other?" she asked.

"We were in the SAS together," the Major said, grabbing Dexter's shoulder and shaking it. "We lived in each other's pockets for a very long time, didn't we, mate?"

"Some would say too long," Dexter added with a grin. "Come on, let me show you to your office. You can get rid of those bags and get to work. I believe time is of the essence, right?"

"Correct," Kate said, looking at the Major and mouthing the word, *"Office?"*

The Major shrugged and walked around her to join Dexter, who was already striding towards the far end of the foyer. Kate jogged a little to keep up and noticed Dexter bore the same determined stride as the Major.

As they walked, the Major filled Dexter in on their situation. Dexter's jovial demeanour had notably changed by the time he stopped and pointed to a door in front of them.

"This is yours for as long as you need it," he said, reaching inside his jacket and pulling out a business card and handing it to Kate. "Make yourselves at home. Just let me know what you need, and I will organise it for you."

"I'm not sure what we need yet, but I'll make sure to let you know as soon as I do," she replied, tucking the business card into a pocket.

"Of course, just call me. Anytime."

The Major grabbed Dexter's hand and shook it again. "Thanks again, Dex. We need as much support as we can get right now."

"It certainly sounds like you do, Dick."

The Major screwed up his face. "Don't call me *Dick*. You know I hate it."

Dexter smirked. "I'll have to let the Prime Minister know about all of this. It sounds like it could become a global issue very quickly, and he needs to know. I'll see you guys later."

Dexter left, rushing away along the corridor.

Kate opened the door to the office and saw several desks with computers and phones on them. A projector hung from the ceiling, and a coffee machine sat on a small table in the corner of the room. Kate's eyes lit up at the sight of the coffee machine, and she bee-lined her way across the room towards it.

The Major pulled out his laptop, attached it to an ethernet cable poking out of a desk, and lifted the screen. "Right. Where do we start?"

"First of all, we need to find out who the Oceania sector leader is and monitor the other operatives around the globe," Kate said, as she made herself a cup of coffee. "Then we need to find out if the operatives I employed have found anything."

Kate cradled her coffee over to a desk and plugged in her laptop. Within seconds of it booting up, a notification appeared on her screen, alerting her she had a new email.

She opened the email and found several from Jesse and Yousef. She opened one from Yousef first. It read—

> We have Gianfranco under surveillance at the Valentino Moretti Hotel in Rome. Waiting further instructions.

"Holy shit, they've found Gianfranco," she said, staring at her laptop screen.

"Excellent," the Major said. "That's a good start, but we can't move on him until we know how to extract the code."

Kate then opened the email from Jesse, which contained two attachments, but all the words were garbled. She screwed her face up.

"What's wrong?" the Major asked.

"This email from Jesse. It's just a mess of numbers and letters," she said, spinning her laptop around so he could see the screen.

The Major leaned over and studied the email. "It's encrypted," he said.

"Encrypted? Why would Jesse encrypt an email, and how do I *decrypt* it?"

The Major shrugged. "I don't know the answer to either of those questions, I'm afraid. What are the attachments?"

Kate clicked on the first attachment. A strange picture of hexagons with numbers and symbols around them appeared on the screen. The second attachment was an RFID scanning app.

"What the hell is all this about?" Kate asked.

"An RFID chip…" the Major said, drifting away into thought for a moment. His eyes then lit up as a smile formed on his face. "Oh my. They're using RFID chips!" he shouted excitedly.

Kate shrugged. "What does that mean?"

"You know the microchips they use in dogs to identify them if they get lost?"

Kate nodded. "Yes," she said. "Are you about to tell me that's what they are using to carry the code?"

The Major pointed to the image of the hexagons on her screen. "That picture *is* part of the code, Kate!" the Major said, waving his arms in the air excitedly.

"They got Min's code?"

"Why else would Jesse be sending you this? They must have! Send that app to Yousef immediately and get them to use it on Gianfranco. We don't have time to waste."

"Are you sure about this, Major?"

"Kate, the worst that can happen is that the app doesn't work."

"But we might lose people. What if Gianfranco kills our operatives?"

The Major stared at her for a moment. "It's a risk we have to take, Kate. The virus is going to be released despite what we do. This app and the string of code are evidence that we are at least affecting something. If this app works, we have bought the team some time. The sun will rise across Australia first, followed by Asia, Russia, and Italy. The last one to see the sun will be the States."

"And we already have Asia's code," Kate said.

"Now you're getting it," the Major said. "The next leader we need is the Russian."

"Alex won't be in Moscow yet," she said, looking at her watch.

"That doesn't matter. Send this app to him and all the other operatives, and let's hope someone else confirms that it works."

Kate created a new email and sent the app to Alex, Yousef and Chuck with instructions attached about what it was for. She pressed send and sat down. "Now we have to find the Oceania sector leader," she said.

The Major nodded. "Yes. We're running out of time fast."

X-RAY

15 Hours Until Virus Release

In the early morning darkness of downtown Rome, Gianfranco paced inside his hotel apartment, preparing his three assassins for what was to come.

"Gentlemen, by this time tomorrow, you will have played a part in the history of the world," he said. "For when the sun rises in the morning, you will release a virus into society that will cleanse the face of the planet, curing it from its crippling disease."

The group of men puffed their chests out proudly.

"Our virus will be released upon five different continents, infecting the Earth's inhabitants and causing unspeakable pain and anguish." Gianfranco glanced at his watch. "Dawn in Australia is a mere 15 hours away, and once the sun has swept across Australia, Asia, and the western half of Russia, it will then be our moment."

The men cheered, punching their fists in the air.

Outside the Valentino Moretti hotel, where Gianfranco was delivering his rousing speech to his men, Fabrizio and Luciano de Angelis sat on a bench inside a bus shelter. For the last five hours, they had taken turns having one-hour naps while the other kept watch over the hotel, waiting on further instructions from Yousef.

Fabrizio's phone rang.

It was Yousef.

"You can move on Gianfranco," he said. "I am forwarding you an app you must install on your phone, along with instructions for how to retrieve the code. Best of luck, gentlemen."

Fabrizio quickly downloaded the app Yousef sent to him through his email and nudged his brother with his elbow.

Luciano sat up on the bench and opened his eyes.

"Green light," Fabrizio said, pointing to his phone.

Luciano nodded as he pointed at something across the road.

Squinting his eyes to see what Luciano was drawing his attention to, Fabrizio saw three men in black emerge from the shadows of an alleyway next to the hotel.

"They must be the assassins," he said, turning to Luciano. "Do you think we should—"

But Luciano was gone. He was already on the move, making his way across the road, heading towards the alleyway.

"Oh…" Fabrizio said, realising he was talking to himself. Luciano didn't speak with his mouth, but he often spoke with his actions.

Fabrizio followed his brother across the road and, moving close to the fence line, crept silently towards the entrance of the alleyway. There, they stopped. They could hear the three assassins' conversation as they spoke together quietly in a huddle.

"I can't wait for this."

"It's going to be excellent."

"We are going to rule the Earth."

"It's about time."

Luciano turned his head and smiled at Fabrizio.

Fabrizio knew that smile and shook his head.

"Don't do it, Luciano," he whispered. *"Not yet."*

No sooner had the words left his mouth than Luciano had leapt to his feet and was sprinting down the alleyway towards the assassins with his pistol raised. He fired a shot into the side of an assassin's head, instantly dropping him to the ground.

The two remaining assassins dissolved into the shadows like cats, blending into the darkness.

Luciano looked around, scanning the building and the alleyway.

Fabrizio ran up behind him. "Up there, Luciano!" he shouted, pointing to the fire escape stairs on the side of the building.

Luciano looked up to see two shadows bounding up the stairs above him. He gave chase, with Fabrizio close behind. Luciano was much nimbler than his older brother and scaled the stairs fast. When he reached the top, he threw open a door and entered the building.

Fabrizio followed his brother, panting heavily.

Making his way down the lavish hallway adorned with gold trim and lush shag pile carpet, Luciano quickly realised he could no longer use the element of surprise to his advantage. Inside the hotel, the assassins could be anywhere. The carpet would mask their footsteps and there were multiple hallways and corners they could hide around.

Luciano's heart pounded in his chest as he crept along the corridor with his weapon raised, watching and listening for the slightest movement or sound.

Fabrizio caught up to him, still out of breath from climbing the stairs. "Can you... can you slow down a little, brother?" he said, panting.

Luciano turned to him and put his index finger to his lips, gesturing for him to be quiet.

Seconds later, a door slammed shut at the end of the hallway. The brothers immediately bolted towards it. Luciano gathered speed, and as he neared the door, he dropped his shoulder and rammed his way through it.

The door was ripped off its hinges as Luciano stumbled into the room awkwardly.

In the middle of the apartment, Gianfranco Ragonesi stood with his hands clasped together at his front, facing them as if expecting their arrival.

"Welcome, gentlemen," he said, spreading his arms out wide. "That was quite an entrance, but you could have simply knocked."

"That *was* knocking," Fabrizio said, helping Luciano up off the floor. "You are Gianfranco Ragonesi?" he asked.

"Yes. I am," Gianfranco replied. "But maybe you should have asked that *before* you knocked down my door."

Luciano aimed his weapon at Gianfranco's head, but hesitated on the trigger.

"Give us the code, and we will leave you alone," Fabrizio said. "Don't make us hurt you."

Gianfranco laughed. "What are you going to do if I don't? Shoot me?" he asked. "You know you cannot kill me if you want your precious code, right?"

Fabrizio didn't answer him. Instead, he quickly scanned the room for the two remaining assassins while Luciano focused on Gianfranco, his pistol locked on his head.

Fabrizio was now Luciano's eyes *and* voice.

And then Luciano spoke. "Are you ready, brother?"

Fabrizio, stunned his brother had chosen this moment to speak for the first time in 20 years, reached into his pocket and pulled out his phone. "Yes! Yes, I am!" he said.

Luciano pulled the trigger twice, firing two quick shots into Gianfranco's kneecaps, causing them to explode. Gianfranco screamed in pain as he collapsed to the floor with blood streaming from his knees, soaking into the plush beige carpet.

"You didn't see that coming, did you?" Luciano said, rushing across the room and pinning Gianfranco to the floor while Fabrizio scanned him with his phone. The phone beeped over the European flag on his right shoulder, and a hexagonal image with numbers and equations appeared on the phone's screen.

"We got it, Luciano!" Fabrizio said. "Let's get out of here!"

"Fab? Don't move," Luciano said.

Fabrizio froze and stared at Luciano, who he could tell was staring at something behind him. "What is it?" he asked.

Luciano snatched his weapon up and fired two quick shots on either side of his head, and two black-clad, knife-wielding assassins dropped to the floor behind him.

"You're lucky I trust you," Fabrizio said, staring at the two motionless bodies behind him. "Why did these guys just let us shoot him?"

Luciano didn't respond.

"Oh, I see. Not speaking again, hey?"

Luciano responded with a wry smile and shrugged.

Gianfranco continued to writhe around in pain on the ground in front of them, clutching at what remained of his knees.

"And what are we going to do with him?" Fabrizio asked, pointing at Gianfranco.

Luciano glanced at Fabrizio before firing a single shot into Gianfranco's head.

"Well, I suppose that's solved that problem," Fabrizio said. "Now, we need to get this code to Yousef."

He pulled out his phone and typed an email with the image of the code attached—

Code retrieved.

Coronado Beach, San Diego, United States
11th February 2021
12:33 am Pacific Standard Time

12 Hours Until Virus Release

The Viribus San Diego operative, Les Wolf, sat on his jet-ski a mile out in San Diego Bay. He had spoken with Chuck a few hours earlier and took the opportunity to do a spot of night fishing while watching for White Cloud.

As midnight passed, he recognised the sound of a helicopter approaching. It was coming from the darkness of the ocean behind him. He turned towards the noise and saw the aircraft approaching him, thundering low and fast across the water's surface. It swooped over him, the downdraft of the rotor blades almost knocking him from the jet-ski.

Once the jet-ski stopped swaying, Les reached for his phone.

"You fly 'em, we prime 'em. Chuck speaking."

"Chuck, we have a helicopter inbound," Les said in a panicked voice. "It came in fast and low off the ocean. It could be them."

"Well, stop talking to me and follow it!"

"I'm on a fucking jet-ski! How far do you expect me to get?"

"Why are you on a jet-ski at this time of night? Do you have a truck there?"

"Yeah, in the car park."

"Then use it! I have another operative in the area. I will get him to you as soon as I can."

Les tucked his phone away, started the jet-ski and chased the helicopter towards the shore, driving it up the beach and ploughing into the sand. Les leapt off it and sprinted up the beach towards his truck in the car park, glancing skywards as he ran, monitoring the helicopter's direction as it disappeared into the distance.

Les quickly reversed his truck out of the car park, crashing it into a parked car behind him. With no hesitation, he shifted the stick into drive and sped off in pursuit of the helicopter.

His phone rang again.

"Hello?" Les said as he drove, watching the sky more than the road.

"Hey man, is this Les?"

"Yeah, who's asking?"

"I hear you need some help. Where you at, bro?"

"Are you Viribus?"

"Of course I am, blood!"

"Good. I'm on the Coronado Bridge, heading east, chasing a helicopter."

"You're doing what now?"

"Chasing a fucking helicopter!"

"Oh shit! Yeah, I see it. A white one? Blue stripe?"

"That's it!"

"Okay, I got it. I'm with you, dog."

Les threw his phone onto the passenger seat and sped up, keeping the helicopter in sight. He entered State Route 94—Martin Luther King Jr. Freeway—and put his foot to the floor as the helicopter banked south.

Mexico was south.

"Oh, no you don't," Les said to himself.

He turned off State Route 94 and headed down Interstate 805, following the helicopter until the Mexican border control came into view.

He could go no further.

Les grabbed his phone off the passenger seat and went to call Chuck to tell him the bad news when the phone began ringing in his hand.

"Hello?" Les said.

"I'll take it from here, bro!"

"Where are you?" Les asked, looking out of his windows.

"I'll be in Mexico shortly, my man. Look up!"

Les looked up and saw a small grey aircraft in the sky heading towards the border.

"Are you in that plane?"

"Yeah, bro! Hahaha!"

Les smiled. "What's your name?"

"Leroy—and you can thank me later. I just saved your ass!"

Les smiled up at the little aircraft in the sky. "Yeah, you sure did."

"I'll let Chuck know where the chopper lands."

"Thank you."

"Not a problem, bro."

Leroy signed off from Les and concentrated on the white helicopter ahead of him. He followed it across the

Mexican border, and a few minutes later, it landed at an airport in Tijuana.

Leroy turned on his aircraft's autopilot, strapped a set of goggles over his eyes, opened the door, and leapt out—arrowing towards the ground at breakneck speed.

With only 1,000 feet remaining on his altitude indicator, he deployed his parachute and descended gracefully to the ground under the cover of darkness.

As soon as he landed, he quickly gathered up the parachute, unclipped it from his back, and ran towards the first car he could find. Wasting no time, he smashed the car's window with his elbow, opened the door and got inside, where he hot-wired the ignition and drove at speed to where he had seen the helicopter land.

As he entered the airfield, he saw three white limousines waiting for a man with a heavily bandaged face emerging from the white helicopter. Leroy followed the limousines into Tijuana Central, where they entered the gates of a Mexican Air Force Base.

Leroy picked up his phone. "Chuck, we have him. He's just entered an Air Force Base next to Tijuana Airport."

"What happened to Les?" Chuck asked.

"He's stuck at the border."

"Okay. I'm on my way. Stay in position. Let me know if this dude moves, alright?"

"Will do, boss."

Chuck immediately emailed Kate.

We have Roman holed up in Tijuana. Eyes on him as we speak. I am going to Mexico to back up the operatives.

Canberra, Australian Capital Territory, Australia
11th February 2021
7:05 pm Australian Eastern Standard Time

11.5 Hours Until Virus Release

Kate's laptop pinged with two emails. One from Yousef and one from Chuck. She opened the email from Yousef and her eyes widened. "Major, you were right. The app works! We've got Gianfranco's code!"

The Major smiled. "Perfect," he said, smiling at her. "Two down, three to go." He returned his attention to his laptop and furrowed his brow. "Now, why on Earth can't we find out anything about this new Oceania sector leader?"

There was a knock at the office door and Dex poked his head inside the room.

"Kate, Dick, I have someone here who would like to meet you."

Dexter opened the door wider and the Prime Minister of Australia stood in the doorway.

"G'day, Kate, Richard," the Prime Minister said, nodding at them both. "Dexter informs me we have some trouble?"

"Yes, Prime Minister," Kate said. "White Cloud is planning to unleash a deadly virus in—" she glanced at her watch "—less than 11 hours. You need to prepare the country and the rest of the world immediately."

"Just slow down," the Prime Minister said, holding a hand up and looking somewhat confused. "Did you say White Cloud? Is this the same White Cloud who has been promoting world conservation and preservation?"

"They *want* you to think they are good Samaritans, sir," Kate said. "That's how they go about their business. They're actually nothing but rebranded terrorists."

The Prime Minister looked surprised. "I must admit, I am rather shocked by this. Do you have any proof to support these claims?"

Kate looked at the Major for help. She knew they had no tangible evidence to back their story up. All they had was what Roman had told her.

The Major shrugged back at her.

Kate looked down at her laptop and opened the email from Chuck. She smiled as she read they had tracked Roman to an Air Force Base in Mexico. She spun her laptop around so the Prime Minister could see the screen. "Why else would their leader be sheltering in Mexico?" she asked.

The Prime Minister took a pair of reading glasses from his jacket pocket, put them on, and leaned over to read the email from Chuck. Everyone in the room watched him read the email and waited for his reaction. After a few minutes of silence, the Prime Minister stood upright and removed the glasses off his face, folding them up and returning them to his pocket.

He stared at Kate for a moment and scratched his chin. "Is this all you have?" he asked.

Kate noticed the Major glaring at the Prime Minister. She could tell he was about to lose his patience. Before the Major had a chance to respond, she jumped in. "We have two pieces of code required to create a formula for the virus, sir," she said. "I'm not sure how much more proof you need," she added, instantly regretting how blunt she sounded.

Her email then pinged with another email from Jesse, which she opened, and saw this one was only partially encrypted—

*Kate*******g*****out***********danger**********************
leader*****frozen*******************

She furrowed her brow and showed the screen to the Major, who screwed his face up in confusion. "Sir, you need to see this," he said, taking the laptop from Kate and showing it to the Prime Minister.

The Prime Minister huffed as he retrieved the glasses from his pocket again and stared at the encrypted email for a moment. "What am I looking at?" he asked.

"Our team in Shanghai just sent us this message. It's a semi-encrypted email. They have previously tried to contact us, but their messages have been coming through in a completely unreadable state. This is the first message containing legible words, and I think you will agree, the words are rather alarming, to say the least."

The Prime Minister took the glasses from his face and put an arm of them between his teeth. He chewed on it as he stared at the ground, pondering the situation at hand.

"I will engage the Americans to assist your people on the ground in Mexico, and I will ensure Australia is on high alert," he said.

He then turned to Dexter. "Lock parliament down immediately and inform the SPS—and get me the Minister of Foreign Affairs on the phone immediately."

The SPS, or Specialist Protective Services, is a highly trained tactical branch of the Australian Federal Police. This unit is usually deployed for domestic and international counter-terrorism purposes and is stationed in Canberra.

Dexter nodded and opened the door for the Prime Minister to exit. Before he left the room, he turned back to them. "Do not leave this office. You will be safe here. If they take me to the bunker, you are coming with me."

Mexico/United States Border, San Diego, United States
11ᵗʰ February 2021
2:27 am Pacific Daylight Time

10 Hours Until Virus Release

Chuck Walters sped towards the Mexican border in his beaten-up, pea-green, ex-US Army Jeep in the dark of night. As the floodlit Mexican border control appeared on the horizon in front of him, he pulled off the road into a roadside lay-by and sent a text.

Within minutes, Les Wolf stopped alongside him in his truck and wound down his window. "Am I coming with you?" Les asked.

"Yeah, man," Chuck said. "It would be *really* stupid to move what I have in the back of this Jeep right now."

Les parked his truck, climbed onto the passenger seat of Chuck's Jeep, and looked in the back. "Holy shit!"

Chuck laughed. "Big trouble gets big weapons," he said.

"How do you think you're going to get all this into Mexico, dude?"

Chuck smiled an impish grin. "Quickly," he said, throwing the Jeep into gear and flooring the throttle, accelerating straight at the barricades of the floodlit Mexican border ahead of them.

Les held on to whatever he could to keep himself from being catapulted out of the vehicle.

The border control personnel manning the gates began frantically waving their arms above their heads, trying to slow down what appeared to be an out-of-control vehicle.

Chuck continued to speed up.

The border control personnel quickly realised the little Jeep wasn't going to slow down and stopped waving, reaching for their weapons instead.

"Oh shiiiiiiiiiiit!" Les screamed.

"Hold on, man!"

The border personnel fired at the Jeep as Les ducked behind the dash and prayed. Chuck laughed hysterically as he crashed the Jeep through the boom gates and continued to speed up.

"You're fucking crazy, dude!" Les yelled with his head behind the dashboard.

"You ain't seen crazy yet, man!" Chuck shouted over the gunshots. "You might wanna sit up for this next part!"

Les sat upright in his seat and looked behind them at the border personnel who were now getting into vehicles. He saw Chuck tightening his seatbelt straps, securing himself into his seat with the racing-style harnesses attached to the racing-style bucket seats.

"What the fuck have you done to this Jeep?" Les asked.

"Better strap in, dude!" Chuck said, smiling mischievously.

Les tightened his harnesses.

Chuck then flicked a switch on the steering wheel, and the Jeep surged forward intensely, forcing Les backwards into his seat.

"What the fuuuuck!"

"Yee-haw!" Chuck roared in delight, smiling as he jostled with the bucking steering wheel.

Les dared to glance over his shoulder. The border force vehicles were falling back, while the Jeep was still pulling away.

Soon enough, the nitrous ran out, and the Jeep slowed down.

"You put nitrous in a Jeep?"

Chuck laughed a roaring belly laugh. "Yeah! Cool, huh?"

"You're a madman," Les said, taking several deep breaths to slow his heart rate down.

Chuck smiled a big toothy grin as the Jeep bounced over the rough terrain.

"Welcome to Mexico, dude!"

Tijuana International Airport, Mexico
11ᵗʰ February 2021
3:10 am Pacific Daylight Time

9.5 Hours Until Virus Release

Roman and his assassins sheltered in a Mexican Air Force Base on the outskirts of the International Airport. Roman knew the Mexican Defence General personally and had called upon a favour to utilise the base and hide from Viribus while he deployed his part of the virus into the Americas. Viribus would expect him to go to the States— South America was close enough to do significant damage.

Roman paced in his quarters, waiting for the sun to rise—his signal to deploy the virus.

Outside, sirens began blaring out around the floodlit compound, and Roman stopped pacing to peer through the small window of the concrete bunker.

He saw Mexican Air Force personnel scattering in all directions, dressing themselves as they ran after being woken rudely by the siren.

Opening the door and grabbing the first Mexican to run past, Roman asked, "What's going on?"

"Air-raid siren, Jefe," the airman said.

"An air-raid siren? What is this? World War Two? Who has air raids these days?"

The airman pointed up at something in the sky. "We do, Jefe."

Roman looked to where the airman was pointing and saw a long horizontal line of red and blue flashing lights in the night sky, coming straight towards the compound.

"Oh, shit," Roman said, running back into his quarters and screaming at his squad of assassins. "Take cover!" he yelled as he scrambled underneath his bed.

The roar of the jet's engines got louder as they closed in on the compound and the concrete walls of Roman's quarters shook as the aircraft unleashed their payloads.

Bombs rained down inside the compound as the aircraft swept across the sky in formation. Roman's bunker wall exploded inwards, collapsing around his bed, and sending cinder block rubble high into the air.

As quick as they had started, the bombs suddenly stopped—the explosions replaced by screams of pain from injured airmen.

Roman pushed away some large chunks of rubble and crawled out from under the bed. He looked up and found himself staring up at the night sky. The roof of the bunker had disappeared. He turned around to see what was left of the room and realised his assassins were now trapped under a pile of rubble that was once the ceiling of the bunker.

As he dusted himself off, he felt a warm, sticky liquid trickle down his neck. He reached a hand up to touch it, and when he pulled his hand away, saw it was covered in blood.

Two of his assassin's began slowly emerging from underneath the rubble, coughing up dust and blood.

"Which one of you has the virus?" Roman yelled.

They glanced at Roman, dazed and confused.

"Well?" he demanded. "Say something!"

One of them slowly reached inside his uniform and pulled out a pouch, holding it up in the air. Roman rushed across the room, stumbling over the debris, and snatched it from the man's hand. He quickly opened it and found the vials were shattered. The liquid was gone. He threw the pouch to the floor in disgust.

"FUCK!!!" he screamed. "Who the fuck are these bastards in the sky?"

Roman looked up through the hole in his ceiling as four C-17s flew overhead, spewing Marines out of their rear cargo holds. Roman watched them fall as their parachutes deployed, carrying the Marines safely to the ground.

It was then that Roman realised Viribus had found him, and he was under attack. He picked up a rifle from a nearby dead airman and began firing at the falling parachutes.

Tijuana, Mexico
11ᵗʰ February 2021
3:35 am Pacific Daylight Time

9 Hours Until Virus Release

Les and Chuck waited for Leroy in a lay-by on the side of the road. A battered old sedan pulled in behind them and Leroy got out. He jumped into the back of Chuck's Jeep, and together, they watched the United States Air Force B1 stealth bombers pass low overhead, unloading their bombs on the military base.

"That's our cue," Chuck said, throwing the Jeep into drive and launching it towards the military compound.

Leroy hung on for dear life in the back of the Jeep. "Damn, brother! Where'd you learn to drive? Stevie Wonder's school of motoring?"

Chuck smiled a wide grin and yelled over the noise of the speeding vehicle. "Look under the tarp! Arm yourself!"

Leroy lifted the tarp he was sitting on in the rear tray of the Jeep, only to find a cache of weapons underneath it.

"Oh, damn, Chuck! You've come to play, my man!"

Leroy handed Les a rifle and some hand grenades, before arming himself with two Uzi sub-machine guns. "Oh man, I look like fucking Rambo," he said.

A few minutes later, the little green Jeep smashed through the boom gates of the Air Force Base and entered the ruined compound as the parachuting Marines touched down in Mexico. The Mexican airmen who had survived the devastating bombing run of the B1s were already firing their weapons at the Marines, with Roman behind them.

It was now a ground war.

Roman and his two concussed assassins armed themselves with whatever they could find, killing as many of the advancing Marines as they could.

The B1s above them were looping around to begin another bombing run when the night sky suddenly erupted with deafening explosions and blinding lights.

Roman looked towards the noise and smiled. His battleship had just weighed into the fight.

The ship launched its surface-to-air missiles at the B1s, plucking them out of the sky one by one—and within minutes, the sky was clear of aircraft.

The ship then turned its attention to the ground attack, firing its stern-mounted Phalanx machine gun towards the shore with violent ferocity. It ripped the American ground assault to pieces, the Phalanx shells slamming into them like missiles and tearing the Marines apart.

The scene was one of absolute carnage. Buildings were on fire, people were screaming in pain, and Mexican airmen were barking orders at one another. Dismembered bodies littered the ground. It was a war zone.

Chuck's Jeep came blazing into the compound with Leroy standing in the back, spitting out bullets from his dual-wielded Uzi 9mm machine guns towards anything that moved. Les assisted him by firing his rifle from the front seat.

A short while later, the American Marines were wiped out by the Phalanx cannon out at sea. It had no further targets and ceased firing its oversized shells.

Roman watched the rogue Jeep loaded with a trio of odd-looking people encircling the compound, bouncing like a bucking bull as it drove over the mounds of rubble and concrete.

Roman flicked a switch on his weapon and raised it to his shoulder, aiming it at the Jeep. He pulled the trigger.

FFFDOOOM!

A grenade shot out of the grenade launcher attachment of his rifle, hitting the ground in front of the Jeep, ejecting its occupants into the air and causing them to disappear into a cloud of dust.

The gunfire around the compound immediately fell silent. No cannon, no gunshots, no grenades. Roman stood in the middle of the devastated arena, totally exposed and waiting for any signs of life. He nodded to his assassins, who ran away in opposite directions, dissolving into the shadows of the ruined buildings around him.

"Give us the code, or we'll kill you," a voice shouted from beyond a semi-decimated wall.

"How does *fuck off* sound?" Roman replied. "Who are you anyway?"

"That don't matter," Chuck shouted. "We know who you are and what you're doing. Give us the code and the virus."

Roman said nothing.

Chuck nodded at Leroy and Les, who dispersed in opposite directions to flank Roman.

As he stood in the middle of his semi-levelled, ceiling-less bunker, Roman reached inside his jacket and pulled out the pouch containing the broken vials and syringes. From another pocket, he produced a different vial—the vial Kate brought with her to Shanghai. He filled the syringe and strolled over to an injured, groaning Mexican airman, who was alive but drifting in and out of consciousness.

Roman held the syringe up to the airman's throat.

"You can't kill me!" he shouted, his voice echoing around the ruined compound. "If you kill me, the code is gone forever, and everyone will die!"

Chuck glanced around the edge of the wall he was hiding behind. Under the compound floodlights, he saw Roman in the middle of a ruined building, out in the open, holding a syringe to a Mexican airman's neck.

"What're you doing, Roman?" Chuck asked from behind the wall, trying to stall him and buy Les and Leroy some time to get into position.

"As soon as I inject this man, the virus will be activated, and he will become instantly contagious.

Everyone will die. *You* will die. Your friends will die. Your family will die. It is now *your* call."

"But won't you die as well, Roman?"

Roman shook his head. "No. I am immune. No harm can come to me."

Chuck took a moment and looked around the wall again. "Your plan has failed, Roman," he said. "The Russian, European and Asian codes have all been retrieved. The virus has not been released anywhere."

Chuck didn't know if he was right, but hoped Roman would buy his bluff.

Roman paused. "What about Australia?" he asked.

"We have operatives on the ground there, too," Chuck said. "I'm sure they have the code by now."

Roman said nothing for a moment. "So, you're with Viribus," he said.

"Yep. Now let the soldier go, Roman. It's over."

Behind a building on the left of Roman, Les reloaded his rifle as he watched Roman in the middle of the ruined building, holding the unconscious airman in his arms while he spoke to Chuck. Leroy waited to the right of Roman and readied his phone.

"Go!" Chuck yelled.

Leroy leapt out from the shadows to the right of Roman, sprinting towards him. Les burst out from behind the building on Roman's left, and together they ran towards him, trapping Roman between them.

A booming shot rang out from one of the ruined buildings, and Leroy watched Les's head explode in front of him. Leroy threw himself into the air, crash-tackling Roman to the ground before he could inject the Mexican airman with the virus, and slapped his phone over the American flag on the White Cloud leader's shoulder.

His phone beeped—

—as another shot fired.

Leroy fell limply on top of Roman. The phone fell from his hand and bounced along the ground, landing amongst a pile of cinder blocks.

Having just witnessed both his colleagues be murdered by sniper fire, Chuck ran for the Jeep and swept a pile of rubble off the driver's seat with his arm. He then jumped in and floored the accelerator.

Driving a wide circle around Roman, he looked up at the buildings to locate the sniper's positions while kicking up vast clouds of dust behind the Jeep, preventing them from getting a clear shot at him.

He stopped behind a semi-destroyed building and reached into the back of the Jeep, pulling out a four-barrel, shoulder-mounted rocket launcher.

Through the dust clouds, Chuck spotted some movement in a building. With no hesitation, he put the launcher to his shoulder and fired. The rocket fizzed through the air towards the building and exploded. The walls of the building disintegrated as body parts of an assassin flew through the air.

One to go.

Chuck returned to the Jeep and continued driving in circles, dodging large chunks of concrete and random body parts strewn over the ground.

Another booming shot rang out, and Chuck snapped his head towards the noise. Through the dust, he saw the muzzle flare above him, perched high on top of a building.

As Chuck was looking up to locate the sniper, his Jeep ploughed into a large piece of concrete and came to a shuddering and sudden stop. Chuck's head slammed against the steering wheel, and he blacked out for a moment.

He shook off the concussion.

He didn't have time for it.

He rolled out of the destroyed vehicle and sheltered behind it, returning the rocket launcher to his shoulder as blood trickled down his face.

He glanced around the corner of the Jeep, and the sniper fired again.

They missed.

Chuck now had the sniper's location, but the sniper also had his.

"You still there, Roman?" Chuck yelled at the top of his voice.

Roman was still in the middle of the ruined building, sitting on the ground against a wall and holding the syringe to the Mexican airman's neck. The airman was now unconscious and lying in between Roman's legs.

"Yeah, I'm still here!" Roman replied. "Are you ready to die?"

Chuck smirked and took a deep breath. He then leaped out from behind the Jeep and fired the rocket launcher at where he had seen the sniper moments earlier. The rocket fizzed its way across the arena, hitting its target and turning the building into a cloud of dust, blood, and concrete.

With the launcher still on his shoulder, Chuck turned to Roman. Roman hadn't moved. He was still sitting behind the Mexican airman, holding the syringe up to the man's neck.

"Don't come any closer," Roman said.

"Come on, Roman. It's over, man. Don't make me kill you," Chuck said.

"Put the launcher down."

"Put the Mexican down."

Roman smiled and shoved the needle of the syringe into the Mexican's neck, pressing down on the plunger.

Chuck shook his head. "Oh, fuck you, man!"

He pulled the trigger of his launcher and fired his last rocket at Roman and the Mexican, ripping them to pieces. Arms, legs, and other body parts rained down around him, landing in the dirt with sickening thuds.

Chuck dropped the rocket launcher and fell to his knees. He was exhausted. As he slowly got his breath back, something lit up underneath the rubble next to him, making him curiously turn his head towards it.

He crawled on his hands and knees over to where the flash had come from and, moving a few large chunks of concrete, he found Leroy's phone.

He picked the phone up, smiled at it, before forwarding the image of Roman's code to Kate.

He then turned to the body of Leroy, lying in the dust next to him and said, "Well done, sir. Your fast fingers may have just saved us all."

What Chuck didn't realise was that he was now carrying the virus.

YANKEE

4.5 Hours Until Virus Release

Dmitri Zagrev gazed out the window of his Moscow high-rise apartment, wearing nothing but a red velvet robe. Behind him, three men in black guarded the door of the apartment with their rifles slung low behind their backs.

"Sasha, Katerina!" he yelled over his shoulder.

Two scantily clad, identical-looking women got up from a huge, luxurious sofa and walked across the room. They stopped on either side of him as he slithered a hand around their slim, bare waists.

Dmitri lowered his voice almost to a whisper. "Soon, I will be in control of all of this," he said, nodding at the city lights of Moscow outside. "And I want you both next to me when it happens. Would you like that?"

"Uh-huh," they said, nodding and smiling wantonly while draping themselves over him and kissing his bare chest under the robe.

Dmitri stroked both of their heads, running his fingers through their long, perfectly straight blonde hair.

"Come with me," he said, leading the women across the apartment towards a bedroom. As soon as he closed the bedroom door behind him, the two women began undressing.

"No," Dmitri said, holding his hand up. "Do not take your clothes off. I do not want your bodies."

The women stopped undressing and looked at him with confusion.

Dmitri then locked the door.

The women glanced at each other with concerning looks on their faces.

Walking over to the bedside table and opening the small drawer, Dmitri took out a rolled-up leather pouch and placed it on the king-size bed. He untied the twine from around the centre of the pouch and opened it. Inside was a syringe with several vials of a clear liquid.

As Dmitri took out a syringe and filled it with liquid from one of the vials, Sasha said, "Er… I'm sorry. We don't do that kind of stuff."

"But you don't even know what it is," he replied.

"It's obviously drugs, and we don't do drugs."

"Well, yes, it is a drug. But this one will not harm you. In fact, it will protect you."

Sasha glanced at Katerina again, and together, they went to leave the room.

Dmitri raised his voice. "Wait! You are not going anywhere. You don't understand. I'm trying to help you."

The twins trusted no one—they simply couldn't afford to in their line of work. They had seen the worst Moscow had to offer.

Dmitri, recognising their growing fear, tried to explain. "Listen to me. In a few hours time, a virus is going to be released into the community that will destroy humanity as you know it," he said, waving the syringe around in the air. "The formula in this syringe will protect you from its effects."

Sasha and Katerina looked at each other before bursting with laughter. "Are you serious?" Katerina asked, giggling. "I've heard some bullshit in my time, but I think this is the best yet. That's a date rape drug, Dmitri. We're not stupid."

Dmitri put the syringe down on the bed.

Sasha walked up to him. "Why would you want to use a *lifesaving* drug on two whores you just picked up off the street? Do you think we're stupid?"

Dmitri took a deep breath and let it out slowly. He then grabbed Sasha by the hair and launched her across the room. She crashed into the wall hard and fell to the floor.

Katerina, upon seeing her sister get thrown across the room like a toy doll, charged at Dmitri and threw a fist at his head.

Dmitri caught the punch with one hand and twisted her arm behind her back, and shoving her face-first as hard as he could into the wall.

Katerina hit the wall the same as her sister and fell to the floor, dazed but not unconscious.

Dmitri picked her up by her hair to beat her some more—when he heard a noise on the other side of the bedroom door.

He froze, turning his head towards the noise with a handful of Katerina's hair.

He heard some scuffling sounds and then—gunfire. Dmitri quickly dropped Katerina and unlocked the door.

He threw it wide open, only to see Alexei filling the space where the door once was, staring down the sights of a Kalashnikov rifle pointed at his head.

"Nice to see you again, brother," Alexei said.

"Alexei? What… what the fuck are you doing here?" Dmitri said, with fear in his voice.

"I have come for you," Alexei replied. "I need you to give me your part of the code."

Dmitri retreated backwards into the bedroom, leaving Alexei in the doorway. "Code? What code?"

"You know exactly what I'm talking about," Alexei said. "The code for the formula."

"I have no such thing."

Alexei noticed the two blonde women in the corner of the room. One conscious, one not. "It's sad to see nothing changes with you, Dmitri."

Alexei then smiled as he lowered his weapon and extended his hand for Dmitri to shake.

Dmitri stared at him warily for a moment before a grin emerged on his face. "Oh, you bastard! You had me scared stupid! Come here, you dog!"

As he went to shake Alexei's outstretched hand, Alexei grabbed his arm and yanked Dmitri towards him, head-butting him hard in the middle of his face.

Dmitri fell to the floor, clutching his nose and crying out in pain as Alexei prowled the ground around him. "You should be more careful, Dmitri. That's the oldest trick in the book," he said. "Now, stop wasting my time. Give me the code."

"Excuse me, sir?" Katerina called out. "Did you say something about a formula?"

Alexei spun around to look at her. "Yes, I did."

"Would this formula be in liquid form, perhaps?"

"Yes, probably."

"He was about to inject us with something a few seconds before you turned up. Maybe that's it?"

"Shut up, Katerina!" Dmitri growled from behind his hands clutched over his face.

Alexei looked down at him. "Is that right? Do you already have the formula, little brother?"

Dmitri looked up at him and said nothing.

"It's over there," Katerina said, pointing to the bed.

Alexei walked over to the bed and picked up the syringe already loaded with liquid.

Dmitri went to get to his feet but stumbled and fell to the floor—face-down—next to the bed at Alexei's feet.

Alexei stood over him and picked his head up, holding it in a vice-like headlock. "What's in this?" he asked, waving the dripping syringe in front of his brother's increasingly bulging eyes.

"It…is…formula," Dmitri croaked through his crushed windpipe.

Alexei lowered his mouth to Dmitri's ear. *"If that's right, then I think you should have some first,"* he whispered.

"No! Wait!" Dmitri screamed as Alexei held the syringe up to his neck.

"What is it, Dmitri? Do you have something else you want to say?"

Dmitri paused.

Alexei tightened the arm around his neck.

"Okay!" he spluttered. "It is not formula! It is virus!"

Alexei dropped him to the floor and stood up. "Girls, get out of here, now," he said without looking at them, his gaze fixed solely upon Dmitri.

Katerina got up off the floor and helped her unsteady sister to her feet before running out of the apartment, stepping over the three men dressed all in black, lying dead in the doorway as they went.

Alexei waited for the girls to be clear of the room. Upon hearing the door close, he grabbed Dmitri around the neck again.

"No, Alexei! What are you doing?" Dmitri shouted, struggling to get out of Alexei's vice-like headlock.

With his free hand, Alexei picked up the syringe and plunged it deep into Dmitri's neck, squeezing the plunger.

Dmitri stopped struggling. He knew the fight was over. Alexei let him go and threw the empty syringe at him in disgust.

"What have you done?" Dmitri croaked.

Alexei remembered his orders in Kate's email—the leaders couldn't die before they retrieved the code.

"How long before you die?" he asked.

"Maybe an hour, maybe two," Dmitri said, getting to his feet and clearing his throat.

Alexei nodded. "I'm sorry it had to come to this, little brother."

Dmitri smiled as he straightened his robe.

"I… am not," he said.

Alexei frowned. "What do you mean?"

"By injecting me with the virus, you have just released it into Russia," he said with a smile. "You have done what White Cloud wanted *me* to do. So, thank you, Alexei. Thank you for taking on that responsibility."

Alexei shook his head. "No. You have it all wrong. I injected you with the virus, so you would have no option but to give me the code. Now stop being so stubborn and give it to me, so I can get both of us the formula."

Dmitri snorted. "Ha! You have made a terrible mistake, big brother. It is not that simple. The formula still needs to be created, and it can only be created in conjunction with the other four codes from the other leaders."

Alexei's phone buzzed in his pocket. "Wait a minute," he said.

"Oh, that's right," Dmitri said. "This is what's wrong with the people of today. The world is about to fall apart in front of you, but of course, your phone is still more important. Typical!"

Alexei ignored him and opened the email from Kate with instructions on how to retrieve the codes from the leaders. He quickly downloaded the attached app and installed it on his phone. "Perfect timing," he said.

"What is?" Dmitri asked.

Alexei tucked the phone away. "I don't need you to give me the code anymore, Dmitri—I can just take it."

Alexei picked up his Kalashnikov and began reloading it, slowly.

Dmitri realised what was about to happen. "No! I will give you the code!" he said, backing away from

Alexei. "You do not need to kill me. We can get the formula codes together, and we will both be cured."

Alexei cocked the weapon. "You just told me that wasn't possible, little brother.

"Alexei! Please stop! You are my brother! I will give you the fucking code!"

"You had your chance, Dmitri," Alexei said, putting the rifle up to his shoulder and following Dmitri around the room as he desperately tried to hide behind the furniture.

Alexei fired the weapon as Dmitri ran for the door of the apartment, shooting him in the leg and sending him clattering to the floor, crying out in pain.

Alexei slowly walked over to his brother lying on the ground, writhing around in agony, and pulled out his phone, placing it over Dmitri's right shoulder—just as Kate had informed him in the email—

—the phone beeped.

An image of hexagons and numbers appeared on the screen, and he immediately forwarded it to Kate.

Alexei put his phone away and looked down at Dmitri. "You stupid bastard," he said. "You could have just given me the code and we wouldn't be here."

"You're all going to fucking die!" Dmitri shouted. "You can all rot in hell!"

"Goodbye, brother," Alexei said, reaching down and grabbing Dmitri's head with both hands and quickly twisting it, snapping his neck with one swift movement, and killing his brother—the Russian sector leader.

Canberra, Australian Capital Territory, Australia
12th February 2021
3:20 am Australian Eastern Standard Time

3 Hours Until Virus Release

It was the early hours of the morning when Moose touched down on the runway of Canberra Airport, carrying Matt, Alaina, and Jesse. They had travelled through the night in a desperate attempt to reach their unsuspecting leader before Sol could get to her. Jesse had tried sending messages at regular intervals throughout the journey to warn Kate of the danger she was in, but had received no response. However, Matt's efforts to hack into the GPS signal coming from her necklace had proved fruitful, and he had successfully directed Alaina to Canberra, where the signal was emanating from.

As Alaina applied the brakes of Moose on the runway of Canberra's International Airport, an airport car shot out from a taxiway and positioned itself in front of the aircraft. The car sported two rotating amber lights on its roof and an illuminated amber sign with the words *Follow Me.*

Alaina followed it into the darkness of a remote parking area to the west of the passenger terminals, where it slowed to a stop, and Alaina applied the parking brake of Moose.

Matt poked his head into the cockpit. "What's going on?" he asked, craning his neck to look out of the cockpit window.

"I'm not sure," Alaina said as she shut down the engines of Moose. "Although these cars coming towards us look very official." Matt saw the two highly polished black cars emerging out of the darkness and stop in front of the aircraft.

They went down into the cargo bay, where Jesse was already arming himself with a rifle from the trunks Alexei had given Kate. Matt took two pistols off him and shoved them into his shoulder holsters while Alaina strapped two huge revolvers to her thighs.

As the entry door of Moose lowered, Matt saw a man standing outside, waiting for them. "Welcome home," the man said.

Matt drew a pistol, looking him up and down.

"My apologies," the man said, extending his hand for him to shake. "My name is Dexter. Dexter Wheatley. Secretary to the Prime Minister of Australia."

Matt holstered his weapon. "What's happened?" he asked, warily shaking Dexter's hand. "Why are you here, and how did you know we were coming?"

Dexter smirked. "The CIA are not the only ones in the world with the ability to gather intel, Mr Knight."

Matt stared at him, uncomfortable with this stranger knowing his last name. He never used it in any capacity if he could avoid it.

"Our boffins saw your aircraft appear on their radars," Dexter said. "So as soon as we had worked out who you were, we concluded that you must be coming here."

"Do you know where Kate is?" Alaina asked from behind Matt.

Dexter nodded. "Yes. She received your messages, but they were semi-encrypted. So, to be safe, we have secured her in Parliament House. I got out of my warm, cozy bed to escort you to her."

"You mean she doesn't know?" Matt asked.

Dexter shook his head. "Know what?" he asked.

"That the Oceania sector leader of White Cloud, her husband, is coming to kill her."

Dexter looked at him and frowned. "What on earth are you talking about?"

Before Matt could explain, Alaina tapped him on the arm. "Look," she said, pointing a finger at an unmarked white business jet with a thin blue line down its side.

Matt stared at the aircraft. "Oh crap. You don't think…"

Alaina shrugged. "It's possible."

Matt turned to Dexter. "How long has that aircraft been there?"

"It turned up about an hour before you did. We watched it arrive while we were waiting for you. Some guy in a white suit got out of it—"

"Oh shit," Matt said. "Dexter, you need to take us to Kate right now."

Dexter looked confused. "Why? What's going—"

"—No time to explain. Get in the car," Matt said, striding past him towards the waiting vehicles.

The Viribus team and Dexter sat in the back of the black limousine as it sped away from Canberra

International Airport and towards Parliament House. Matt was glad it was the early hours of the morning. The roads were void of any other traffic, which made getting through Canberra a lot easier than it normally would.

Dexter's phone rang as they sped down the highway at a speed greater than the posted legal limit. He promptly fished it from his jacket pocket and answered it. Matt watched him hold the phone away from his ear slightly as the person on the other end of the call screamed and shouted something through the phone at him. Dexter suddenly went pale and ended the call.

"What's wrong?" Matt asked. "Who was that?"

"It's uh… uh…"

"Come on. Spit it out."

"That was my PA. Parliament House is under attack," he said as the colour drained from his face.

"Oh shit," Matt said, sinking into his seat. "We're too late."

Canberra, Australian Capital Territory, Australia
12ᵗʰ February 2021
3:30 am Australian Eastern Standard Time

3 Hours Until Virus Release

Sol launched a rocket-propelled grenade at the locked front doors of Parliament House, blowing a hole in the front of the building. Before the assembled SPS had time to react, one of Sol's three black-clad assistants carrying duffle bags full of weapons over their shoulders lobbed several smoke grenades into the foyer of the building as they marched inside it. The grenades exploded in front of them, allowing Sol and his assistants to enter the parliamentary building under a veil of smoke and remain out of sight.

"I'm here for Kate Fabianski," Sol yelled in his strange digital voice. "Hand her over and I leave here in peace."

None of the SPS responded. The smoke was too dense for them to see or do anything. Sol switched on the thermal vision of his mask, watching for any movement inside the smoke cloud.

Sol saw one of the SPS members stand up and randomly fire his weapon towards them, hitting one of his assistants in the shoulder. Sol snapped his rifle up and returned fire with a volley of bullets. Pieces of flesh and blood were launched into the air as the SPS member was ripped to pieces and his body fell to the floor.

Sol glanced at the wounded man behind him, clutching at his shoulder with blood trickling down his arm and onto the floor.

"Get out of here," he said. "You are of no use to me now. Get the car ready."

The assassin did as he was ordered and left.

"If anyone else tries anything stupid like that, this is what you'll get!" Sol shouted.

Down the hallway, and inside an office, Kate and the Major had instinctively ducked at the noise of the rocket-propelled grenade hitting the front of the building and remained crouched behind the office door, listening to what was happening outside.

Kate soon grew impatient and slowly opened the door to see what was happening on the other side of it.

"Stay in here, Kate. This doesn't involve you," the Major said, putting a hand on her shoulder.

"With all due respect, Major, I would put money on the fact that it does. This guy could very well be here for us, and here we are, hiding in an office, waiting for him to find us. I'm going for a look."

Kate opened the door a little further and moved out into the hallway.

"Kate!" the Major said through gritted teeth. "Fucking hell," he groaned before reluctantly following her through the door.

The smoke cloud surrounding Sol and the SPS members in the foyer began to dissipate, and Kate could see the SPS surrounding a man with a mask on his head wearing a uniform she recognised. This man was with White Cloud.

The Major noticed the Australian flag on the man's shoulder. *"I think we've found the Oceania sector leader,"* he whispered into Kate's ear.

"No. It's worse," she replied. *"He found us."*

Sol looked at the SPS surrounding him. "I do not wish to harm any of you," he said. "I am here for Kate Fabianski, the leader of Viribus. Hand her over to me and I will leave you alone. There will be no further casualties."

The SPS captain yelled, "Put the guns down and we can talk! There's no need for the weapons, sir!"

"You don't understand," Sol said, laughing behind his mask. "This is not up for negotiation. I am aware that as soon as I put this weapon down, you will kill me. I am not stupid, *sir*."

The SPS captain held his weapon aloft. "Look, I have no intention of harming you. If you put your weapons down, we can talk."

Sol sighed and raised his weapon to his shoulder.

The entire SPS detail mirrored his movement—but before chaos could break out, Kate stepped out from the safety of the hallway with her hands in the air, behind the wall of SPS members.

"Wait!" she yelled.

"Kate, what the *actual fuck* are you doing?" the Major hissed at her desperately.

Several SPS members forming the wall in front of her turned their heads to see who was speaking.

"Are you the Viribus leader?" Sol asked over the wall of SPS standing between him and Kate, seemingly unperturbed by the fact they had their weapons trained on him.

"Yes. I am," Kate said, walking into the centre of the foyer with her hands in the air. "And I will come with you peacefully. There is no need for anyone else to be harmed."

Sol dropped his weapon, but the SPS kept theirs up to their shoulders. "You need to tell these people to stand down," he said.

"I cannot do that," Kate said. "I have no jurisdiction over them. But I will come with you peacefully if you turn around and leave this building right now."

Sol took a moment before breaking out in laughter. His two remaining assistants behind him each dropped a smoke grenade to the ground, which detonated on impact, enveloping them in a dense cloud of smoke. Once safely out of view, the assassins began hurling more smoke grenades into the foyer, filling it with another enormous cloud of blinding smoke. Only this one was thicker, and *much* denser.

Kate watched the smoke billow out between her and the masked man quickly and she looked over at the Major.

He waved his hand at her, beckoning for her to return to the safety of the hallway.

As she turned to him, the man in the white uniform burst out of the cloud of artificial smoke, charging straight at her from behind.

"Kate! Look out!" the Major yelled—

—But it was too late.

Sol's shoulder connected with her spine, sending her clattering forward on her front and hitting the ground hard enough for the impact to expel all the air in her lungs.

Sol flipped her over and straddled her chest, pinning her to the ground by digging his knees into her biceps.

Kate looked up at him as she gasped for air—and for a moment, she noticed something familiar.

A smell.

An aroma she had not smelled for a long time.

Kate went to speak, but her voice was non-existent. Her lungs felt like they were on fire, and she couldn't get enough air in them to make a sound. Sol never heard her utter his name under what breath she had.

"Sol?"

Sol's assistants appeared from the smoke cloud behind him, carrying the duffle bags full of weapons.

"Cable ties," Sol demanded, holding his hand out.

One of his assistants set down a duffle bag and pulled out a bunch of cable ties, handing them to him.

Sol knew it was only a matter of time before the cloud dispersed and his cover would be gone. He could hear the SPS yelling at each other inside the cloud, and with the thermal mode of his mask turned on, he could also *see* the disorientated SPS searching for him. They hadn't seen him enter the cloud of smoke as it enveloped them and weave his way through the wall of people to reach his target.

One of the assistant's produced a ball gag from one of the bags and shoved it into Kate's mouth. He then secured it to her head, preventing her from making any noise, while Sol tied her hands and feet together with the cable ties.

From his vantage point in the hallway, the Major could do nothing but watch as the small group of men quickly bound Kate up and covered her head with a bag. He had no weapons at his disposal and desperately hoped the cloud of smoke would disperse in time for the SPS to see what was happening behind them and react. Except, the cloud of smoke was much denser than the previous one and didn't seem like it was dispersing at all.

He needed to do something.

"Fuck it," he said, bursting from the safety of the hallway and charging at the men who were now attempting to lift Kate's hog-tied body off the ground.

The Major crash-tackled the two assistants simultaneously, knocking them off their feet and smashing their heads into the marble floor. He heard one of their skull's crack, rendering them unconscious instantaneously. The other assistant's head bounced off the ground, causing him to howl in pain as he clutched at his skull.

The Major got to his feet quickly and went to stand up—only to find himself staring down the barrel of Sol's Desert Eagle revolver, aimed at his head. Sol's stunned assistant got to his feet groggily, shaking away his concussion and rubbing at his head.

The Major froze as he stared at Sol along the barrel of his weapon.

"Get her out of here," Sol said, staring at the Major but directing the order at his assistant. The assistant slowly walked over to Kate, hauled her up onto his shoulder, and picked up the duffle bag of weapons.

The Major slowly raised his hands into the air.

"You have no reason to kill me," he said.

Sol breathed heavily. "Who are you?" he asked in his imposing digital voice.

"That doesn't matter," the Major replied. "Please. Let her go. I beg you. There are two young children waiting at home for their mother to return."

Sol paused for a moment. "And what are you going to do if I don't let her go?"

"Then you will cross a line that you cannot come back from. Viribus will hunt you down until you and every member of your disillusioned organisation are wiped out for good."

Sol lowered the revolver and began chuckling to himself behind the mask. "That's funny," he said as he laughed. "But you know what? I really don't give a shit."

He snapped the revolver back into position and pulled the trigger. The noise of the Desert Eagle reverberated around the foyer as the Major fell backwards, hitting the floor with a perfect, bullet-sized hole in his forehead.

The gunshot immediately got the attention of the disorientated SPS in the smoke cloud, and one by one, they began emerging out of it. Sol and his one remaining assassin, carrying Kate over his shoulder, turned and ran for the elevator at the rear of the lobby.

As the doors of the elevator closed behind them, Kate got some air into her lungs and began wriggling and squirming on the man's shoulder as they ascended in the elevator. "Let me go!" she screamed. "You will not get away with this! What did you do to the Major?"

Sol spun the Desert Eagle around in his hand and struck her with the butt of the revolver, knocking her out cold.

"That's better," he said calmly.

Sol glanced at the toned, middle-aged Asian man standing next to him. "I never asked you your name," he said as he reloaded his revolver.

The assassin's lifeless eyes stared straight ahead at the elevator door in front of him.

"My name is Tao," he said.

Canberra, Australian Capital Territory, Australia
12th February 2021
3:58 am Australian Eastern Standard Time

2.5 Hours Until Virus Release

As Sol and Tao made their way towards the roof of Parliament House in the elevator, the SPS captain spun around in the lobby below. "They're going for the roof!" he shouted, his voice echoing around the marble-lined, chasm-like foyer. "Follow them!"

The SPS detail responded to the order and, with their extensive knowledge of the layout of Parliament House, began running from the lobby in several directions—however, all of them held the same destination—the roof. Some ran for the fire exit stairwells, while others filed through the multiple front doors of the building.

The SPS captain watched his detail disperse until its last member had vacated the building, and then he went to follow them. He stopped as he passed by the body of the Major and crouched on one knee. "I don't know who you were," he said, closing the Major's eyes. "But it's obvious you weren't one of the bad guys. Rest in peace, my friend."

On the rooftop, the elevator doors slid open, and Sol emerged first. Close behind him, Tao carried out the limp and unconscious body of Kate draped over his shoulder, along with the duffle bag full of weapons.

Australia's New Parliament House is built into a hillside and is considered an underground structure. Its roof is covered in lush grass and sloped on all sides, excluding the front of the building, making it entirely possible to walk over the parliamentary headquarters from one side to the other.

The SPS, who had exited the building through the front doors, were already storming up the hillside, making their way towards Sol and Tao.

Sol saw the SPS racing towards him and threw his Desert Eagle revolver away, sliding the M-16 assault rifle strapped to his back around to his front. He raised the semi-automatic weapon to his shoulder and fired at the advancing SPS, callously cutting them down as they charged towards him. He slowly stepped towards them as he fired, gradually making his way down the western slope. The SPS returned fire, but Sol was fast and devastatingly accurate. As soon as any of them fired a shot at him, he would shoot back, cutting them down with a wicked volley of bullets.

Behind him, Tao put Kate down on the ground and joined Sol in firing at the SPS, backing him up. When Sol needed to reload, Tao took over, making it difficult for the SPS to advance up the hillside.

Suddenly, some of the SPS members burst out of a fire escape exit door behind them. Tao stopped firing at the SPS to his front and reached for two of the grenades he had attached to a belt around his torso by their arming pins. Yanking them from the belt and activating the grenades, he hurled them at the fire exit doorway where they detonated, blowing the SPS members into pieces.

Sol quickly realised this was a battle he would not win. The SPS were outnumbering them, and they would both run out of ammunition soon. The sound of helicopters approaching in the distance confirmed his decision to run.

"Get her in the car!" he shouted. "We need to get out of here! Now!"

Tao hurriedly picked up Kate, along with Sol's Desert Eagle revolver he had thrown to the ground, as Sol continued to fire at the SPS with the M-16 while retreating to the top of the hill. When he reached the top, he and Tao raced down the other side of the hill as a car with the injured assistant at the wheel screeched to a halt in front of them. Tao quickly bundled Kate into the trunk as Sol dove into the passenger seat through the window. The injured driver floored the accelerator and sped away, steering the car with one hand, while the other hung limply across his lap, covered in blood.

The SPS continued to fire at the vehicle as it sped away from the Parliament House complex; bullets peppering the car and causing its occupants to duck for cover.

The SPS helicopter arrived on the scene, illuminating the car with its high-intensity searchlight, pinpointing its location. Tao pulled down the rear seat and reached into the trunk, producing a long, cylindrical metal case. He flicked open the latches and pulled out a shoulder-mounted FGM-148 Javelin anti-aircraft rocket launcher.

The driver flicked a switch on the dash, and the sunroof retracted automatically. Tao stood up on the back seat and poked the Javelin through the sunroof, taking aim at the helicopter and firing. A sudden flash of light and a violent hiss emerged from the launcher as the rocket locked onto the hovering helicopter above and propelled itself rapidly towards it.

The rocket plunged into its target and detonated, illuminating the early morning sky with a tremendous explosion, and turning the helicopter into nothing more than pieces of burning metal.

Tao sat down in his seat and placed the Javelin next to him. "We need to find cover," he said. "And fast."

ZULU

2 Hours Until Virus Release

The black limousine carrying Matt, Alaina, Jesse, and Dexter arrived outside Parliament House as the night sky was succumbing to the dawn. Bodies of SPS members lay strewn around the parliamentary complex, and the burning wreckage of a helicopter lay in the middle of a nearby car park, creaking and moaning from the intense heat. Sirens wailed in the distance as local authorities scrambled their fire trucks and police cars to reach the scene of chaos.

"What the hell happened here?" Dexter asked as he emerged from the limousine and stared at the surrounding carnage.

"White Cloud happened here," Matt said, pushing his way past the gawking Dexter and sprinting towards the entrance of Parliament House with Alaina and Jesse close behind him.

Matt barged his way through a door and burst into the foyer of the building. "Kate!" he shouted before coming to an abrupt stop to stare at the devastation in front of him. He didn't receive any response—except for his own voice echoing around the empty building. Several injured SPS members lay on the ground to his left, moaning and groaning in pain, while others were not groaning at all.

"Kate!" Alaina shouted, walking past Matt and deeper into the foyer of the building. "It's us! You can come out!"

"There's no one here, Alaina," Matt said. "We're too late. She's gone."

Alaina turned to him with tears in her eyes. "No, she isn't. She has to be here somewhere. We have to look for her. What if she's hurt and can't respond?"

Matt nodded. "Wait. I have her GPS transmitter signal. We don't need to run around like headless chickens to find her." He turned to Jesse behind him. "Fetch your laptop. Plug in Kate's GPS details and locate her as quickly as you can. While you're there, grab Dexter and bring him in here. If Kate isn't in this building, we need to find her laptop to see what she was up to." Jesse nodded and ran out of the building to the limousine parked outside.

Alaina and Matt trudged across the marble floor, surveying the situation with terror still hanging in the air. As they approached the elevator at the rear of the foyer, they simultaneously recognised the body of the Major lying on the ground in front of them, and froze.

"Fuck," Matt said.

"Oh, my God! No!" Alaina shrieked, crying into her hands as she fell to her knees next to the Major's body.

Jesse returned into the foyer with a laptop in his hand, and Dexter behind him. "I think I know where she is!" he shouted with excitement in his voice. He ran towards them with the laptop cradled in his arms. "You're not going to believe—"

Jesse stopped as he saw Alaina on her knees and sobbing into her hands next to a body.

A body he recognised.

"Dad?" he said under his breath, while choking back tears. He handed Matt the laptop as he stared at the Major's body. "She's at the airport," he said, his voice cracking as he said the words. "We need to move."

Matt put a hand on Jesse's shoulder. "We need to find Kate's laptop first. We'll find that while you have a moment alone with him."

Jesse looked up at Matt and nodded. "Thank you."

"He was a great man," Matt said, tight-lipped.

Jesse nodded and forced a smile as a tear trickled down his cheek. "He sure was."

Dexter stood behind Matt at a distance. "Is that…"

"You knew the Major?" Matt asked.

"He was my partner during Operation Desert Storm," Dexter said. "We fought alongside each other in that sandpit shoulder to shoulder. He saved my life."

"Let me promise you this; I will make sure he gets the send-off he deserves," Matt said. "But right now, we have to find Kate and get the bastards responsible for all of this. I need you with me, Dexter."

"Of course," Dexter said.

"Show me where Kate was working."

"Sure. Follow me."

Dexter marched towards a hallway, closely followed by Matt and Alaina, leaving Jesse to have a few minutes alone with the Major to say goodbye. No one else knew the Major was his father. As far as they were concerned, he was

Jesse's flying instructor. It was a secret Jesse had sworn to keep between him and the Major.

Dexter entered a side office. "That's all their gear over there," he said, pointing at the laptops, phones, and bags piled in the corner of the room. "Take what you need."

Matt and Alaina rushed across the room and gathered up as many of Kate and the Major's belongings as they could carry in their arms.

"Do you want to come with us, Dexter?" Matt asked as he went to leave the room.

"No," Dexter said, shaking his head. "We have secured the PM in the underground bunker for his safety. My place is here with him. But if you need me for anything, please call." He produced a business card from his jacket pocket and handed it to Matt. "The Prime Minister of Australia authorises you to use whatever force is necessary to bring these guys to justice. You have his complete backing."

"Thank you, Dexter," Matt said. "We'll keep you informed. Can we take your car back to the airport?"

"Of course, be my guest," Dexter replied.

With that, Matt and Alaina returned to the foyer and met up with Jesse.

"You all done, kid?" Matt asked.

Jesse nodded.

"Good," Matt said, shoving Kate and the Major's laptops into his arms. "I need you to find out what Kate and the Major were doing and who they had been speaking to. I need everything, and I need you to do it before we get back to the airport."

"Sure, I'll do my best," Jesse replied.

Canberra, Australian Capital Territory, Australia
12th February 2021
5:17 am Australian Eastern Standard Time

One Hour Until Virus Release

Sol, Tao, and the injured driver drove the bullet-ridden car into an old, abandoned hangar on an unused part of Canberra International Airport. Outside, a business jet waited for their return—only Sol had other ideas.

Once the vehicle was inside the hangar, Tao handed Sol his Desert Eagle revolver and exited the car, rushing across the hangar floor to close the enormous sliding doors behind them.

As the hangar doors banged together, Sol lifted the Desert Eagle and pointed it at the head of the injured assistant sitting behind the steering wheel next to him. "I have no further use for you," he said.

Before the man could plead for his life, Sol pulled the trigger. The man's head burst open inside the car, splattering it with blood and little pieces of brain.

Outside the car, Tao flinched as the booming gunshot echoed around the empty hangar. Sol climbed out of the vehicle, his white uniform now covered with blood and small pieces of the unsuspecting assistant's skull.

Tao popped open the trunk and stared at Kate's body lying lifelessly inside it. Sol joined him at the rear of the car and stared down at it as well. "Let's get on with this," he said, reaching for her bound ankles. "We don't have much time. Help me get her out."

Together, they carried Kate's body into the middle of the hangar and dropped it onto the cold concrete floor. Sol reached for a control pad hanging from the ceiling and pressed a large red button upon it, lowering the overhead crane jig down to the floor.

While the jig was lowering, Tao cut away the cable ties around Kate's wrists, replacing them with a length of thick tow rope he had found in the trunk. As the jig came within reach, he ensured her new binds were taut before placing the rope knot over the jig's hook.

Sol pressed the green button on the control pad and the jig elevated Kate's body by the wrists until it was entirely suspended in the air, her feet mere inches off the floor.

"Wake her up," Sol said as he let go of the control pad. "And take the hood off her head. I want to watch the life drain out of her."

Tao hurried over to the side of the hangar, picked up the fire hose, and roughly unfurled it before twisting the faucet handle and allowing the water to gush out. He walked back to the dangling body of Kate and splashed her with the freezing cold water.

Kate sprung into life, thrashing around in shock as Tao doused her with the water from the hose. She instantly felt an immense pain in both her shoulders as she hung in the air with a ball gag lodged firmly in her mouth, preventing her from speaking.

"That's enough," Sol said, holding a hand up. "You can leave us now."

Tao stopped splashing her with the water and went to turn the faucet off. Before he left, he stopped and stared at Sol for a moment. "If you kill her now, how is the virus going to propagate? There is no viable host in here for it to spread to."

Sol pointed at Kate. "Viribus will come for her, Tao. Mark my words. And when they do, *they* will be the ones who will propagate the virus—"

Tao smiled. "—Killing the key members of Viribus in the process," he said, realising Sol's plan. He threw the hose to the floor. "I guess you'll be needing this then," he said, reaching into his jacket and producing a small black pouch.

Sol took the pouch from him and slid it into his pocket. "Thank you. Please, prepare the jet."

Tao nodded before taking one last look at Kate and exiting the hangar.

Kate shook the water from her face and opened her eyes. She saw a sinister-looking man in a blood-soaked uniform, with a strange-looking mask over his head, staring back at her.

Sol waited for Tao to exit the hangar, and the instant the door banged shut behind him, he began walking towards Kate.

Amidst her terror, Kate recognised the walk.

It was Sol's walk.

She tried to scream but could only manage a useless muffled noise with the ball gag in her mouth. The masked man paced towards her slowly. His heeled shoes and the hangar's enormous empty space exaggerating his footsteps, making them sound ominous and terrorising.

He then stopped in front of her and clasped his hands together behind his back as he looked her up and down for a few seconds.

"Mrs Fabianski," he said, his strange, digitised voice echoing around the hangar just as much as the heels of his shoes had. "How nice it is to finally get you all to myself."

Kate wriggled like a worm on a hook and desperately tried calling for help, but she couldn't make enough noise, even if there was someone to listen.

The man held a hand up. "Mrs Fabianski, stop. Or this is going to end far too quickly for my liking."

She stopped wriggling and began sobbing in frustration and fear.

"That's better," he said. "Crying is much better than screaming."

Kate stared at him, studying his features. She realised that even though she was suspended from a crane, he could still look her in the eye. This man was tall. Just like Sol used to be. *It couldn't be him, could it?*

The man turned around and peeled the mask off his head as if he had heard her thoughts. When he turned to face her again, Kate's eyes went wide.

It was Sol.

Although she recognised the scarred face, this wasn't the real Sol. It was his face and body, but his brain was clearly that of someone else entirely. He didn't recognise her, and she couldn't tell him who she was.

She started wriggling again, trying to dislodge the gag to speak and tell him who she was. But it was of no use.

Sol held his hand up to calm her down again.

"Do you see my face, Mrs Fabianski?" he shouted over the noise of her struggling in his now non-digitised voice.

Kate stopped at the sound of his voice as tears began rolling down her cheeks uncontrollably.

He repeated the question. "Do you see my face, Mrs Fabianski?"

Through her tears, Kate nodded her response. She wanted to do so much more. How she would have loved to hold him and tell him about the sons he'd never met.

"You did this to me, didn't you?" he asked.

Kate shook her head, staring at him through the tears.

"Liar. The last time you saw this face, you had it in the crosshairs of your sniper rifle. And then you left me to burn in the wreckage of a helicopter, didn't you?"

Kate paused for a long moment and then nodded slowly. There was no point lying. There was nothing she could do.

Turning around and standing with his back towards her, he inhaled deeply. "I appreciate your honesty," he said. "But I already knew the answer. I just wanted to make sure you knew the reason why I'm about to kill you."

Sol then took out a six-inch hunting knife from inside his jacket, spun on his heels, and quickly marched towards her. He grabbed the hair on the back of her head and yanked it backwards before plunging the knife into her chest.

"Goodbye, Kate," he said, staring into her eyes as the life drained from her body.

As her eyes closed, she smiled, revelling in being so close to her husband for one last time.

Kate's body went limp, and Sol let go of her hair and the knife. He took a step back and opened the pouch that Tao had given him, filling the syringe full of the liquid and injecting Kate with the virus.

As he cast the syringe to one side and turned to leave the hangar, something on the ground made him stop.

He stared at the object on the ground in front of him for a moment before momentarily glancing back at Kate's lifeless body hanging in the air.

He then picked up the necklace.

Canberra, Australian Capital Territory, Australia
12th February 2021
5:54 am Australian Eastern Standard Time

30 Minutes Until Virus Release

As Dexter's car sped through Canberra towards the airport, Jesse successfully hacked into Kate's laptop.

"Jesus Christ," he said, staring at the screen. "Kate and the Major got the code out of Roman and Gianfranco. Dmitri's is also here in an unopened email from Alexei. Kate never opened it, which means—along with the code we retrieved from Min—the only one we need is Sol's."

Matt and Alaina glanced at each other.

"Shit," they said in unison.

"Everybody needs that app on their phone," Alaina said. "If any of us get close enough to him, we need to be able to retrieve it."

They soon arrived back at the airport and stopped next to Moose.

"Where is she now, Jesse?" Matt asked.

Jesse looked down at the laptop he was cradling in his arms and tapped a few keys. "It says she's in that hangar over there," he said, pointing towards the abandoned hangar in front of the white business jet they had seen earlier.

"All right. Jesse, I need you to wait in Moose. Hide the best you can. We'll be on the comms," he said, pointing at the earpiece in his ear.

Jesse nodded and got out of the car, heading towards Moose.

Matt turned to Alaina. "You ready for this?"

Alaina nodded enthusiastically back at him and cocked her pistol. "You betcha skinny white ass I am," she said.

Together, they crept towards the hangar with their weapons raised. As they neared the hangar's large sliding doors, one of them began slowly creaking open.

Matt and Alaina froze, aiming their weapons at the opening of the door.

A man wearing a white uniform covered in blood and carrying a mask in his hand appeared through the gap in the doors. His face was badly scarred, and he had no hair—but Matt and Alaina still recognised him—it was Sol.

Sol saw them and froze.

"Don't move!" Matt shouted. "Stay where you are!"

"Where is she?" Alaina shouted.

Sol glanced into the hangar behind him. "Where is who?" he asked.

"You know who we mean," Matt said. "And we know who you are."

"Is that right?" Sol said, turning to face him.

"You're Solomon Barrett, the Oceania sector leader of White Cloud," Matt said. "You are also the husband of Kate Barrett—the leader of Viribus."

Sol looked at him quizzically. "Who?"

"The woman you kidnapped from Parliament House is your wife."

Sol stared at him for a moment before shaking his head. "No. You're wrong. I took Kate *Fabianski*. She was the one that did this to me," he said, pointing at his face.

"She killed me and my family, and now she has got what she deserves."

"What are you talking about, Sol?" Alaina asked cautiously. "What have you done to her?"

Sol turned around and slid the door of the hangar open further. "See for yourself," he said, ushering them inside.

Alaina and Matt peered around him to look inside the old hangar. Amidst the darkness, they could make out a body hanging from a ceiling-mounted crane hook.

"Kate!" Alaina shrieked, abandoning everything and instinctively running into the hangar.

Matt stared at the lifeless body swinging from the crane, his brain failing to comprehend what he was looking at. *Oh, shit. We're too late,* he said to himself.

While the discovery of their dead leader distracted them, Sol slipped away into the shadows, running for the white business jet as its engines began whirring into life.

Matt saw him running in his peripheral vision. "Sol, stop!" he yelled, a finger hovering over the trigger of his pistol. As much as he wanted to kill him, Matt knew he couldn't. He still had a piece of the code they desperately needed. "Jesse!" Matt yelled into his earpiece.

Jesse's face appeared in the doorway of Moose.

"Stop him!" Matt shouted, pointing at Sol running across the apron towards the small aircraft. "But do *not* kill him!"

"On it!" Jesse yelled, leaping out of Moose and charging after Sol, as Matt followed Alaina into the darkness of the hangar.

Sol glanced over his shoulder to see Jesse closing in on him fast. The small aircraft up ahead was waiting for him with its door open as Tao appeared at the top of its in-built set of steps, brandishing an M-16 assault rifle.

Tao fired at Jesse, who ducked and weaved as he ran, dodging the bullets. Tao's rifle quickly emptied as Sol closed in on the aircraft.

Jesse saw his opportunity and launched himself onto Sol's back, crash-tackling him to the ground and wrapping himself around him. Before Sol could get away again, Jesse whipped out the phone from his pocket and slapped it over the Australian flag on Sol's shoulder.

The phone beeped.

Sol jolted his entire body upwards, throwing Jesse off him like a bucking bronco. He quickly got to his feet, punched Jesse hard in the face, and bounded up the steps of the aircraft, closing the door behind him.

Despite his throbbing face, Jesse leapt up at the aircraft, latching himself onto the door handle before Sol could close the door. He pulled as hard as he could to prevent Sol from closing the door—and then—the jet's brakes released, and it began to move, with Jesse hanging on to it.

The aircraft wasted no time, speeding up quickly and racing towards the runway with Jesse hanging from the door handle, desperately trying to prevent the aircraft from taking off.

And then Jesse's time ran out.

The aircraft lined up on the runway and the engines roared to full take-off power, despite the open door. It charged along the runway, with Jesse clinging to the door, until the g-force became too great, and he was forced to let go.

Jesse hit the tarmac of the runway at speed, rolling along the ground as the wings of the aircraft swooped over him and took to the air.

Jesse reached for his phone, hoping it hadn't been damaged in the tussle with Sol and the subsequent fall on the runway. He looked at the image of hexagons and numbers on the screen, picked himself up off the ground and ran across the airfield to the hangar where Matt and Alaina were.

"Matt! Alaina!" He shouted as he entered the hangar. "I got the last piece of the—"

He froze at the sight of Matt and Alaina kneeling next to Kate's body. "—code."

Matt and Alaina looked at him with tears in their eyes.

"Oh no," Jesse said.

A few moments later, Kate's body jolted and inhaled a large breath of air…

Tango-Hotel-Echo   Echo-November-Delta

EPILOGUE

2 Hours After Virus Release

Alexei trudged along a dark, empty alleyway in Moscow, pinching his oversized trench coat around the neck to keep out the falling snow. He coughed as he waited on the side of the road for a taxi to return him to the airport, and had begun to feel nauseous.

He had successfully completed his mission.

Russia was safe.

Within minutes, Alexei's cough worsened until he started struggling to breathe and fell to his knees.

A passer-by ran to his aid, propping him up against an alleyway wall while calling the emergency medical services. Alexei continued to cough, violently and consistently, while clutching at his chest, his lungs failing him as he gasped for air.

He was suffocating.

An ambulance arrived quickly. The paramedics laid him down on the ground, attempting to open his airway—but it was too little, too late. Alexei's face turned a sickening shade of purple as he coughed up blood.

Moments later, Alexei's body suddenly convulsed and his battle to survive was over.

Over the next few weeks, the virus spread exponentially throughout Russia before moving across the border into Eastern Europe and parts of Asia. On the West Coast of the United States, the virus was also on the move, spreading throughout South America, North America, Canada, and many other surrounding islands.

In Australia and China, there were no reports of any infections. Instead, both countries had closed their borders to the world as a plan was being devised to save the world from total annihilation.

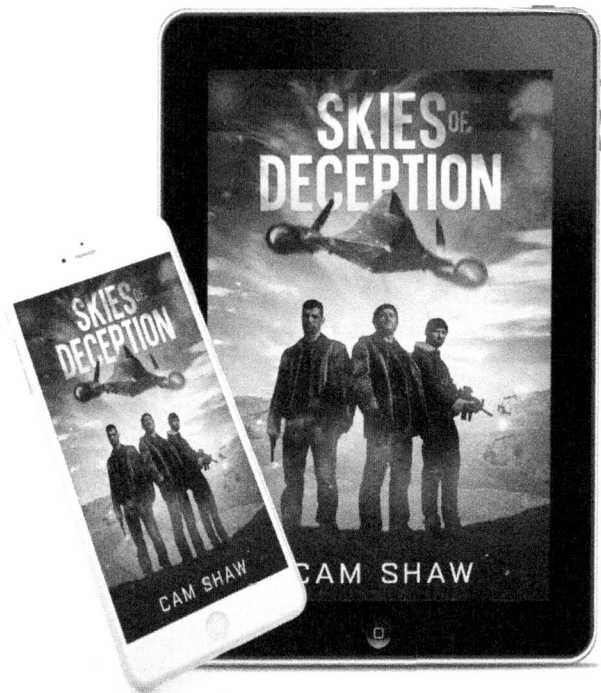

Don't forget to sign up for my monthly newsletter to receive a digital copy of the novella—*Skies of Deception*—obligation free and exclusive to subscribers.

This title is not available in any store!

www.camshawauthor.com

ACKNOWLEDGEMENTS

The first lot of thanks must go to you, the reader, for picking up this book and reading it. If you have enjoyed what you've just read, please give it a review! And for those who follow me closely, I'd like to thank you for sticking with me as I navigate this extremely steep learning curve. I know I have been slow, but I think I'm finally reaching the pinnacle now, and I can move forward and finish this series. There are plenty of other ideas queuing up behind this one, just itching to get out onto paper!

This is my second attempt at this story, and I am happy to say it didn't receive as much of an overhaul as what *Skies of Destruction* did, which is a good sign. It means I am finally beginning to stomach my work, although there is always room for improvement, but with sufficient practice, I know I will only get better.

I would also like to thank Craig Martelle and Chris Cartwright for their kind words of advice at a writer's conference I attended in Adelaide. They met me in an overwhelming self-doubting phase of my journey, but they convinced me I *could* do this. I just needed to *keep* doing it. A rising tide really does float all boats, and I can't thank you enough for your inspiring words.

Thank you to my wonderful fiancé, Sarah, and my two beautiful daughters, Georgia and Olivia. You all mean so much to me, and I appreciate all of your support immensely. I couldn't do this without you.

As always, the biggest thanks go to Karen, my editor, and the reigning godparent of the *Kate Barrett* series. She has supported me through my low (and my high) moments since 2020 and is truly my guiding light. I think she would agree when I say—this one is my best book yet.

Acknowledgement must also be given to my little team of beta readers, Samantha, Leanne, and Cathy. Your help in polishing this book up before release is greatly appreciated. Hopefully, you can see exactly where you helped!

Please, please, please give the book a review on Amazon and let me know what you think. Good or bad constructive feedback is priceless, and reviews mean everything to an independent—*indie*—author. It really helps us float to the surface in the oceans of novels out there.

And finally, if you liked this story as much as I enjoyed writing it, let me know! Anyway, that's enough waffling from me. I have another book to write.

Until next time…

Cam.

ABOUT THE AUTHOR

Cam Shaw was born in Melbourne, Australia and moved to the UK with his mother, June, when he was very young. Cam completed all of his compulsory schooling in the UK before securing a job at Manchester Airport as a baggage handler. It was here his interest in aviation developed.

Upon reaching his late teens, Cam returned to Melbourne, Australia, to live with his father, Graeme. His working life in Australia began as a bartender at the Rosebud Hotel on the Mornington Peninsula before signing up to serve his country as an avionics technician in the Royal Australian Air Force in 2004. Cam served in the RAAF for 7 years before leaving in 2011 to pursue other ventures. He is now applying his trade with a large aircraft maintenance contractor based at RAAF Amberley.

Cam currently lives in the suburbs of West Brisbane with his fiancé, Sarah, his daughters, Georgia and Olivia, and Sarah's two sons, Ryan and Luke. Together they own two dogs and a parrot: Roxy, a Rhodesian Ridgeback x Bull Arab, Queenie, a Great Dane, and Rosie, an 11-year-old talkative Eclectus parrot.

In his spare time, Cam plays guitar and is a devout follower of Formula One, MotoGP, and Manchester United. He was inspired to write by another Australian author: the best-selling, internationally acclaimed, Matthew Reilly.

Website - www.camshawauthor.com
Facebook - @camshawbooks
Instagram - camshawauthor
TikTok - @camshawauthor
Email - camshawbooks@gmail.com

Please leave a review on Amazon!

Skies of Deception
(Only available to mailing list subscribers)

Deception tests their friendship, war will define their destiny.

Sam Rosenberg and Jimmy Garcia are two highly skilled individuals who form an unbreakable bond during their CIA pilot training. Their future looks bright as they are both posted to an elite SR-71 Blackbird Squadron. However, what Sam doesn't know is that his closest friend has a hidden agenda.

Jimmy's true colours are revealed when he coerces Sam into participating in a diabolical plan involving a weapon of mass destruction hidden deep in the desert. As Jimmy's plan unfolds, Sam finds himself in a precarious position that his life, as well as millions of others, are at stake.

The fate of the world rests in Sam's hands as he battles his own inner demons and uncovers the truth behind Jimmy's betrayal. Will he be able to stop his friend's evil plot, or will he succumb to his own inner turmoil?

"No matter which book you are up to in the series, this novella slides right into place with twists, turns, and "No way!" moments. It's a must-read for those thrill-seeking fiction readers out there!"

— Sarah

Visit www.camshawauthor.com to sign up today!

Skies of Destruction

The skies have become a deadly arena...

Kate Barrett, an Australian nurse, is kidnapped by a twisted global alliance and discovers her husband, Sol, is walking into their trap. If he does not comply with their demands and use his aircraft maintenance skills to assist them with their plans, they will kill her, along with the rest of their family.

Except they didn't know who they were dealing with...

A rogue group of vigilantes rescue Kate, and realising her potential and determination, train her in the deadly art of the sniper. But with the clock ticking, she must learn quickly, and prevent Sol from committing a crime so foul, it will change the face of the world forever.

Embark on an electrifying journey with Kate Barrett, a healer turned hunter, fighting against an organisation that threatens to reshape humanity. It is a journey where nothing is as it seems...

"Loved this book, full of twists and turns and thoroughly riveting until the finale!"

— *Matthew*

Visit www.camshawauthor.com to buy today!

Printed in Great Britain
by Amazon